SURVIVE THE COLLAPSE BOOK ONE

BRINK OF DARKNESS

T.L. PAYNE

Brink of Darkness
Survive the Collapse Series, Book One

Copyright © 2022 by T. L. Payne
All rights reserved.

Cover design by Deranged Doctor Design
Edited by Lone Road Publishing
Proofread by Joanna Niederer

No part of this book may be reproduced in any form or by any electronic or mechanical means, including information storage and retrieval systems, without written permission from the author, except for the use of brief quotations in a book review.

Don't forget to sign up for my spam-free newsletter at www.tlpayne.com to be among the first to know of new releases, giveaways, and special offers.

❦ Created with Vellum

Contents

Preface	vii
1. Sam	1
2. Lauren	10
3. Sam	18
4. Lauren	22
5. Billy Mahon	31
6. Lauren	36
7. Sam	44
8. Becky	49
9. Sam	53
10. Sam	61
11. Vince	72
12. Lauren	77
13. Billy Mahon	85
14. Vince	89
15. Lauren	95
16. Sam	102
17. Sam	110
18. Vince	119
19. Sam	128
20. Vince	134
21. Sam	144
22. Lauren	154
23. Sam	163
24. Sam	169
25. Lauren	174
26. Vince	178
27. Sam	184
28. Vince	194
29. Becky	199
30. Billy	202
31. Sam	205
32. Lauren	216
33. Lauren	225

34. Billy	236
35. Sam	239
36. Lauren	244
37. Lauren	251
38. Lauren	259
39. Lauren	264
40. Sam	273
41. Billy	279
42. Sam	282
43. Lauren	289
44. Becky	295
45. Sam	303
46. Lauren	310
Acknowledgments	315
Also by T. L. Payne	317
About the Author	319

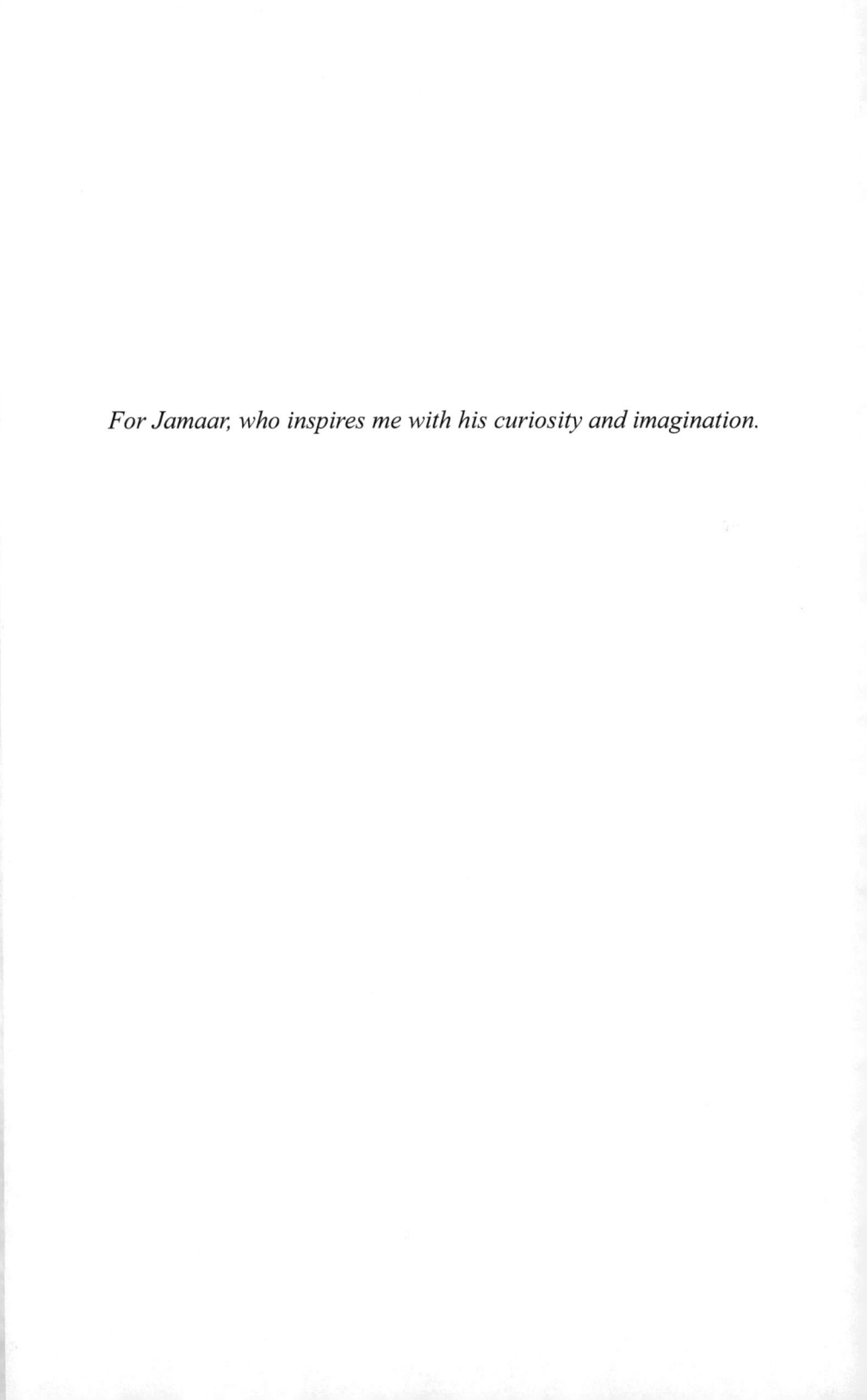

For Jamaar, who inspires me with his curiosity and imagination.

Preface

Real towns and cities are used in this novel. However, the author has taken occasional liberties for the sake of the story.

While the Unicoi Board of Aldermen, Unicoi Police Department, and Johnson City, Tennessee Commission are real institutions, versions within these pages are purely fictional.

Thank you in advance for understanding an author's creative license.

ONE

Sam

Midtown
Atlanta, Georgia
Day of Event

Sam Wallace pulled his cell phone from his pocket and dialed 911 as he bolted across a parking lot after his murder witness, Tara Hobbs, and the three armed Russo brothers chasing her.

"Atlanta 911. What is your emer...." The call cut off so he pocketed the phone, drew his pistol, and ran diagonally between the apartment buildings with the aim of emerging around the far corner just as Tara passed, cutting off the hitmen in the process. He timed it perfectly.

"Stop right there and put your hands in the air," Sam shouted, pointing his pistol at the men.

The men dove in different directions and began firing. Sam spun back around the corner and dropped to the ground as bullets whizzed past. He rolled and returned fire, dropping the perp closest to him while the other two concentrated their fire in Sam's direction. Sam stood and took off in the opposite direction in search of Tara. As he rounded the far end of the next building, he collided with her, knocking her to the ground.

"What the—not you again. Leave me alone," she said, rolling away from him.

"The District Attorney sent me to offer you protection," Sam said, reaching down and yanking Tara to her feet.

"That's what you said last time and look where I am now." Tara pulled herself free and stood looking around with her hands on her head.

As the criminal investigator for Unicoi County, Tennessee, Sam had often made that offer to witnesses. Unfortunately for Tara, she had run off to Atlanta, and Nigel Corbin's hired killers had caught up to her before Sam could get her into protective custody.

"Let's go," Sam said, grabbing her wrist.

Tara resisted but only briefly before giving in and running with Sam back the way he had come. He led her into the nearest stairwell.

"What are you doing in Atlanta? I told you I'm not going back to Tennessee, and I'm not testifying against Nigel."

Tara Hobbs was the prosecution's star witness. They needed her testimony to put her lover away for the murder of Misty Blue and bring justice to Misty's family.

Sam looked at his cell phone's blank screen. He tried swiping, then held the power button on the side of the phone for several seconds, waiting to see the familiar fruit logo appear, but the screen remained stubbornly black.

"It's dead. Do you have a phone?" Sam asked.

"Yes," she said, pulling her phone from her pocket.

"Call 911 and report this. We need to get some police presence over here," Sam said, peering around the door jamb into the long hallway.

Tara swiped her screen and tapped on it a few times. "It's dead."

Sam clenched his jaw and cursed. "Follow me—let's see if we can get to my Bronco. I have a burner phone there." He tried to recall when he'd last charged the phone. If it was dead too, he would need to drive Tara to the police station to keep her safe.

Sam and Tara sprinted to the end of the hall, and Sam stuck his head out of the entrance doorway to look for the two remaining Russos. "Stick close," Sam said. He and Tara flew out the door and across the front yard toward the apartment complex's playground, dropping to a crouch behind a row of shrubs that enclosed the play area. Seeing neither of the Russo brothers, Sam rose slightly and fished inside the front pocket of his jeans for his keys, wishing he could just press a button on a modern key fob to unlock his 1973 Bronco. He handed the keys to Tara. "You go first—you'll have to unlock it. Make it quick. We need to jump in and get the hell out of here. We'll call the police on the way to the station."

Alarm flashed across Tara's face. Sam touched her shoulder. "You can do this," he said in a low, even tone. "See that blue Bronco?" he asked, pointing. She nodded. "We're going to run like hell and drop down behind the front fender by the driver's door." She started to put the keys into her pocket, but Sam stopped her. "No! Hold onto them. Have them ready to slide into the lock the second you get there. Unlock the door, then jump in and start the engine."

"What are you going to be doing?"

"Watching our back—I'll be right behind you, ready to fire at those guys if they pop up," Sam said. "After you start the truck, climb over into the passenger seat and pop open the glove box. The phone's in there. Call 911, tell them there's been a shooting, and give them this location."

Tara swept her hair away from her face. Fighting back tears, she took a deep breath and gripped the key to the Bronco in her right hand.

"We're getting you out of this, Tara," Sam said.

She nodded.

Sam nudged her with an elbow. "Go!" he said, slicing through the bushes after her. He turned, moving backward with his pistol in both hands and his eyes whipping back and forth, searching for the Russo brothers.

Squatting by the tire, Tara struggled to insert the key into the lock. The Bronco's old, rusty suspension squeaked as she climbed into the driver's seat. Sam dropped down behind the Bronco's front fender when he spotted movement near the apartment building. "Start the engine, Tara!"

As the Russo brothers came into view, the Bronco roared to life and the contract killers began running toward them.

"Move over," Sam said, pushing her gently toward the passenger seat. She climbed past the shift levers as Sam climbed into the driver's seat. "Get the phone," Sam barked over the sound of bullets striking the Bronco. He threw the vehicle in gear and mashed the gas pedal. As he turned the first corner, Sam looked back and saw the two brothers jump into a 1970 Chevelle SS. He knew the old Bronco would be no match for the Chevelle's 454-cubic-inch big-block V-8. He could only hope the brothers would wreck the poor handling old street rod before they caught up with the Bronco.

A million things ran through his mind as they raced away from the apartment complex. Sam was mentally routing their way to the Atlanta Police Department when two cars slammed into each other at the intersection ahead. Sam barely slowed, making a split-second decision to turn left on a side street to avoid the accident. He glanced in the rearview mirror as the Chevelle turned the corner after them. Sam turned right, punched the gas, and sped away, losing sight of them.

"Open the glove box," Sam told Tara again.

Tara leaned forward, popped the glove box open, and grabbed the burner phone.

"Turn it on and call 911. Tell them we're heading to the police station."

He made another turn, attempting to get back onto a familiar road, but had to slam on the brakes instead, throwing Tara forward into the dash. A truck was sitting diagonally in the middle of the street.

"What the hell?" Sam said, driving onto the sidewalk to get around it.

"Have you dialed yet?"

"It won't power up," Tara said.

"Push the button on the side and hold it until the home icon appears."

Sam drove another two blocks and turned right, intending to get back on the main thoroughfare where he could pick up the highway and head to the police station.

"It's not working," Tara said, handing him the phone. Sam took it and tried to dial, but the screen wouldn't even light up. "It's dead, too."

The road ahead was blocked with stalled cars. People were standing in the street everywhere, and they lined the sidewalks on both sides of the road. Sam twisted and looked over his shoulder. There was no sign of the brothers.

"Hold on," Sam said as he took off across the front lawns of homes along the street, running over flower gardens and children's toys to make his way around the mess of cars and people.

"Look," Tara said, pointing toward a gas station. There were multiple vehicles with the hoods up and drivers wearing puzzled looks. Some were holding battery jumper cables. "What's going on with all the cars?"

EMP? It was the only thing that made sense.

Putting two and two together, Sam's mind was racing. He and his brother, Vince, had studied the effects of such a situation where the power grid, phones, and cars stopped working and had spent years preparing their family and small prepper community back home in eastern Tennessee to survive. The loss of modern technology was just one of many things that could have apocalyptic consequences on society. The consequences of an EMP event were enormous. His thoughts shifted to his wife and son. Had Charlie's plane landed safely? Had Lauren picked him up at the airport? Had they made it back to Unicoi before the shit hit the fan?

"Ever heard of an EMP?" Sam asked.

"No. What's that?"

"It's our ticket out of here, but it's also probably the end of life as we know it unless something even weirder is going on," Sam said, flying around a stalled car in his lane and blowing past the driver who was waving his arms trying to get Sam to stop.

"What? Something weird is sure going on—look at all the cars everywhere. Why did they all stop running at the same time?"

"An Electromagnetic Pulse—EMP, or a Coronal Mass Ejection—CME, caused by the sun, can take out everything electronic, like phones and cars. The traffic lights are out, and I noticed the power was out at the convenience store we just passed, too."

"But your truck is still running."

"That's because this is an older vehicle without anything electronic—everything under the hood is mechanical," Sam said. He'd selected the Bronco specifically to withstand an EMP. The vehicle, along with his get-home bag were his insurance policy for making it home. Sam had tested his pack several times by hiking on the Appalachian Trail from his home in Unicoi County, Tennessee, to the Virginia border. He was confident he had what he needed to make it home to his family.

"Hang on. We've got to get out of this populated area as fast as possible before we're stopped by people who want my truck."

"You're crazy. There's no way you could know something like this for sure."

"Well, all the signs point to an EMP or a CME, and whether that's what happened or not, we've still gotta get the heck outta town, pronto," Sam said, swerving around cars and people in the street as fast as he considered safe.

"Are you some sort of doomsdayer?" Tara asked, disdain dripping from the phrase.

Doomsdayer? He'd been called all sorts of things by family and friends who didn't understand when he and Lauren had purchased their homestead outside of town and begun raising and storing food.

"I'm a realist. My wife and I read the news. We understand how quickly the world can go to shit. The pandemic and everything following it showed us that."

"You're not part of some survivalist militia or something, are you?"

Lauren had had a similar reaction to him and Vince at first, but the pandemic and following supply chain shortages had convinced her that good preparation went a long way. Even after they'd moved into town to care for her elderly parents, they'd continued to prepare for an apocalyptic event. It hadn't been easy, but Sam was now grateful they had. "We're college-educated professionals who saw the writing on the wall, Tara."

Tara choked back something unintelligible as Sam reached under the seat. He retrieved two full magazines for his 1911, opened the dashboard ashtray, shoved them inside, and pushed it closed with the magazines sticking out the top at an angle. Then he reached under the seat again and came out with a box of .45 ACP rounds and two more empty magazines.

"Do you know how to load these?" Sam asked.

"No—I don't play with guns. They're dangerous," Tara said with a scowl.

"Well, Tara, you're right. Guns are dangerous—but only in the hands of bad people or those who aren't proficient in using them," Sam said.

Sam knew all too well what they could do in the hands of bad people. He had been working the beat as a cop in Johnson City,

Tennessee, when a group of perps surprised him and his partner, Jon. Sam had been behind the wheel. As they ate lunch in their patrol car, a bullet ripped through the windshield, striking Sam in the left shoulder. Their burritos flew everywhere as they scrambled to draw their service pistols, which were wedged between their hips and the seat belt latches.

By the time Sam had drawn his pistol, another bullet had punched through the windshield and struck Jon in the neck. Jon's carotid artery had pumped blood all over the windshield and all over Sam. As bad as Hollywood would have portrayed this kind of scene, the reality was much worse. The blood had soaked Sam's face and arms and the entire right side of his uniform. Its coppery smell and taste had created a memory that still made him physically ill five years later. The past frequently traveled with him. At night, it caused fitful sleep. Sam had worn a cross-draw holster ever since to ensure his pistol was always within immediate reach.

Stop. Stop it.

Sam tried to shake off the trauma and focus on the current situation.

"I don't care—I don't like guns," Tara offered, crossing her arms and sticking her nose in the air.

Sam rubbed his brow and put the empty magazines on the seat between his legs. "This is going to be a long trip."

Sam figured they'd have to stop one way or another, so he kept pushing on through whatever they encountered as fast as possible. As he weighed his options, he looked over at Tara. If this was the apocalypse, he probably didn't need to get her back to Unicoi. So far, he had no confirmation the EMP effect was widespread. It could just be localized. Things could be perfectly normal in Tennessee. Until he knew otherwise, he still needed to bring her back to testify as planned.

Sam accelerated and was about to make another turn toward the police station when he spotted movement out of the corner of his eye. "Hang on!" Sam yelled, swerving around an overturned pickup lying next to a Prius on the side of the road. The centrifugal force shoved Tara against her door as something struck the side of the Bronco.

The last thing Sam remembered was the windshield exploding into a million shiny little diamonds and the panicked screams of his frightened witness fading into the distance.

TWO

Lauren

Interstate 26
Unicoi, Tennessee
Day of Event

After meeting with the board of aldermen for a long morning of budget meetings, Lauren Wallace slid behind the wheel of her Honda Pilot SUV and headed to McGhee Tyson Airport in Knoxville, Tennessee. As the mayor of Unicoi, Tennessee, she really needed to be at city hall handling the latest crisis, but picking up her stepson at the airport one hundred and thirty miles away came first.

Lauren pulled up next to the fuel pumps at the travel center just off Interstate 26 on the west side of Unicoi and got out to fill her tank. After inserting her card and placing the nozzle into her fuel tank, she turned back toward the pump and came face to face with her nemesis, Billy Mahon, a ruthless drug dealer and sex trafficker. She fought to keep her face from twisting into a mask of disdain.

Billy Mahon sneered back at Lauren, holding the machine's opposite pump nozzle for a second, then turned away and began filling his motorcycle. Lauren chewed her bottom lip, dying to say something to the piece of human garbage standing behind the machine. Billy operated his illicit businesses out of the Unicoi Inn adjacent to the travel center's truck port. The inn's owner, Corbin Industries, had turned a blind eye to the crimes committed on its premises for years.

Lauren reflexively balled her hands into fists and battled to hold her tongue, but finally lost the battle. "You off to groom more little girls, Epstein?"

Mahon turned to face her, his mouth forming something more aggressive than a smirk. Lauren's upturned face dared him to say something, her hand wanting to draw the Colt single action revolver holstered in dark-brown tooled leather hanging around her waist. Billy's day was coming—just not soon enough for Lauren.

Billy finished filling up his motorcycle, hung up the nozzle, and climbed onto his bike. As he turned to pull past the back of Lauren's Honda Pilot, he flipped her the bird, then made the image of a gun with his fingers and dropped his thumb as if firing it. Lauren took it as another threat from the Corbins. It wasn't the first one she'd received, and it wouldn't be the last—even after Nigel had been sentenced to death and sent to Riverbend to rot until his date with the executioners.

"I can't wait to put handcuffs on that piece of shit and haul his ass off to jail," said a voice behind Lauren. The voice belonged to Sam's friend and Unicoi town cop, Benny Jameson.

"The DA won't charge him—not until he uses him to make his case against the Corbins," Lauren said.

"We'll be closer to that day after Sam locates Tara Hobbs," Benny said.

"We'll see."

The DA's refusal to prosecute Mahon had been a source of conflict between Lauren and Sam, but Sam had no control over his boss's prosecutorial decisions. Sam always wound up seemingly siding with his boss whenever he reminded Lauren why Mahon couldn't be prosecuted.

"Isn't Charlie coming in today? Are you headed to Knoxville now?" Benny asked.

"Yeah. Do me a favor. Drive by my parents' house while I'm gone."

"Sure thing. I'll keep an eye on things," Benny said.

Lauren climbed into her Pilot. As she pulled from the parking lot, she called the Unicoi city clerk to discuss the upcoming news release for the publicity she knew in her heart was just around the corner about the overdose of a young girl the night before at the Unicoi Inn.

In Lauren's mind, the town hadn't been able to shut down the inn or put Mahon behind bars due to District Attorney Coleman's political ambitions. This time, the media attention alone should be enough of a catalyst for him to put Billy Mahon away—before another life was lost.

∼

McGhee Tyson Airport
Knoxville, Tennessee
Day of Event

As Lauren drove her SUV into the airport parking lot, she pressed the call button on her steering wheel.

"Call Brent Jenkins," she said.

She knew Sam was good at his job—he'd find Tara Hobbs, but Nigel Corbin had high-priced attorneys from Nashville working to get him off. As an attorney herself, Lauren was only too aware of how often money bought an acquittal. DA Coleman was willing to take his time to make his case against the rest of the Corbin family, but Lauren refused to wait that long to deal with the crime at the Unicoi Inn.

"Lauren, it's been a while," Brent said.

"It has." It had been over six years, in fact. She'd left a job at a prestigious law firm in Boston, Massachusetts to move back home to Unicoi County, Tennessee, to care for her parents after her mother had been diagnosed with dementia and her father's health had declined. Shortly after, she and Sam had started dating and eventually married.

"I need a favor."

"Sure, what can I do for you?" Brent asked.

"I need to purchase a motel," Lauren said.

"You need me for that?"

"The Unicoi Inn isn't for sale."

"You don't need me. You were the best mergers and acquisitions attorney in the firm," Brent said.

"I need my name left out of it."

"I see. Email me the details and I'll take care of it."

Before the ink had even dried on the contract, she intended to serve Billy Mahon and his crew an eviction notice and have that hell hole leveled to the ground.

Lauren spotted Charlie walking down the ramp toward the baggage claim carousel. She checked her watch. The flight had arrived early. She waved. If Charlie was disappointed to see her there without Sam, he didn't show it. On the way back to the car, Lauren sent Sam a text to let him know Charlie had landed safely, but the message never went through. She hit the button to resend the message several times without success.

Charlie threw his backpack and suitcase into the back of the Honda and plopped himself into the passenger front seat without a word. She was fine with that. Lauren had no idea how to talk to a teenage boy. She'd stopped playing video games before law school and wasn't up on the latest pop music. She preferred country music. Lauren turned on the radio, dialed in a local pop station, put the SUV into drive, and headed north toward the interstate.

The traffic was heavier than when she'd arrived. Living back in Unicoi for the last six years, Lauren had almost forgotten what rush hour traffic was like. It was still a little early for the bulk of the evening commuters, but the congestion was more than she had expected. Lauren turned the SUV toward Highway 129 and headed north. "You should call your mom and let her know you made it here safely."

"I already did when I was waiting for you."

Sam's ex-wife, Bekka, had likely already called him to complain about her being late, even though Lauren had been on time and it was Charlie's flight that was early.

Lauren turned on her blinker to pull into a convenience store. "I'm going to stop and get a soda. Do you want anything? Are you hungry? We could drive through McDonald's or something."

"No, thanks."

"You sure? It's no trouble. We could get some ice cream or pie, maybe. I saw a diner on my way."

"Mom has me on this diet. She told Dad about it. Gluten-free, dairy-free, flavor-free." He was talking with his hands like his father. Charlie was taller than Lauren's brother had been at thirteen. He was nearly her height at five foot eight inches. He looked like Sam, except Charlie's hair was a little darker and more like his mother's.

"I can try to find some gluten-free and dairy-free snacks at a health food store, maybe some banana chips or something?" Lauren thought she saw a slight smile form at the corners of his mouth, but then it faded.

"Mom says they have too many preservatives or additives. I don't know. I'm just not allowed to eat them."

This summer was going to be more difficult than she thought.

Now Sam would end up on the phone arguing with his ex-wife about Charlie's diet. Fun. Charlie had asthma. It had been hard to control when he was younger, but as far as Lauren knew, they'd found the right meds and avoided the things that triggered attacks.Charlie's mother would never have let him out of her sight if it wasn't for the court's visitation order.

"I can talk to the owner. They should be able to find you something tasty to eat that works."

"It's okay. My mom packed me some organic kale chips."

As Lauren pulled into the fast food parking lot, her phone rang. It was Benny. Her heart lurched for a moment as her mind conjured up images of her husband bleeding from a gunshot wound. She pressed the Accept Call button on her phone. "Hi, Benny. Say hello to Charlie." She wanted to warn Benny that Sam's son was listening.

"Hey there, Charlie. How was your flight?"

"Boring."

"They usually are," Benny said. "Lauren, Chief needs to speak with you as soon as you're back in town."

"Is everything all right?" she asked.

He hesitated."Millie found a note on your desk."

"A note? What kind of note?"

"From the Corbins."

"The Corbins left me a note?" Her mind raced. Nigel Corbin knew her husband was the prosecution's investigator on his case. "Did you tell Sam?"

"I left him a text. He didn't respond to it yet."

Lauren drew a deep breath and let it out. She glanced over to see whether Charlie was listening. He was staring straight ahead with his headphones in his ears. She could hear his music playing. He couldn't hear her conversation. "Was it about Sam? Was it another threat?"

"Yeah," Benny said.

"Did anyone see who left it?"

"I had Steve in IT get me the video feed from the hallway outside your office."

Lauren changed lanes, avoiding slower traffic. "And?"

"It was one of Corbin's associates from the motel. Chief Avery and Officer Cordell went to talk to him about the note, but he wasn't there."

"How did they get into my office?" She always locked her office door. Usually, she kept a revolver in a safe in her bottom drawer.

"It was hard to say from the angle of the video, but he might have had a key."

"Avery?" Lauren asked. Despite the lack of evidence, she was sure he was on Corbin's payroll.

"I'll look into it, but it might be hard to prove."

"I don't need proof."

"Okay," Benny said, making it sound more like a question than a statement.

"I'll drop Charlie off at home, and I'll be there as soon as I can. We're just leaving the airport now."

Lauren put on her blinker and moved into the eastbound lane. She was two hours away from Unicoi. There was nothing she could do from her car to keep Corbin or his goons from going after Sam.

"Could you call that detective at the Atlanta Police Department and tell him about the note? Maybe he can tell Sam when he stops by there."

"Done. Sam's already...." Benny stopped mid-sentence. The line just went dead as the car in front of Lauren slowed suddenly. Lauren attempted to yank the wheel to avoid rear-ending it, but the steering felt stiff—the power steering had failed. Lauren tried to apply the brakes, but they weren't slowing the vehicle. She stomped on them harder.

"Lauren!" Charlie screamed, pointing at the windshield.

Lauren gasped. "What the hell!"

All she could see was the nose of a jetliner. The aircraft was attempting to land on the highway. It was no more than 100 feet off the ground, coming down fast and headed straight for them. Lauren leveraged her weight onto the pedal and yanked the steering wheel to the right. Her SUV struck and slid along the guardrail until it stopped. A pickup stopped fifteen feet in front of her and a man jumped out waving his arms wildly. He was shouting something, but Lauren couldn't hear what he was saying.

"Get out, Charlie," Lauren yelled as she opened her door.

"Get out!" she heard the man shouting. "Get the kid out of there!"

He was pointing behind them. Lauren twisted in her seat and gasped as a tractor-trailer slid sideways toward them.

"Charlie!" Lauren screamed. "Get out, Charlie!"

As the semi-truck slid toward the shoulder, its trailer went sideways, striking a sedan and splitting the big rig's trailer in two.

"The plane!" someone screamed. Lauren spun back around just in time to see the plane's left wing strike a row of vehicles, tossing them around like matchbox cars. Metal screeched against concrete. The sound was deafening. Pieces of metal and debris flew into the air. The right wing struck a power pole, tearing it from the fuselage. The nose of the plane dug into the dirt in the median but kept on coming. Flames rose from the back where it had scraped along the concrete highway.

Lauren's mind went blank as her brain tried to process what was occurring around her. In her peripheral vision, she saw Charlie opening his car door. She dropped her gaze and struggled to unbuckle her seat belt. The guy from the pickup was yelling something, but she couldn't hear him over the screaming—her screaming. Adrenaline flooded her brain, making it hard to think clearly.

What the hell is going on?

After untangling herself from the belt, Lauren threw open her car door. She lifted her gaze just as something large and metallic struck the back of her SUV.

THREE

Sam

South of Downtown
Atlanta, Georgia
Day of Event

Slender fingers dug into Sam Wallace's armpits. Someone was pulling him, but he lacked the strength to resist. His hands scraped the concrete, gathering tiny bits of sand under his nails. Pieces of glass tore through his shirt and ripped at the skin on his back. When the dragging stopped, Sam opened his eyes and was blinded by the scorching afternoon sun. He squinted and tried to turn his head as stiffness gripped his neck. Sam fought to remain conscious. He tried to sit up, but a searing pain lanced his skull. A thunderous noise echoed around him repetitively like a jackhammer.

What is happening?

Had his patrol car come under fire? Sam reached for his lapel mic, but it wasn't there. It should've been. He always wore it with the cord threaded under his shirt and then out between the top and second shirt button so that if his mic came loose, it would end up hanging in front of him, not down his back. "Jon!" He called his partner's name as darkness overtook him.

"Wake up—we've got to get out of here!" a woman yelled. "Wake up!" she screamed in his face. The woman grabbed his hand and yanked desperately, trying to pull him to his feet. He could feel her warm breath on his skin.

"What happened?" he asked, managing to open one eye. He slowly turned his head. His Bronco lay on its side next to him. "Where the hell am I?"

"Let's go!" the woman yelled, yanking on his arm. "We have to go before the Russos come for us."

"The Russo Brothers?" Sam asked. He jerked upright, his green eyes whipping back and forth, searching for the contract killers. "Where are they?" Sam asked.

Tara pointed toward the other side of the Bronco. "They're over there shooting at us!"

"Did you call 911?" Sam asked, drawing his 1911 from its holster.

"Our phones are dead." She held up her phone for him to see. "Something happened. Don't you remember?"

Sam stared back at her with a blank expression.

"All the cars suddenly stopped. You don't remember that?"

"What?" Sam asked, bewildered.

The EMP!

A bullet struck the Bronco right above Sam and Tara. "We've got to get outta here," Sam said, putting a hand to his bloody brow. He tried to stand, but barely made it to his knees. His head swam and bile rose into his throat. Another round struck the underside of the Bronco as Sam heard the crack of its report.

"Follow me." Sam dropped to the ground again, then did his best to crawl to the front of the Bronco and peer around the front bumper, ready to return fire, but the Russos were nowhere to be seen. Sam turned toward Tara and spotted his get-home bag lying behind his driver's seat. He needed that bag to make it home to his family. He wouldn't stand a chance of surviving the two-hundred-mile journey on foot without it. Sam scrambled back inside, snatched the pack and the two full magazines lying near it, and climbed out. Sam took Tara's hand and pulled her to her feet. "Follow me."

Sam and Tara sprinted toward a row of parked cars along the curb, keeping the Bronco between them and the Russo brothers. More shots rang out, and they dove for cover between two sedans. Bullet holes appeared in the parked vehicle in front of them. They'd be exposed if they left the protection of the vehicles to cross the street.

"We have to move," Sam said, but there was nowhere left to go. A tall stone wall ran along the entire block next to the sidewalk. Sam preferred to avoid a full-blown gun battle on a city street with just a pistol.

"My ex-boyfriend lives a couple of streets over—we can go there," Tara said.

That wouldn't work. The Russo brothers had the same information he had on Tara. "They know where he lives. They'll head straight there," Sam said. "We have to get you to the police station."

"What good is that going to do? They're never going to stop looking for me. Nigel and his family won't stop until I'm dead."

Sam could understand why Tara would feel that way. Nigel Corbin was from one of the most prominent families in eastern Tennessee. They were also the most corrupt and dangerous, as he'd discovered after Nigel had killed one of the girls he'd been sex trafficking along Interstate 26.

"Let's keep moving," Sam said. He winced as he swung his pack onto his back and tightened its traps. He was sore from the crash and the gash on his scalp was bleeding, but there was no time to tend to it now. They ran along the grass between the parked cars and the sidewalk.

At the next intersection, Sam grabbed Tara's arm. "Now!" He and Tara sprinted across the street and crouched behind an SUV. Sam turned and looked behind them around the rear bumper. The Russos were checking for them between all the cars parked along the curb.Gunfire suddenly ripped through the silence with a clapping echo from the wall. Sam grabbed Tara's hand, and they ran to the next street, then crossed left into an alley behind a corner house. They needed to put distance between themselves and the Russos. Sam's head was pounding. He was not in any shape to play this game of escape and evasion.

Sam surveyed the buildings to their left. They were mostly single-family homes and apartment complexes. There was a long row of business down the block, but that would require crossing the street in the open. *Too risky.*

Voices grew closer. Sam inched his head above the wall to find Skip Russo rounding the corner.

"We have to move." He yanked Tara to her feet. She craned her neck, trying to see behind them. "Stay low and don't stop for anything. Don't look back."

They ran as fast as they could down the block, weaving in and out of parked cars. Sam's pack was heavy on his back, making it awkward to run. He spotted a narrow alley at the back of a parking lot and headed for it. Tara was exhausted. Sam knew she couldn't keep up their current pace. After scanning the adjacent parking lot and seeing no sign of the Russo Brothers, he and Tara crossed it and headed north.

"We need to keep heading north," he said.

At the intersection, there had been a collision. Traffic was backed up in all directions. The police, fire, and possibly an ambulance should have been dispatched to clear the scene. It was clear no one was coming to help. Everyone was on their own.

FOUR

Lauren

Highway 129
Knoxville, Tennessee
Day of Event

Lauren awoke disoriented on the ground several feet from where her vehicle had stopped against the guardrail. She struggled to pull herself up onto her knees. She was dizzy. All she could think to do was run—she had to get away from there. As she got to her feet, there was a thunderous explosion. The shock wave moved through her body and back out again, sucking the air from her lungs. She fought to remain upright. She could feel the heat from the explosion on her back, intense and angry, and getting hotter. Lauren willed her feet to move, but it felt like her legs were filled with lead. The putrid smell of jet fuel and burning debris filled the air. She couldn't catch her breath. She stole a glance over her shoulder as her legs began to move. All she saw were flames as she ran toward the metal guardrail, where she dove for cover.

On her hands and knees, struggling to take in oxygen, she realized she didn't know where Charlie was. While her brain screamed for air, her mind told her body to get up and find him. Gasping, fighting to expand her lungs and draw in life-sustaining oxygen, she put one foot on the ground under her intending to stand, but felt a hand on her back.

"Stay down," a male voice said. "Take deep breaths."

"Charlie," Lauren croaked.

"He's right here," the male voice said.

"Sam?"

"Dad's not here. He's in Atlanta," Charlie said, standing beside her, brushing his hands on his pants legs.

Lauren's ears were ringing. Everything sounded like her head was inside a drum. She stuck a finger in her ear and then pulled on her earlobe. Nothing helped. Her stomach felt queasy as the brain fog began to lift, and the magnitude of what had occurred mere minutes ago struck her.

"Are you okay?" Lauren asked Charlie, moving to a seated position.

"I think so."

He was bleeding from a gash in his chin.

"Let me have a look." She reached for him, cupping his face with her hands, and tilting it sideways. The cut looked deep. It would need a few stitches. If it hurt, Charlie didn't show it. His wide-eyed gaze was fixed on the burning plane.

Lauren scanned the wreckage. It was hard to tell what was from the plane and what were damaged automobiles. She surveyed the area for survivors and expected to see the plane's emergency exit doors open and people sliding down the emergency ramps, but nothing happened.

"Are they...." Charlie stopped to catch his breath and then continued. "Are they going to make it out?" he asked.

The heat was intense. She wasn't sure how anyone could get close enough to rescue them.

Charlie touched her arm. "You're bleeding." He pointed to a crimson smear on her forearm. A droplet of blood fell on the blacktop next to her hand, and she realized it had come from her head. She touched her temple, her fingers coming away wet and sticky.

"I have a first-aid kit in my truck. I'll be right back," the man said, running back to his pickup.

"Here," he said as he returned with the medical kit. "There should be something in there to put on it until you can get to the emergency room."

Lauren pulled out a gauze pad and reached for Charlie's chin. "We need to get this wound irrigated, but first, let's stop the bleeding." Charlie winced as she touched his chin. "Sorry."

"I'm fine. You need it more than I do," Charlie said, grabbing the gauze pad from her hand. He ripped open the wrapper and pressed the four-inch pad against the side of Lauren's head. It didn't hurt. She felt no pain.

"I'll be right back. I need to go check on the driver of that semi," the man said.

A slender young woman climbed over the guardrail holding a bottle of water. "Here, take this to flush the wound."

"Thank you," Lauren said, taking the bottle from her. "Let's take care of your chin first, Charlie." Lauren tipped Charlie's head. "This may sting a little," she said as she poured the water over his chin.

Charlie nodded toward the plane. "Do you think anyone could have survived that?"

Lauren didn't answer him.

"I tried to call 911, but my phone isn't working," the young woman said.

"I imagine someone has called already," Lauren said.

"My boyfriend's phone wasn't working. He went to find one and call for help."

"The airport should have alerted emergency services by now. They had to have seen the plane go down."

"What's taking the fire and ambulances so long, then?" the young woman asked.

It was odd. A plane goes down on a highway near the airport, and emergency services don't immediately rush to the scene. They had to have seen it drop off the radar or seen the smoke from the control tower. Why weren't they here yet? Lauren didn't have an answer.

Charlie was taking quick, shallow breaths. Lauren reached over and lowered his shirt collar slightly to reveal his jugular notch just below his Adam's apple. Sure enough, it was retracting with every breath. She lifted his shirt. His chest heaved in and out as he struggled to take in air. Charlie was in respiratory distress. He needed his medication now before it progressed to respiratory failure.

"Where's your inhaler?" Lauren asked.

Charlie felt his pants pocket. A panicked expression came over his face. "I put it in the bin to be x-rayed. I think I forgot to pick it up."

No! No! This is not happening.

"You brought an extra one, right? In your carry-on?"

"Yes," he said, nostrils flaring.

"Sit here and take deep breaths." Lauren stood and approached the roadway, but then stopped in her tracks. Her SUV was entangled in the guardrail with the semi-truck behind it on its side. Spiderweb cracks covered the SUV's windshield. Lauren squinted and peered through the rear driver's side window. She attempted to pull open the car's door, but it wouldn't budge. Charlie's pack was wedged between the back seat that had been pushed forward and the front passenger seat.

"I've got something to open it," the man said. He returned a moment later with a tire iron. Lauren snatched it from his hand. "Step back," she said before smashing the window. The hole was big enough for her to reach inside the SUV and pull the bag through. She dropped it to the ground next to her feet, then rummaged through it, searching for the inhaler. She unzipped every pocket and inspected every pouch. She turned it upside down and shook it, spilling the contents onto the pavement. Dropping to her knees, she went through everything on the ground, then went through his bag again. Socks, briefs, deodorant, and toothpaste, but the inhaler wasn't there. She rechecked each pocket, ensuring she hadn't missed it.

Oh my God, this is not happening right now.

"It isn't here, Charlie. Recheck your pockets."

Lauren checked on the ground again and again. Full-blown panic wound its way around her head. Her heart began to break. She had to call someone. She needed to find a pharmacy or get Charlie to the hospital before it was too late.

Lauren felt her pocket for her phone. It had been in the center console of the Pilot. She'd been on a call with Benny when all this had happened. There was no telling where her cell phone was now. "Was your phone in your backpack, Charlie?"

"No, it was in my hand when I jumped out," he said through gasps.

Lauren searched the ground. The back part of her SUV was under the guardrail.

"I doubt it would do you any good, anyway. Cell phones don't seem to be working either," the man said. He adjusted his hat, a blood-smeared ball cap with a blue Ford logo.

"What do you mean?" Lauren asked.

"I can't explain it, but something's happened. No one's vehicle will start. Mine just died before the jet crashed," Ford Guy said.

"None of the cars will start?" asked Lauren.

"There was this guy who had an older model truck that worked. He just weaved his way through everything without stopping."

"Nobody's phones are working?" the young woman asked. "What happened to everyone's phones?"

Ford Guy shrugged. "Whatever killed the cars took out the phones too, I guess."

"You think that's what happened to the plane?" the young woman asked.

No one answered.

Lauren stared at the black smoke. She needed to get to a working phone and let Sam know his son's plane was already on the ground. If he saw the news before Lauren could call him, he'd freak thinking it was Charlie's plane that had crashed.

"Do you think it could have been a cyberattack? The government has been warning about Russia and China attacking our infrastructure with a massive cyberattack for a while now," Ford Guy speculated.

"I could see them taking down the power grid, or even disrupting cell signals, but being able to stop cars from working and cell phones from powering up?" Lauren asked.

"Maybe. Everything is connected to the internet these days," he said.

"If that's what happened, how long will it take to get it fixed?" the young woman asked. She swiped tears from her cheeks, causing mascara and dirt streaks on her face.

"I'm not sure," Lauren said. Bile rose in her throat. She turned, ran toward the metal barrier, leaned over, and spewed vomit. Everything was spinning. She straightened, wiped her mouth with the back of her hand, turned, and took in the scene. Her mind wanted to reject what she was seeing. It was too difficult to accept. Even though she and Sam had tried to prepare for the worst, she never really thought anything like this would ever really happen.

"I don't know. I can't say if the cars or phones are destroyed or if there's just some force or signal preventing them from operating," Ford Guy said.

"It could be a laser weapon or something. I read China was working on stuff like that," Charlie said through ragged breaths, wheezing loudly now.

"Could they really do that?" the young woman asked.

"I don't know," Ford Guy said. "It could be a CME or an EMP. That would explain this."

"A what?" the young woman asked. Again, no one answered her.

Sam's words played in her head. He called them Shit-Hit-The-Fan situations. EMPs were one of the things for which they had prepared. Lauren had thought cyberattacks on the financial sectors and electrical grid were more likely. They were now in an actual SHTF scenario if this was an EMP.

Sam would be home before she and Charlie made it back. Would he stay and look after her parents or come searching for them? Questions began running through her mind. Would Angela, her parents' nurse, stay with her parents, or would she abandon them to take care of her own family? How would she care for them without electricity? She forced herself not to consider what this could mean for all of them in the long term. Instead, she focused on getting Charlie to a doctor and dealing with one issue at a time.

Lauren was suddenly aware of the magnitude of their situation. It was over one hundred and thirty miles to Unicoi. Although the thought of walking home sucked, she hoped Sam would stay and look after her parents. Her parents would need him. She thought of her brother Josh out in California. Her father would be beside himself with worry when he couldn't get ahold of him. Thankfully, the dementia her mother lived with now didn't allow her to remember that Josh had left home, let alone that he was two thousand miles away.

Lauren couldn't afford to think about all those things now. She had to focus on getting Charlie medical help and getting them both home to Unicoi. It was difficult to shake off all of the intrusive thoughts. Her mind wanted to make sense of things, to analyze and compare the situation with known facts stored in her brain to understand what was going on, but nothing like this had ever happened. All she could do was to follow Sam's training as best she could.

Get yourself together, Lauren. You're all Charlie has right now.

Lauren grabbed the tire iron, raked it over the remaining glass still hanging in the window, and climbed inside.

"What are you doing?" Ford Guy asked.

"I have to get my bag." Somehow she managed to pry up part of the collapsed roof just enough to feel her get-home bag in the rear of the SUV. Lauren tugged and pulled on the bag until it was partially exposed, but try as she might, she couldn't yank the bag free of the tangled metal. Unwilling to abandon its contents, she unclipped the extra keys she carried from her pack and hammer-fisted the dangling kubaton, allowing the three rings of keys to dangle between her thumb and index finger. She had the Munio keychain for self-defense when she couldn't carry her revolver in places like the airport and the courthouse.

Lauren dropped the kubaton. It wasn't what she needed now. Reaching inside her pack, she found and extracted a paddle-holstered Glock 19 and two extra magazines, then wiggled her way back out of the window.

She shoved the holster paddle around Charlie's belt and inside the waist band of his jeans, then dropped the two magazines into his front pockets. "Remember your gun safety training. Never take this off."

Charlie nodded.

"Whoa! What's that for?" the young girl asked, backing away. "You two are loaded for bear!"

Lauren ignored her, unholstered Charlie's pistol, racked the slide to chamber a round and re-holstered it. She would have felt better about their chances if she could retrieve the entire get-home bag, but there was no way of prying it out.

"So, what are we supposed to do now?" the young girl asked.

"Do you live in town?" Lauren asked.

"Yes."

"I'd start walking home, then."

"But my boyfriend went to get help."

"Leave him a note," Ford Guy said as he turned back toward his truck.

Lauren hurried to Charlie's side. She took his hand in hers. "Deep breaths, Charlie. Like this." She inhaled deeply and slowly, and then exhaled. He attempted to do the same. However, deep breathing alone wasn't going to help him. There was no point in waiting for help that would likely never come. They had to get moving. Lauren glanced down at Charlie's feet. Thankfully, he was wearing running shoes and not open toe sandals. Lauren stepped onto the roadway. "We should go."

"Go where?" Charlie asked, gasping.

She pointed north. "We have to get you to the hospital."

FIVE

Billy Mahon

Corbin Industries Headquarters
Johnson City, Tennessee
Day of Event

After being summoned to Corbin Industries by the boss's assistant, Billy Mahon expected an ass-chewing. He'd never been to the office before. As far as Billy knew, the boss wanted to keep his connection to the company on the down-low.

"Emmet will be right with you," the secretary said as she placed the water bottle down next to him.

The door to the old man's office was open just enough for Billy to see Corbin sitting behind his desk. Billy envisioned himself sitting in that chair someday if his plans worked out.

Although Preston Corbin was in his early eighties, he still worked six days per week. Preston was all about making money—he lived and breathed it, but he didn't really have a choice at the moment. With his only son in jail awaiting trial for murder, Preston had to keep his father's business running smoothly.

He picked up the receiver on the black rotary phone and pushed the button to buzz his secretary. "Lisa, where's my paper?"

"Emmet is bringing it in now, sir."

Preston's assistant, Emmet Pollard, was a punk. Preston would bark orders, and Emmet would piss his pants. The family had employed him for over forty years. He'd been hired when the family patriarch, Thomas Corbin, controlled the business.

Thomas had started in construction before getting his own firm off the ground. The business grew and expanded into land development and eventually to banking and investment. Under Preston Corbin, the company had expanded into even more lucrative trades, such as drug dealing and sex trafficking—Billy's specialty. He was responsible for Preston's success, he thought. Someday, Billy planned to cash in and cut the Corbins out of his enterprise.

"Tell him to hurry it up—and get Nigel's lawyer on the phone."

"Yes, sir," the secretary said.

Emmet Pollard ran past Billy and cautiously approached the oversized mahogany desk. "Your paper, sir."

"What took you so long? I've been here for twenty minutes."

"I'm sorry, sir. I was on the phone."

"Did you call our guy in Unicoi?"

"Yes, sir. He's in the lobby."

"What excuse is the lowlife making today for his ineptitude? If he can't find a way to deal with one stupid broad, why are we trusting him to handle our Interstate 26 operation? Wait, don't tell me. It was that damn female mayor again."

Ineptitude? He must be talking about his son, Nigel. At least I haven't killed a girl and left a witness.

"What was the phone call about? Tell me it wasn't more trouble with that Unicoi mayor?" Corbin asked.

"It wasn't about the Unicoi mayor, not specifically," Emmet said.

"Well, what then?" Preston asked, unfolding his copy of the Wall Street Journal and spreading it across his empty desktop.

"It's her husband, the ex-cop—the DA sent him down to Atlanta to locate Nigel's girlfriend." Emmet took two steps back and stood behind the leather club chair in front of the desk.

"That girl is still alive? Do I need to fire the lot of you and find someone who knows how to get a job done? For Pete's sake, you boys are letting a couple of little women lead you around by the nose." Preston's face was flush with anger. "You sure you even got a pair of balls in those drawers of yours?" He pounded a wrinkled fist on his desk, stood, and pointed to the oversized, ornately carved wooden door. "Get out there and kill that girl before the cop finds her. Kill them both. I want this mess with Nigel over and my boy home by the end of the week, or heads will roll."

Emmet was already backing away before Preston had finished his sentence. He would probably have to head straight to the bathroom to change his panties. Emmet stood in the doorway. "Yes, sir. I have the Russo brothers down there now. I expect to hear from them at any moment."

The Russo brothers? Those dudes don't play. That girl is as good as dead.

"You better."

Emmet turned and exited without closing the door. Preston called out. "Send Herbert Mooney's boys, too. I want this over today."

"You said...."

"I don't care what I said. I don't care if it connects back to Herbert. We'll burn him if it does. I want results. Mooney's boys get results."

"I'll go make the call, sir."

Emmet ran back past Billy without acknowledging he was still sitting there. Billy was okay with that. He was enjoying the show.

The secretary's phone rang. She placed the call on hold and then pushed the intercom button. The intercom buzzed in Preston's office, and he picked up the receiver. "What?" he yelled into the phone.

"Sir, I have Mitch Kenner on the line for you," the secretary said.

"Who the hell is Mitch Kenner? Does he have an appointment?"

"Mr. Kenner is your son's attorney, sir. You asked to speak to him."

"Oh, right. Put him through," Preston said.

"Mr. Corbin. This is Mitch Kenner. What can I do for you, sir?" Preston had put the call on speaker, and it was loud enough for half the town to hear. So much for attorney-client privilege.

"You can get my son out of that jail and back home to his mother. That's what the hell you can do for me. That's what I'm paying you for, isn't it? What the hell is your problem?"

"I'm working on it, sir. These things take time and...."

"I'm not paying you for excuses, Kenner. I'm paying you for results. You do whatever the hell you have to do, but you best have my boy home by the end of the week. Are we clear?"

"Yes, sir."

"Kenner, I want something done with the lady mayor in Unicoi. She's hurting my business there and impeding the expansion of my operations along the I-26 corridor."

"I'm not sure what I can...."

"You're a creative guy. Come up with something. If you can't, I'll have to call for help. Help is expensive. If I have to call someone else to do the job, it will come out of your fee."

"Understood, sir. I'll take care of it."

"Good. That's what I like to hear." Preston took a long sip of his coffee. "Now, how's your mother?"

Billy was growing bored. He stood and stared out the window, admiring how the sun shone off the tank of his Harley Davidson.

The secretary's phone rang and she picked it up and listened. "Emmet will see you now, Billy," she said.

Billy winked at her and strode across the hallway to Emmet's office. It was more of a closet compared to the old man's space.

"Have a seat, Billy," Emmet said.

Billy strolled across the room and slid into a chair across from Emmet. "Trouble in Atlanta?" Billy asked.

"Nothing we can't handle. I've brought you in today because after meeting with the accountant, it appears that your first-quarter earnings were down by twenty percent. The boss is going to want to know why."

Billy stared back over the desk and lied through his teeth. He couldn't tell him that earnings were actually up thirty-five percent but that he'd taken his commission off the top. Billy had invested it in a new enterprise with new partners. Everything was coming together for him. Soon, he'd own the I-26 corridor, not the Corbins. For now, though, he'd play along. "Well, the cops are breathing down my neck because of Nigel's murder investigation. Cops hanging around scares off customers."

"We're handling that." Emmet stood. He'd changed out of his khaki pants and put on a pair of blue dress pants. Billy suppressed a chuckle. "It will be over soon. You better find a way to make up the lost revenue, or you'll be out of a job."

Out of a job was slang for dead, but Billy wasn't worried. He and his new partner, Stuart Russo, were going to make their move soon, and Emmet would be the one out of a job.

SIX

Lauren

Highway 129
Knoxville, Tennessee
Day of Event

"Which way are you two headed?" Ford Guy asked as they walked past his truck.

"East." Ford Guy seemed nice enough, and he'd saved Charlie's life, but Lauren didn't know him and she wasn't about to tell him where she lived. She heard Sam's voice in her head. Operational Security means you don't give away details about where you are, where you're going, or what you have.

"I'm headed east too," Ford Guy said.

Charlie stared back at her with pleading eyes, his chest heaving in and out with each breath. If he collapsed, she wasn't sure how she'd carry the teenager all the way to the hospital on her own. Despite her misgivings about the stranger, she needed him. Charlie's life could depend on it.

"It's a public road," she said, stepping onto the roadway. Her perception of him thus far was mixed. He'd handled himself well in the immediate emergency, but things were different now that they understood the gravity of the situation.

Lauren and Charlie walked side by side except when they needed to avoid vehicles. Ford Guy walked several paces ahead of them, his arms swinging like he was power walking. A few other travelers had decided to abandon their cars and head out on foot, likely to get away from the plane and the smoke. They were all walking quickly, heads down.

They walked past people with shrapnel injuries from the plane, others with charred skin and torn, scorched clothing. Had they been on the plane or in the automobiles crushed by it? Lauren couldn't tell. The highway was filled with twisted metal, chunks of broken sections of the cabin, suitcases and carry-on bags, and fabric and wiring were everywhere. Pieces of paper flew around in the air. Clothing was strewn everywhere. Computers, books, makeup kits, and all types of personal belongings littered the roadway stretching for at least a mile.

Cars had been sheared in two. In the back seat of one, a small child was still buckled into his car seat. He wasn't moving. His head rested against his chest. Blood covered his shirt. Ford Guy ran over, reached in and checked for a pulse. Without a word, he stepped back and kept on walking. It was a heart-wrenching scene beyond anything Lauren had ever witnessed. There were bodies everywhere. Some were still strapped upside down in their seats, dangling from the plane, their charred arms reaching toward the ground.

A few bystanders moved from body to body, checking for signs of life, but no one had survived. Charlie stared at them as they passed. Lauren thought to shield him, but death was everywhere. The only thing she could do now was get him away from there as fast as possible.

As they got farther from the plane, more people had given up on help arriving and had taken off on foot. Those who still remained with the vehicles sat with their doors open, fanning themselves with anything they could find. Their expressions ranged from bewildered to frightened, much like her criminal clients' had back in her public defender days. Even the big guys who thought they were badasses looked the exact same way when they heard their guilty verdicts.

Babies cried, small children bounced in back seats, an elderly man fanned his wife with a folded newspaper. Lauren stopped making eye contact with people. She couldn't bear the thought of telling them that help wasn't coming.

As Lauren stepped around two vehicles jumbled together in the middle of the roadway, she glanced back at her crumpled Honda. Past it was the remainder of the burning plane. She glanced skyward. How many more were up there circling the airport waiting to land or crash?

We aren't safe here.

As bad as her body hurt, they needed to get as far from there as possible.

Lauren touched Charlie's shoulder. "How's your breathing?"

"About the same," Charlie said.

"You're taking deep breaths, right?"

"Trying."

How long did he have? Lauren was trying to remain calm, but as the minutes passed, Charlie's need for help grew. She took his hand and sped past Ford Guy. A second later, he was by her side. "You sure pushing him like this is a good idea?"

"Charlie needs medical attention. He lost his inhaler. Besides, I'm not sticking around waiting for another plane to drop from the sky," Lauren said. Her head was pounding and blood dripped down her face as they walked north, weaving in and out around stalled cars. Charlie was holding his chest. Neither of them could keep up this pace, but she wasn't sure what a safe distance from the airport was or how far it was to a pharmacy or hospital. The incline as they approached the Tennessee River was too much for Charlie. He had to stop every few feet to catch his breath.

"It's not much farther. The hospital is just ahead," Ford Guy said.

Lauren knew it was more like a mile or more. She wished she was strong enough to carry Charlie. She feared she might have to before they reached help. When she saw the sign for the University of Tennessee Medical Center, she pointed to it. "There. Hold on, Charlie. We're going to get you fixed up."

Lauren looked around to see whether anyone was near enough to see her ditch the pistols she and Charlie carried. She didn't want to be stopped by security guards for carrying weapons into the hospital. "Charlie, I'm going to take your pistol from you," she said. Lauren removed the paddle holster holding Charlie's 9mm from his belt and shoved it, along with her tooled holster and pistol, into a storm drain. "Come on—let's go," she said, grabbing Charlie's hand.

The red brick building appeared in the distance on the other side of the Tennessee river. She breathed a sigh of relief at the sign for the children's hospital as they crossed the bridge. Then she gasped as they approached the emergency room entrance. Dozens of people stood out front blocking the double door entrance. Injured adults as well as children sat on the curb waiting to be allowed inside for treatment.

"Stick close, Charlie," Lauren said, taking his hand.

"I'll make a hole; you get him inside," Ford Guy said.

He stepped in front of them, pushing a middle-aged man out of the way. "Pardon me. Excuse me."

They made it to the door, only to discover that the dark hallway was packed as well. Ford Guy peered back and began making his way through the crowd.

"Wait your turn," a young mother said. In her arms, she held a young girl with a gash above her left brow. "We have a kid having an asthma attack," Lauren shouted. "Let us through, damn it."

Lauren wrapped her arms around Charlie's shoulder and

shoved her way through to the nurses' station. "My son is having an asthma attack."

The short, thin woman behind the counter told her someone would be right with them. Lauren glanced over at Charlie. His head bobbed as he struggled to take in air. He was running out of time. "He needs a doctor now!" she said, rounding the counter and pulling Charlie with her. Ford Guy was right on their heels.

The receptionist grabbed Lauren's arm. Lauren glanced down at the woman's hand. "Do you want to keep that hand?"

"All the doctors are busy with other patients. If you'll just take a seat and...." She stopped herself. There were no seats left to take.

"Where are the nurses? He needs help now. He is struggling to breathe." Lauren didn't wait for a reply. She pushed on down the dark corridor, through a set of double doors, and pulled back curtains until she found a fifty-something nurse in cartoon character scrubs. Lauren grabbed her arm. She tried to pull away.

"My son is having an asthma attack. He needs attention now." Lauren shoved Charlie into the nurse's arms. He was gasping for air. The nurse's gaze shifted from the tiny patient in the bed with a piece of glass stuck in her foot to Charlie. A second later, the nurse rounded the bed and starting opening drawers. "Take a seat in that chair."

Lauren stood beside Charlie. Ford Guy took a position in the doorway with his back against the wall while he stared down the hall, the tire iron tucked in his armpit. The chaotic situation at the medical center had him on edge, too.

The nurse pressed a handheld mesh nebulizer to Charlie's face and dispensed the super-fine particles into his bronchi and lungs. Luckily the device functioned when she switched it on. Within one minute, Lauren could already see a difference in Charlie's breathing. The furrows in his brow eased and the retractions of his chest nearly ceased. They'd made it to the hospital in time to save him. She felt bad for all the other parents out there who wouldn't be that lucky.

Children cried down the row of emergency room beds, and parents shouted for someone to attend to them. Lauren wasn't sure whether the events near the airport had brought so many people seeking help or whether it had been other things. Did they need to be worried about biological or chemical weapons, too? How would they know, without communications coming back online?

Lauren touched Charlie's hand. "Are you feeling better?"

He nodded.

"We're going to need a couple of inhalers," Lauren said as the nurse walked by again. She plucked two from her shirt pocket, tossed them to Lauren without a word, and disappeared behind the curtain across the hall. Charlie stood.

"We'll stay here as long as you need, Charlie."

"I'm feeling better," he said. He turned and set the nebulizer on the chair behind him.

"No, let's take it with us," Lauren said.

"But...."

Lauren walked over and snatched it from the chair. "You may need it again."

People were growing desperate as the medical staff became more and more overwhelmed with patients. Not just children, but adults, all in need of treatment. Gurneys lined the hallways as the staff triaged patients and dealt with the most critical first. Ford Guy made a path through the crowd again as they tried to locate the exit.

At the end of the dimly lit corridor was a man dressed in a suit jacket and expensive shoes. He was holding a towel to his head with one hand and his gut with the other when a man carrying a bloody child shoved him out of the way and ran toward a set of double doors. The father struck the door with the palm of his hand, but it didn't open. He yanked on the handle, rattling the doors, but they held firm. He placed the child on the floor and pounded with both fists. "Open these damn doors. My baby needs help. She's going to bleed to death out here."

A second later, a man in scrubs rushed down the hall and grabbed the man's arm. "Stop. They're in surgery. Let me help."

"Are you a doctor?" the man asked, hope in his voice.

"No. I'll show you to the receptionist and she can get you a nurse."

"You aren't a nurse?"

"No. I'm an x-ray technician."

Ford Guy tugged on Lauren's arm. "This way."

They exited through a side door and onto the main street leading back to the interstate. People needing medical treatment blocked their way and were pushing and shoving each other trying to get into the hospital. Several fistfights had broken out.

"He's got a knife," a young woman yelled, and the group scattered, revealing a teenage boy with a little girl on his back. He was holding a kitchen knife out in front of him, waving it back and forth. Lauren and Charlie stepped aside and let him pass. The boy glanced back as he opened the door and went inside. "My sister's sick. She can't breathe. She has asthma."

"Wait," Charlie said, stepping back onto the walkway.

"Charlie, no!" Lauren said, reaching for him.

It was too late. He closed the distance and approached the other teen. "Here. I have asthma, too." He handed the boy the nebulizer and one of the inhalers. "They can't help her in there. It's crazy. Take her home and keep her calm," Charlie said.

The boy nodded and thanked him. Lauren couldn't help but feel proud that Charlie was so compassionate, but he'd now risked his own life. She prayed the inhaler would be enough to stave off another major episode. If he had another attack, they wouldn't be able to find a second nebulizer. They had supplies at home. They just had to keep him healthy until they got there. "Come on, Charlie. Let's go back and pick up our weapons from the storm drain and get back on the interstate," Lauren said, gently putting her hand on his shoulder.

"Yeah. We need to get out of here before things really explode," Ford Guy said.

Lauren and Charlie followed Ford Guy back across the Tennessee River to the storm drain, where they gathered their weapons, then walked up the on-ramp of Interstate 40, heading northeast. The lack of mechanical noise was eerie. Lauren was amazed at how unsettling it was. It was so foreign and ominous. It reminded her of her time on the Appalachian Trail in her gap year between college and law school. But they weren't in the middle of a forest or on top of a mountain range. They were on a highly trafficked interstate in the heart of Knoxville, Tennessee—a city of almost two hundred thousand people. Soon, it would be a city of two hundred thousand desperate people. She didn't plan on being around there at that point.

SEVEN

Sam

Midtown
Atlanta, Georgia
Day of Event

After skirting the historic Oakland cemetery, the final resting place of many of Atlanta's most famous residents, Sam and Tara weaved through neighborhoods, pushing north toward the police station and safety for Tara.

Sam stopped once more to check his map. "We'll have to cross the railroad tracks to get to Little Five Points. We're going to be exposed. It's dangerous, but we'll take the tunnel."

"What tunnel?" Tara said.

"Krog Street Tunnel. We'll cross Cabbagetown Park and then slip into the tunnel."

Tara nodded.

Across from the park, the street intersected with the graffiti-tagged tunnel. The entrance was blocked with stalled cars. Covered in colorful graffiti-style street art, there was barely an inch of unpainted space on the walls, ceiling, and floor. Sam stopped beside an SUV and surveyed the scene. People were milling about outside their cars. He took Tara's hand and was about to cross the intersection when multiple bullets flew past them and into the side of the SUV. The people near the tunnel all dove for cover at the sound of the gunfire. A young man peeked out from behind a silver Prius. Sam quickly rolled onto his knees and returned fire, then scrambled to his feet.

"Run, Tara, get to the tunnel," Sam yelled, helping her to get moving.

Sam spun around and fired two more shots, causing Corbin's goons to hit the ground. He didn't wait around to see whether his bullets had struck them. He ran as fast as he could into the dimly lit tunnel.

The crowd at the entrance screamed as more gunfire echoed through the underpass. Sam and Tara dashed to the opposite side.

"Let's go," Sam said as he and Tara exited the tunnel and found themselves at an intersection. Without glancing back, they crossed the intersection and ran north another block before heading northeast toward the police station.

Sam set a pace that he thought Tara could manage, and they arrived at the police station in about an hour. The waiting room was standing room only, and the parking lot just outside was packed with people. When the power had gone out and communications and vehicles had ceased to function, frightened civilians had apparently turned to the police for help, just like Sam had predicted.

"We'll be right with you," said the desk sergeant behind the glass, who was busy trying to respond to two very animated people. Sam waited a few seconds, spotted Laverick behind the desk sergeant, and said too forcefully, "I need to speak with Detective Joe Laverick—he's right there behind you. Buzz me in."

The desk sergeant turned toward Sam and gave him a stern stare. "I can't. No electricity." The sergeant called the detective's name and a moment later, the glass door opened.

"Joe, this is Tara Hobbs, the witness we discussed."

"Nice to meet you, Tara. I'm afraid we've gotten a bit busy today with the power out. Let's go to my office, where we can talk," Joe said.

They meandered around people as they headed toward Joe's dimly lit office. Joe raised the blinds, allowing light to enter.

"It's crazy out there," Joe said, jutting a thumb over his shoulder. As he slid behind his desk, he pointed to the two empty chairs opposite it. "Have a seat. What can I do for you?"

Sam pulled out one of the chairs for Tara. She lowered herself onto the seat and crossed her arms over her chest, hugging herself. She was shivering. Joe removed his sports coat and handed it to her. She stared at it for a moment before wrapping it around her shoulders.

"First, I need to report a shooting," Sam said, taking a seat across from Joe.

Joe's eyes widened. "A shooting? Where was this?" he asked, grabbing for a notepad.

Sam gave Joe the address of the apartment complex. "It was one of Corbin's guys. The ones I told you about earlier. His two brothers took off after Tara, so I didn't stick around to see what condition he was in."

"We got away in Sam's truck, but they followed us," Tara added.

"I wrecked my Bronco about two miles from there. They were on top of us in seconds, firing," Sam said

"You wrecked your vehicle? Was anyone else involved?" Joe asked.

Sam didn't know. He had no memory of the crash itself. He likely had a concussion. He should be in bed letting his brain rest, but that wasn't happening.

"The Russos plowed into the side of us. The car flipped," Tara said. She turned to Sam. "I think that's when the EMP thing happened. All the cars just suddenly stopped."

"When the EMP happened?" Joe asked.

"Electromagnetic pulse. With the phones out and cars all dead, we came straight here. I could use your help. Tara needs your protection. I have to find a way to get back to Tennessee," Sam said.

"Wait. What?" Joe waved his hands in the air. "You think an EMP is what caused all this?"

"It's the only thing that makes sense." He didn't have time to explain everything to Joe. "You see how crazy things are out there."

Realizing there was no way he could just dump Tara at the police station, Sam stood and reached his hand out to her. "Joe, you're too busy here. I'm just going to take her with me."

Joe stood as Sam and Tara walked to the doorway. "You've gotta do sworn statements on everything you've just told me so we can get a case started," Joe said with his hands on his hips. "Go back to the waiting room. The desk sergeant will call your names when he gets to you. I'll give him a heads-up," Joe said.

Sam and Joe locked eyes.

"Go on," Joe said. "It's only getting busier out there."

Sam and Tara went back the way they'd come. When they neared the doorway to the waiting room, Sam turned and looked back toward Joe's office. Joe was still standing there watching them, but he raised one hand in the air as a wave as Sam and Tara entered the waiting room.

"Let's go. No one here can help us," Sam said.

Tara stood, scanning the room wide-eyed. "We're going back out there? Really?"

"We can't sit around here. We have to find some form of transportation and get the hell out of Atlanta before nightfall."

∼

"What now?" Tara asked as they sliced their way through the crowd outside the station and crossed the street.

"We're going to look up an old friend of mine. See if he can help us with our transportation problem. Last I heard, he was rebuilding vintage muscle cars."

"Where does this guy live?" Tara asked, hurrying to keep up with him.

Something he'd said recently must have changed her mind about leaving town with him. In a way, it would be best if she refused to go. It would be much quicker and easier to travel without her.

"I don't know where he lives," Sam replied.

"You don't know? How are we going to find him?"

"He works security at the CDC."

"That's six miles from here. What if he's gone when we get there?" She scanned the road crowded with people. "It looks like everyone is walking home."

"He won't leave. It's the CDC. They wouldn't leave it unguarded. It's highly likely he'll be there," Sam said.

EIGHT

Becky

Nantahala Outfitters
Franklin, North Carolina
Day of Event

Nantahala Outfitters was sparsely packed with Appalachian Trail hikers purchasing supplies for their hike. Cashier Becky Shelton was ringing up the purchases of another grungy, albeit fit-looking man in his early twenties. The man held out a credit card. Their eyes met. He smiled and held onto the card as she attempted to take it from him. A smile tugged at Becky's lips. She tucked a strand of bright blue hair behind her ear and tugged harder. Their fingers touched, and she felt electricity surge through her body.

Even with a week's worth of trail dust on him, he was a gorgeous specimen of a man. She glanced at his perfectly toned thighs. How long had it been? A year? Two years? She couldn't remember the last time she'd felt an actual attraction to anyone. Of course, she would pick a tourist, though it wasn't as if she had many options in town. This time of year, the store saw fewer thru-hikers. Most of them had already passed by Franklin. Now, they mostly saw section hikers heading out to the AT trailhead at Windy Gap. She had to take her chances on companionship where she could find it. With her bright blue hair, nose ring, and sleeve tattoos, she stood out in the community, and her "don't mess with me" vibe kept most suitors away.

Becky froze when the lights cut out, waiting for the power to come back on. The lights didn't flicker on and off again as they normally did in a power outage. Power issues were fairly common in the rural western North Carolina town. After a few seconds, it was obvious the power had a mind of its own. They would need to close the store.

Becky checked the name on the man's card—Wolf Ellison— and noticed the screen on the credit card machine was blank. "I'm sorry, Mr. Ellison. I'm gonna need cash. The reader's down."

Wolf dug into his backpack, pulled out his wallet, and peeled off two twenties and a ten. He smiled. "Keep the change."

"I can't." Becky counted out his change and pushed it into his hand. Her boss didn't allow them to accept tips.

"Must be a storm somewhere," he said.

"Must be."

"I sure hope the power is on at the hotel. I really could use a hot shower," he said.

Becky smiled. "Fingers crossed." She wanted to offer him her shower, but that would have further branded her as an undesirable in the small community. She considered slipping him her cell phone number. "We're going to need to close up, Becky," her manager said, interrupting her chance for romance.

Becky wasn't from Franklin. Her home had been deep in the Blue Ridge mountains. Love had brought her to the tourist town. Becky had fallen hard for a soldier in her brother's unit in Afghanistan, but she'd lost them both to a roadside bomb.

Even though she had married a local, Becky was still considered an outsider. She wasn't sure why she'd stayed. There just hadn't been much to go back to in her tiny Appalachian hometown.

Unlike Franklin, her home in the Shelton Laurel Valley didn't have a thriving tourist industry.

"If you get there early enough, the lodge should still have hot water for a while longer."

"Good to know," he said, sliding the cash into his pocket. "You working tomorrow?"

"I work every day," Becky said.

"Maybe I'll stop by on the way back to the trail," he said as he turned to go.

She watched him through the window as he crossed the parking lot and disappeared.

"You got cash?" She asked the next guy in line. After settling up with everyone who had cash for their purchases, she closed the store and walked up the hill to her garage apartment.

She dropped her keys on the table by the door and picked up the phone to call home. It had been days since she'd spoken to her mother. She pressed the buttons on the handheld phone but couldn't get a dial tone, so she walked into the bedroom, opened the top drawer of her nightstand, and retrieved her cell phone. She rarely carried it anymore. Why bother? Her mother was the only one she spoke to now. She wasn't sure why she even kept putting minutes on the cell phone. She pressed the button to power it up, but it was dead. Without thinking, she plugged the power cord for the phone into the wall, expecting to see the charging indicator light come on. To her surprise, it didn't.

Becky had just returned to the living room when there was a knock at the door. It startled her, and she jumped. No one visited her. Becky didn't have friends in town. She crept over and peered through the peep hole. She gasped, and her hand flew up to cover her mouth. She stumbled backward several steps, trying to think what she should do. How in the world had he found out where she lived? She smiled. She knew there had been a connection. It didn't matter how he had found her. He was there—right outside her door. All she had to do was reach down, turn the knob, and open it. It felt like she was moving in slow motion as she did just that.

"Hello," the hiker said. "The lodge was closed."

Becky stepped back, flattened herself against the open door, and arched her back in silent invitation. She held her hand out to him. "That's too bad."

NINE

Sam

Midtown
Atlanta, Georgia
Day of Event

As Sam and Tara continued north, he was starting to feel the pain from rolling his Bronco. His left elbow was throbbing and his right ankle was screaming at him with every step. They weaved in and out around stalled cars trying to avoid the bulk of the crowd on the sidewalk. They were forced to veer around vehicle wreckage and onto the sidewalk near the intersection.

As they passed a bicycle shop to their left, Sam got an idea. He grabbed Tara's hand, pushed his way through the crowd of people, and approached the door to the shop. He tried the knob, but it was locked. A man appeared in one of the aisles. In his right hand, he held a pistol. The man raised it, pointing it at Sam. Sam raised both hands in the air and backed away. The message was clear. His store was closed.

"We need to find bikes," Sam said, stepping back into the street.

"You want me to bike all the way to Tennessee? You're crazy. I'm not riding a bike two hundred miles," Tara said.

"No, just to the CDC." Sam wasn't sure how far they'd have to travel by bike. Even if Matt had a vehicle that ran and was willing to loan it to them, there was no telling how far away he lived. It was a shot in the dark, but at the moment, Matt was their best hope. If they were going to travel two hundred miles on foot, they'd need many more supplies than he carried in his get-home bag.

"What was it?" Sam asked as he led Tara back through the crowd and across the street.

"What?"

"What persuaded you to come back with me?"

Instead of answering, Tara asked him a question. "Is it all lost?"

"Life as we knew it? Probably—at least for a very long time."

"Will the lawless really take over?"

"In some places. In others, good people will do their best to prevent it. Some will succeed."

"You're no optimist, are you?" Tara said, restraining a chuckle.

"I told you. I'm a realist. As a cop, I saw the worst of human nature. I know what mankind is capable of."

"So, in your mind, there's no goodness in the world?"

"There is. It's just harder to find," Sam said. He pointed to his right. "Let's get off the street. We'll take the walking trail through the park." They weren't the only ones walking in the Atlanta heat. Unaccustomed to such high temperatures, the heat was taking its toll on Sam. It was slowing them down. Dehydration was a real danger. "Let's take a break under that shade tree there. I have some water in my pack, and I want to study this map more closely." Sam pulled out two water bottles and handed one to Tara. As they drank, Sam went over his map.

Sam heard the rustle of clothing behind him and shot to his feet, drawing his pistol as he stood. He spun, pointing it at the chest of a twenty-something man dressed in basketball shorts and a T-shirt. Beside him was a young woman holding an empty sports water bottle.

"Whoa, dude. What the hell are you doing with a gun in the park?"

This guy is clueless.

Sam lowered the weapon, pointing it at the man's feet.

"We just wanted to see if you could spare some water," he pointed to his girlfriend's water bottle. "We've been walking for a long time and we're getting dehydrated."

Tara slowly rose and stood behind Sam.

"We can't spare any water," Sam said, his eyes darting between the man and the woman.

"But you have two full bottles. That's like a liter a piece," the young woman said.

"How far away do you live from here?" Sam asked, his eyes on the man's hands.

The guy was repeatedly clenching his hands into fists. Sam raised the pistol, aiming it at the center of the man's chest. He got the message and backed up two paces.

"About two miles from here," the girl replied. "I don't think I can make it without a drink of water."

"I'm not giving you my water. You can make it two miles. It won't kill you," Sam said.

The man opened his mouth to counter him and Sam held up his left hand. "Don't! I said no. Now get the hell out of here."

With that, the young man and woman backed away and continued on their way. Sam would have gladly given them his water in different circumstances, but he and Tara still had nearly five miles to walk to the CDC and didn't even have enough water for themselves. They could easily become dehydrated in this heat. Sam couldn't afford to share his with a couple who were merely thirsty.

Tara puffed out a breath of air and leaned against a tree. "What the hell was that?"

"A precursor," Sam said.

"Precursor to what?"

"How the entitled will behave. It won't be long before we get to see how people behave when they're desperate."

"Wouldn't it have been easier to just give them some water?" Tara asked, taking a sip from her bottle.

"No. No, it wouldn't. If we gave them our water, where would we get more? We have a long, long road ahead of us. We won't make it if we start giving away our supplies, Tara."

"I don't believe it will get that bad."

"Not accepting reality will get you killed." Sam holstered his pistol and picked up his pack, stuffing the map and water bottle back inside. "Are you familiar with this park?" Sam asked.

Tara clutched her bottle to her chest. "No, why?"

"We need to find more water."

"I don't think there are any vending machines in the park."

"I'm not looking for a vending machine."

"Bathrooms?" Tara asked.

"That or a pond or other water feature."

"Pond? I'm not drinking dirty pond water."

Sam pulled out his Sawyer MINI Filter. "We'll filter the water and it'll be as clean as any tap water you've tasted. You should never drink ground water that hasn't been filtered or purified, no matter how clean it looks. You can get some nasty stomach issues from non-purified water. Luckily, I have three means to make water drinkable."

"Why can't we just get bottled water from the store?" Tara asked.

"We could, if we find one taking cash, but all the chain stores will have locked their doors the moment the lights went out."

"That Quick-Trip didn't."

"I bet they have by now. They couldn't even get their cash

drawer to open. They were dumping cash into a safe under the counter. I bet some idiot will try to rob them to take it."

Sam spotted a young man and woman in running attire walking toward them. "Hey, is there a pond or water fountain in this park?" he asked them.

The guy stepped around his girlfriend and pushed her to the edge of the path, away from Sam.

"No," he said.

"How about a bathroom?"

The woman leaned around her boyfriend. "You might find one at the golf course. It's on the opposite side of the park," she said, pointing west. Sam was heading north. It could be a wild goose chase leading them in the wrong direction.

"Thanks," Sam replied.

"Let's keep walking north. Hopefully, we'll come across something," Sam said. Time was ticking. Before they knew it, the sun would be setting. The last place he wanted to be after dark was in midtown Atlanta. They walked without talking for another mile. Then Sam broke the silence.

"How'd you get involved with the Corbins?" Sam asked.

There was a long pause before she answered. It was a touchy subject. Sam had read the statement she had made to the police. She'd been vague about their personal relationship. Sam's gut said her relationship with the Corbins had been more than she'd bargained for.

"I was a waitress at Pizza Palace. He always asked to sit in my section. He was an attractive, successful guy, so I was blown away when he asked me out."

"Did you know who he was—before he asked you out?" Sam asked. Corbin's family name bought him numerous privileges in Unicoi County. Young, pretty girls were just one of them.

"I was new to the county. When I told my friends his name, they all warned me to steer clear of him. But did I listen? No, I didn't."

"What did your friends say about him?"

"That he was a player, and he'd use me and then dump me. One of the other waitresses said he was into some kinky stuff, but that didn't bother me. I was blinded by his good looks and money. I thought I could handle him—I was such a fool."

"Did you ever learn where his family's money came from?" He sounded like a cop now. He thought that might make her clam up, but she didn't.

"I did. The grandparents made their money legitimately. It was Nigel's dad who got greedy. He made some questionable investments for quick cash that came around to bite him. He found himself in deep with some shady dudes, and now they own him. He's laundering money for them. They're running their drugs and prostitutes through businesses technically owned by the Corbins."

This was all new information for Sam. He'd been left out of that side of the Corbin case. The DA had some financial gurus working on it. He must have had that part of Tara's statement redacted to keep Nigel's defense team from learning about the deeper investigation into the Corbin family. If that came to light, it could jeopardize the whole case. Why would Coleman risk that? Sam doubted he'd ever get his answer. There'd be no trial if the shit had really hit the fan. Coleman would have bigger problems to deal with than court sanctions for withholding evidence in a murder trial. With Nigel free, Coleman had better hire some damn good security.

"Knowing all that, it was brave of you to come forward and give a statement to the police," Sam said.

"They didn't give me a choice. They were threatening to charge me with Misty's murder, too. They said I helped." Tara stopped in the middle of the sidewalk and turned to face him. "I had nothing to do with that girl's murder." Tears were streaming down her cheeks. She lowered her head. "I tried to help her get away." She turned her back to him and lifted the tail of her shirt, revealing red, angry looking stripes across her lower back. "This is what I got for it."

Sam winced, feeling pain in his gut at the sight. His heart twisted at the thought of the mental and physical pain she'd endured.

"The cops promised me protection, but all they did was put an officer outside my apartment for a few days. I got the first warning from Nigel in the form of a threat scribbled on a napkin one of his crew left on one of my tables at work. The second was days later when they killed my cat. I wasn't about to stick around until they killed me, too."

Sam could see why Tara would be hesitant to return to Unicoi County. The danger to her would likely be even greater now. Nigel would want revenge—likely against everyone involved in putting him behind bars. His father had openly made threats against the judge in the case.

They continued walking north past Colonial Revival, Craftsman, and Tudor Revival homes. Most of the area residents downtown were likely stranded there.

"Where will you go?" Sam asked.

"After we're out of the city?"

"Yeah."

"I don't know. All my folks are here or in Unicoi County." She thought for a moment. "I have an ex-boyfriend who lives in Gainesville. He's in Dubai for work right now, though." She stopped again. Sam stopped beside her.

You have an ex in Gainesville? After an extensive background search of all Tara's friends and family, Sam hadn't learned of this ex-boyfriend. If he had learned of him, maybe Corbin hadn't either.

"Did you ever tell Nigel about this guy?"

"NO! Tara hung her head. "No one knows about me and Everett. I was dating his cousin at the time and Everett was married. I'm not proud of it. I promised him I wouldn't tell anyone." She swallowed hard. "I moved to Unicoi County and he eventually divorced and took the job in Dubai."

"How will he get home? Will planes still fly?" Tara asked.

"No. I don't think they will."

She dropped her gaze.

It was too much to contemplate. The concept that someone was so far away that you might never see them again was rather foreign in the days of planes and automobiles.

Tara raised her head and looked off into the distance. "He has a couple of acres and a pond. I guess I could stay there for a while." She threw her shoulders back and continued walking.

She was thinking now—trying to form a survival plan.

"You won't make it long on your own, Tara. Even if you have everything you need at this boyfriend's place, someone bigger and stronger will come and take it from you. It could cost you your life."

Tara said nothing.

"Are you sure there is no one else—a former co-worker, school teacher, a coach, someone that might have a large family, maybe?"

"I don't know where any of them live."

"You can stay with me and my wife." The words came out before Sam had thought them through. Having her in their home would put them within the Corbins' crosshairs, but Sam was pretty sure he already was. He'd poked around in the Corbins' closets and found a few skeletons they'd like to keep quiet. He wasn't sure any of it would make a difference now with the world gone to shit.

"In Unicoi County? That's a death sentence for me, for sure. I'd rather take my chances here," Tara said.

"I'll help you get to Gainesville, then. It's on my way. It's safer to travel together."

"That's fine," Tara said.

TEN

Sam

Midtown
Atlanta, Georgia
Day of Event

The street Sam and Tara were on was well traveled, and they continued to encounter confused residents trying to make their way home from wherever they'd found themselves when the lights went out. Most walked with their heads down, refusing to make eye contact with anyone. Many people avoided eye contact with strangers in large cities out of habit. Nonetheless, Sam was suspicious by nature. He was trained to look for anything out of the ordinary. When someone stopped to talk to them, Sam was always ready to draw his weapon.

"Could you tell me where Brantly Street is?" a blonde-haired man in his forties with a foreign accent asked.

"Sorry, I don't know. I'm not from here," Sam said, and kept on walking.

The man spun and followed them. "Do you know what happened to the vehicles and mobile telephones?"

EMP. An electromagnetic pulse took out the power grid and most things with electronics." Sam continued to walk away from the man.

A second later, he was at Sam's side. Sam rested his hand on his belt buckle, ready to draw. "Where should I go for help?"

Sam stopped walking and pivoted to face him. "Sir, all I can tell you is that you need to get out of the city as fast as you can. This is not the place you want to be—it's about to get ugly here."

Sam started to walk away, but the man grabbed his arm. Sam stared down at the man's hand and unholstered his pistol, letting it rest at his side. The man's eyes grew wide, and he removed his hand from Sam's arm like he'd been stung. "Where am I to go? I'm from Norway. I was only here on business."

"I'd suggest going south. Stay away from large cities," Sam said. Sam resumed walking and this time the man didn't follow.

Tara glanced back. "He's just standing there."

"He let fear paralyze him. A lot of people will die for the same reason," Sam said.

"They'll let fear stop them from acting?" Tara asked.

"Exactly."

"This isn't much different from the streets where I'm from," Tara said. She choked back tears. "Misty Blue froze."

Sam said nothing. He'd read Tara's police statement. She'd tried to help Misty escape Nigel's house of horrors, but Misty had panicked and only Tara had gotten away. Tara slowed and Sam matched her pace. Although they couldn't afford to, Sam knew he couldn't push her. She was dealing with survivor's guilt, and he needed to get her mind into a better place. Surviving any situation began in the mind. He needed her focused on the here and now or she wouldn't have a future.

"That wasn't your fault."

Tara said nothing.

"It's not your fault that you're a fighter and a survivor. You were a hero that day," Sam continued.

She stopped walking.

"How so? Did you see what they did to her? They punished her for what I did—for me getting away."

"They're to blame for that, Tara, not you. You did nothing wrong. You had a right to live."

"Did I?" She was sobbing now. Sam had seen this in victims so often that it no longer affected him like it used to. He'd been concerned about how he would deal with feelings like these in the early days of his career. An older, more seasoned officer had told him it was part of the job. Detaching himself from those feelings didn't mean he was cold and unfeeling. It meant he had the capacity to empathize but still separate himself from it in order to function and do his job. His job wasn't to be a friend, it was to find the perpetrator and bring him or her to justice. He couldn't take away someone's trauma or pain, but he could stop it from happening to the next person—and that was his focus.

Tara crossed her arms over her chest and hugged herself. "I was wrong for ever getting involved with Nigel Corbin. I should have known."

"You should have known he was a sadistic serial killer?"

She tilted her head up, her blue eyes glistening with tears. "I knew he was a sociopath after the first date. In my heart, I knew."

"That would've prevented what happened to you, but he would've never been caught if you hadn't escaped and gone to the police."

She dropped her gaze. "That didn't help Misty."

Sam softened his tone. "No, but it saved the next girl, and the next one after that. It gave her family a chance at justice."

"Justice?" Tara dropped her chin. Her eyes bore into his. "Justice would have been if I'd blown his effing head off when I'd had the chance."

Sam placed a hand on her shoulder. He needed to calm her down. They couldn't afford a meltdown now. "We can't go back and undo what's been done, Tara, but you're stronger now. You know what you're capable of. It'll help you survive in this new world." He needed to bring her back around to the present and their current situation.

"Survive? That's all I've ever done." She turned her head, taking in the crowded street. "Now, it looks like my chance for anything more has passed."

Tara stepped into the street to avoid three people walking toward them. Sam quickened his step and walked up beside her. He took her by the forearm and led her around an SUV parked at the curb.

"Tell me about this place your ex-boyfriend has in Gainesville," Sam said, attempting to get her mind on something more positive. She needed hope. Hope was essential for the will to survive. Lack of hope would likely be the cause of the death of many in the coming months.

"I've only been there a few times. Everett moved there after his divorce. He grew up on a farm. He was trying to get back to his roots or some shit. I thought he was crazy. Who wants to get their hands dirty and play in chicken poop all day, right?"

"You said he had a pond. Are there fish in it?" Sam gestured ahead for her to keep walking.

"I don't know. Maybe." She stepped between two cars and, for a moment, disappeared from view.

Sam stepped out to catch up with her. "It would be good if there was. If not, there will be frogs and other things you can harvest to eat," Sam said.

"Harvest? Harvest frogs?"

"When you get hungry, you'll eat whatever you can find," Sam said.

"I'm not eating frogs."

Sam snorted. Three days without food and she'll be hungry enough. "Frog legs are good. They taste like chicken."

Sam nudged Tara and pointed to a house on their right. "Follow me," he said. Sam opened the gate to the three-foot wrought-iron fence surrounding a well-manicured lawn.

"Where are you going?" Tara whispered.

He pointed to a large three-tiered outdoor water fountain.

"What?" she asked.

"There's our water," Sam said, dropping his pack beside it and retrieving his Sawyer MINI filter and water bottle. "Keep an eye out for the homeowners." He wasn't likely to get shot for trespassing in this neighborhood, but he wasn't taking any chances. He filled three sixteen-ounce collapsible water pouches with the filtered water, handed one to Tara, and slid the other two into his pack.

Tara wrinkled her nose. "Are you sure this is safe to drink?"

"Hikers use this filter to drink from mud puddles," Sam said.

"Yuck!" Tara scrunched her face. "I don't think I can drink water from a dirty fountain."

"I just filtered out the stuff that will make you sick, but sometimes it still tastes off. I have some flavors you can add if you like."

"You sure?"

"I've used it hiking many times. I never got sick."

"Okay, but I sure hope we find bottled water soon."

Sam opened and held the gate for Tara. Before she could exit, Sam heard screams. "Stay down," he said, shoving Tara to the ground. "Get behind that truck." Sam unholstered his pistol and moved toward the vehicle. As they reached the back bumper, a man ran from the house next door. Under his arm was a laptop computer and in his opposite hand was a camera. A woman in her sixties ran after him, screaming for help. Normally, Sam would have run after the perp, but he wasn't risking his life for some useless electronics.

The thief made it halfway down the block before someone grabbed him. The perp dropped the camera, spun around, and produced a knife. With lightning speed, he stabbed the man several times. As the thief ran off, the man who'd tried to stop him crumpled to the ground.

"Come on—let's go," Sam said, tugging on Tara's arm.

"Should we do something?" Tara asked as they passed the man writhing in pain on the ground. The homeowner sprinted over to the injured man. She bent over him, applying pressure to his stomach. Blood oozed between her fingers.

"There is nothing we can do for him. We have to get off these streets. Things are only going to get worse."

∽

Sam quickened his pace, weaving in and out of stalled cars and pedestrians. Much to his frustration, Tara continued to lag behind him. Near the driveway to the Callanwolde Fine Art Center, he stopped and waited for her. "Tara, you need to try and keep up."

"I'm trying."

Sam took in the road behind and ahead of them, then looked down the driveway toward the art center. He wondered how long it would be before people were in the frame of mind to appreciate art again. He was pretty sure it wouldn't be lost forever. Art had been a part of the human experience since time began. It would continue in some form. People would carve, sculpt, paint, and find ways to express themselves in other ways again at some point.

"That's a real-life haunted mansion," Tara said, pointing to the Briarcliff Mansion across the street on their left. "My aunt said she saw a ghost when she worked there, back when there was a mental hospital on the grounds."

Sam said nothing. He was deep in thought about finding the supplies he'd need to make it all the way home to Tennessee.

"There are underground tunnels connecting all the buildings. They used them to move the mental patients back and forth," Tara said. As they walked past the mansion, she asked, "Do you believe in the supernatural?"

"I don't know. God is supernatural, so I guess, yes. As far as ghosts and such, no."

"They've made scary movies and TV shows there."

"It looks like it would make a good location for it," Sam said.

Continuing north, the only hint of possible trouble was gang-related graffiti on a power transformer that seemed out of place in the well-kept neighborhood. If a gang had claimed this area as their territory, someone had to be around to protect it. There was likely an apartment complex or some multi-family units nearby where they conducted their business. Sam would steer clear of areas like that. No need to borrow trouble at this point.

A light rain began to fall as they continued to make their way north toward the CDC. They were soaked to the bone by the time they reached the Fox 5 Atlanta television building. Sam stopped in the driveway. He could see the tops of the Centers for Disease Control buildings from there.

"I think we can cut through here and save some time," Sam said.

"What about the fence?" Tara asked, pointing to the four-foot-high, black, wrought-iron fence surrounding the station.

"The gate arm is up," Sam said, heading up the drive toward the gate. The barrier arm was stuck halfway up with an abandoned mid-sized sedan just beneath it. Sam ducked and went under it, spun, and held his hand out to help Tara under as well.

From there, they walked to the southeast side of the Fox 5 property and climbed over the fence, where they followed a trail down to a creek. The ground, littered with decaying leaves, was slick from recent rains, even in the heat.

"It's moving too fast for us to cross. Let's continue north and see if we can find a bridge or more shallow place to cross," Sam said.

They traveled north along the swollen creek for several minutes before reaching a road. Turning right, they encountered people milling about outside an SUV in the middle of the street.

Sam pointed to the shoulder and stepped off the roadway. The rain-soaked ground was soft, causing his boots to sink into the mud. As they approached the vehicle, the rain began pouring down, quickly soaking the ground. Sam lost traction, and they both began to slide on the slippery grass. Then Tara's feet slipped out from under her and she slid toward the swollen creek below, taking Sam with her. He struggled to hang onto Tara as they descended the incline. Sam's fingers slipped on Tara's moist skin, causing him to lose his grip on her hand. The two tried to stay on their feet but immediately began tumbling head over heels. Gravity dropped them into the swift-moving water below. Sam held tight to his pack as they were swept toward what looked like a giant water slide.

"Can you swim?" Sam yelled.

Sam saw terror in Tara's eyes as she floundered in the churning surf. She screamed as she went over the edge, dropping toward the creek below. As Sam went over, the distance he fell before crashing into the water surprised him. It must have been a ten-foot drop. The fast-moving current carried them downstream about a hundred feet or so before Sam was able to catch up to Tara and pull her ashore. Lying on the muddy bank, Tara gasped for breath between coughs and spat up water.

"It's okay. Just cough it up," Sam said. As the fluid exited her lungs, Tara began to cry. She curled into a ball, sobbing into her knees. Sam lay next to her, shielding his eyes from the rain. He was spent. He tried to think of something he could say to comfort her, but came up empty. He could tell her everything would be all right, however, that would be a lie. Sam was well aware that things would be far from all right for a long time. They may never be right again. So, all he could do was lie there and be present.

Eventually, the tears faded to sniffling. Sam glanced over and she was staring up at the grey sky. They lay quietly on the bank, staring up at the sky for several minutes. The rain eventually stopped, and the sun began to shine through the clouds.

"I'm starving. You hungry?" Sam asked.

Tara sat up. "What? We just almost died again, and this is what's on your mind?"

"Well, I haven't eaten lunch," Sam said, glancing down at his watch, a gift from his wife on their last anniversary. He was grateful it still worked—it was a wind-up, and it was waterproof. He let his arm flop down on the grassy bank. It would be dark in less than two hours. They couldn't afford to just sit there. They were in a dangerous city, and time was ticking.

Sam's head swiveled, searching for a place to climb back up the bank. He thought of how close they'd come to drowning—he would have never seen his wife and son again. He thought of Charlie and a palpable fear crept up his spine. He felt bile rise in his throat. Not being able to call his son to know whether he had made it off the plane alive was almost debilitating. His only solace was that Lauren was there at the airport. If Charlie's plane had somehow landed safely, she'd find him. She'd keep him safe and find a way to get him back to Unicoi.

What a wonderful woman.

Sam clenched his jaw to hold back his emotions. He'd make it home to them. He didn't care what he had to do to get there.

"We should go," Sam said, rising to his feet.

"I almost died. Do you think I can have a minute?" Tara said.

"We really can't afford to rest, Tara. Dwelling on things won't help, I promise."

"Do you have a family, Sam? You said you were married. Do you have kids?"

Sam didn't immediately reply. He didn't want to be outright rude, but he didn't want to discuss his family with her.

"I have a wife and son back in Tennessee."

"Do you think they're okay? I mean, are they going to be okay without electricity and stuff?"

His stomach tightened. Had they been home, they'd be in a far better position. Sam and Lauren were better prepared than most, but he knew no amount of preparation could insulate them from everything. But they weren't home—they were at the airport where he should have been, guilt reminded him once again.

"Yes, they're fine," Sam said, hoping his positive words would help to make it so. In truth, his heart had ached for them since the moment he'd left for Atlanta. Sam got to his feet and offered a hand to Tara. "Come on—let's go."

She stared at it a moment before pushing herself to her feet, brushing dirt from her factory-torn jeans, and following him up the bank and into the trees. As they went, Sam held tree branches up out of her way so she could pass under them as they progressed, but gradually Tara began falling behind again. He was pushing her too hard. They were both exhausted and he recognized they needed a break.

"You asked me for my story. What about you—what's your story?" she asked, twisting her hair to one side of her head to wring out the river water.

"I don't have a story. I'm just here to keep you safe and get you back to Tennessee." Sam again pointed toward the road. "We should...." The sound of single gunshots, followed by automatic fire, filled the air. Sam dropped to the ground, pulling Tara down with him. He rolled away from her and began searching for the shooters before realizing that the gunshots were for someone else, and no one was shooting at them.

"Where did that come from?" Tara asked, again brushing leaves and debris from her jeans.

"I don't know. It kind of sounded like it came from the direction of the CDC."

"Why would anyone be shooting there?"

"I don't know," Sam said, but it had him worried. He was already concerned with how he was going to contact his buddy, Matt. If the guards were already jumpy, he might never get close enough to ask.

"Are you sure we should go there? It doesn't sound very safe," Tara asked.

Sam needed to think of a way to ensure they weren't shot by security guards with itchy trigger fingers before they found Matt. While he dropped his pack and knelt down to open it, Tara sat on a rock and pouted.

"What are you digging for in there?"

"My badge. They won't shoot a cop."

"I thought you weren't a cop anymore."

"I have a sheriff's department law enforcement badge through the district attorney's office," Sam said, pulling it from a side pouch.

"So your plan is to run up there flashing that badge? You think they'll just open the gate and let us walk on in?" She was mocking him, but he wasn't going to let her bait him into a distraction of useless dialogue.

Sam slung his pack over his shoulder. "I am going to ask to speak to my friend. I'm not interested in going inside."

A few minutes later, she stopped in the middle of the road. "Wait a minute!" Tara said.

Sam put his hand on his pistol and scanned the area. "What is it?"

"It's not that. I want to know what happens to all the nasty germs they keep at the CDC with the electricity out. We could already be contaminated just being this close to the place."

"They have hardened generators to keep things contained—at least until the diesel runs out. By the time that happens, I plan to be far, far away from here." Sam passed her and pointed. "Let's move it. Time is ticking."

ELEVEN

Vince

Vince Wallace Residence
Unicoi, Tennessee
Day of Event

Lindsay Reynolds screeched to a halt. She had her car door open before even putting the vehicle into park.

"Where's the fire, Lindsay?" Vince Wallace joked.

"Where the hell have you been? I've been trying to reach you all day," Lindsay said, sprinting toward him.

Vince shut the hood of his 1970 Jeep Wagoneer and turned to face his on-again, off-again girlfriend. "My phone's inside on the charger. What's the emergency?"

"Emergency? Just the shit hitting the fan, that's all." She was out of breath and panting, but damn she looked good in her black leggings and hot pink crop top. Lindsay was normally fairly dramatic, but her level of distress seemed over the top—even for her.

"What happened? Did you get fired—again?" Vince wanted to

laugh. She'd recently been fired from her bank job for cussing out her boss. It was justified—the guy was a jerk—but unwise since she really needed the money. Lawyers were expensive and without cash, Lindsay would have to settle for a public defender or plead guilty to the assault charges she now faced. She had the temperament of a rattlesnake and was just as deadly.

"You really don't know?" she asked with her hands on her curvy hips. She gave him the death stare like she did when he'd forgotten their anniversary—their day-they-met anniversary. But, now, they weren't technically an item, so she didn't have any right to be upset if he had missed some supposed anniversary.

Vince wiped his greasy hands on a shop towel and stuck his thumbs through the straps of his bib overalls. "You know what, Lindsay. I'm too busy for games." He ran a hand over his close-cropped brown hair and leaned back against the fender of the Wagoneer. "I got Timmy down there manning the counter at the gun range. I need to get this belt put in and get back. I have a survival tactic training course starting this afternoon and a YouTube post to make." He had a full schedule and would have already been at the range meeting clients had he not had to unexpectedly replace a belt on his truck.

"You really don't know." This was a statement. Her expression changed from anger to sadness. "It's happened, Vince. The end of the world shit you always talk about—an EMP."

Vince chuckled for a second. But her expression said she was deadly serious. "What makes you think we've been hit by an electromagnetic pulse?"

"No phones, the electric is out, and my dad's new truck won't start."

"Did you try your car charger on the phone?" Vince wasn't ready to accept that there'd been an EMP strike—not based upon such an unreliable source.

"You should try the radio," Lindsay said.

Vince opened the door to his truck and turned the key. The engine roared to life. Vince reached in and turned the dial on the radio, expecting to hear his favorite classic rock songs playing through the speakers, but all he heard was static. He turned the dial over and over and all he heard was silence. Not picking up any radio stations was concerning, but he needed to get inside and onto his Ham radio for positive proof.

He raced inside his cabin, down the hall, and into the back room where he kept his survival gear and amateur radio station. He pulled back the chair and sat in front of his microphone. In minutes, he had his proof. The event was widespread—at least as far away as Colorado and as far north as Michigan. That was the report from the other Ham radio operators. It was time to implement their SHTF survival plan. Members of his group and those who'd taken his survival course knew what to do. Now, all he had to do was manage his freaked-out girlfriend.

Vince signed off and pushed himself away from the desk. He had things to do. Things that were time-sensitive. "I need to get to town," he said.

Shit—Sam!

His brother was in Atlanta. He'd spoken to him that morning. Sam had asked him to check in on Lauren and his son, Charlie.

Vince checked his watch.

"What time did the lights go out?"

"Somewhere around two-thirty," Lindsay said.

"Lauren went to the airport in Knoxville to pick up Charlie. His flight was due in around 3 o'clock." Vince let out a string of four-letter curse words as he raced around the house, collecting the items he would need. He changed out of his greasy coveralls and sneakers into tactical pants and pulled a black T-shirt over his hulking frame, his muscles straining against the fabric at the forearms, biceps, and chest. He holstered his open-carry Glock 17, put four spare magazines in the side pockets of his cargo pants, and grabbed his AR-15 rifle.

"Change your shoes and grab that go-bag. We need to get to town. I'm going to drop you off at Bill and Edna's, and then I'm going to find Lauren and Charlie."

Lindsay didn't question him—that was a good thing. She could be a little flaky at times, but she knew how to pull it together when it counted. She'd trained with him and Sam enough to know he couldn't waste precious time explaining things to her.

Vince reached down and pulled on the strap to the hidey-hole in the floor where he kept the safe containing his end-of-the-world-as-we-know-it cash. He punched in the combination and pulled out a wad of one-hundred-dollar bills. He peeled off five bills, placed the rest back in the safe, and closed the hide door.

"What's that for?" Lindsay asked.

"Fuel, food, ammunition, and whatever I can find to buy for cash." Vince headed toward the door. "I'll drop you off at Bill and Edna's on my way."

He was putting a large tote of supplies in the back of his truck when Lindsay exited his cabin with her pack slung over one shoulder. Her hair was pulled back into a tight bun, and her Glock 19 hung on her hip. Lindsay was in tactical mode. She was unusually quiet on the ride into town. The gravity of the situation had obviously sunk in. This was no drill. The decisions they made now could determine not only their survival but that of everyone they knew and loved.

There was virtually no traffic on the roads into Unicoi. Vince did see a few people out and about driving lawn mowers and riding bicycles, and even a rider on a horse as he got closer to town. Vince drove past Jim Horn, a local drunk who regularly drove his lawn mower into town, waved, and then turned on his blinker to make the turn into Bill and Edna Taylor's driveway.

"You taking Dave with you?" Lindsay asked.

"And Steve Armstrong, if he'll come."

"He'll come. He's never said no to you. Millie will throw a fit, but he'll go, anyway."

"We'll see." Steve was young, and he'd never seen him fall for a girl like he had with Millie. Vince would understand if he chose to sit this one out. It was a lot to ask. But Sam was his brother and Sam's wife and son were stranded in Knoxville.

TWELVE

Lauren

Interstate 40
Knoxville, Tennessee
Day of Event

Once they made it to Interstate 40, Lauren checked her watch. She was relieved to see the Seiko still worked. It was nearly six o'clock. They had maybe two or three more hours of daylight. She glanced skyward, shielding her eyes from the sun. The eighty-five-degree heat would cause them to go through the water she was carrying very quickly. They needed to find fluids or they'd dehydrate. In the next hour, they covered maybe two miles, weaving in and out of stalled traffic and trying to avoid close contact with the people milling about.

"Ford Guy," Lauren said, pointing to the Pepsi delivery truck parked on the westbound shoulder. "What do you think?"

"You got cash?"

Sam's voice in her head told her to maintain OPSEC.

"I have some," Charlie chimed in. "Mom gave me my allowance for the summer."

Lauren shot him a look. He should have remembered his father's warnings to always maintain OPSEC, though he hadn't taken many of their actual survival courses yet. She needed to have a talk with him—sooner rather than later.

"I bet the ole boy will part with a few cans for some pocket cash," Ford Guy said. "My name is Cody, by the way, and I don't drive a Ford."

Lauren pointed to the man's head. "Your hat."

He removed it and stared at the logo. "Damn!" Cody threw it to the ground like it was poisonous. "That ain't my hat. Ugh!" Blood coated the inside and was smeared on its brim. He shuddered like an arctic blast had struck him. "Mine fell off when I poked my head inside the cab of the semi to check that trucker for a pulse. I must have picked up his cap by mistake."

"You better find another hat pretty quick or that chrome dome of yours is going to look like an overripe tomato," Lauren said.

"Your mom's a comedian," Cody said.

"She's not my mom."

The words stung like acid on her skin. She wasn't his mother—it was true. She had a hard enough time just figuring out the stepmother thing, but she was in this for the long haul, and there wasn't anything she wouldn't do for him. Maybe it was the way in which he'd said it or something in his tone. Lauren dug her short fingernails into the palms of her hands. Feeling the pain, she counted to ten and then turned her attention to the task at hand. She didn't need feelings right now. She had to focus. Survive now, analyze her feelings later.

Lauren marched up to the driver's door on the Pepsi truck. A man was seated in the passenger seat with his head back and eyes closed. At first, Lauren thought he might be dead. She knocked on the window of the driver's door. He didn't stir. She knocked again —harder this time. He woke, startled and wide-eyed with his mouth open. She gestured for him to roll down the window. Pepsi

Guy threw both hands in the air. "I can't. The battery's dead. No power."

"Open the door, then." Lauren barked.

He leaned toward the driver's side, tugged on the handle, and pushed open the door. "What?"

It had already been a crappy day, so Lauren was in no mood for this type of attitude.

"Charlie?" Lauren extended her hand. "Your allowance." Charlie rushed to her side, handing her a twenty-dollar bill. "We'd like six cans of soda, please," Lauren said, holding the money out to the scrawny guy. She would have asked for more, but they didn't have a way to carry them—which was something they had to remedy very soon.

The driver stared at the cash in Lauren's hand. "Do I look like a vending machine to you, lady?" His greasy hair hung over his collar and his fingernails were dirty and needed to be trimmed. From the size of his biceps, Lauren doubted he could lift a case of soda. There must have been a shortage of delivery drivers for a company to hire this guy.

Lauren's hands balled into fists. "Take the money and give us the drinks," Lauren said, shoving the money into the guy's bony chest. The muscles in his jaw tightened. Lauren raised an eyebrow and lifted her chin. Her right hand rested on her holster as he grabbed the cash.

The driver immediately dropped his pissy attitude, took the twenty, and backed out the passenger door. He disappeared around the back of the truck without another word and returned with the drinks, handing them to Charlie and Cody. He shot Lauren a dirty look before returning to his truck. She heard the truck's roll-up door close as they walked away. It wouldn't be long before the rest of the stranded travelers discovered his merchandise and took it from him. If he was smart, he'd walk away right now.

As they popped the tops on their drinks and drank, Lauren kept her eyes open for any sort of bag to carry them in. Even a plastic shopping bag would help and give them the ability to carry more fluids. She knew caffeinated soda wasn't the best thing for hydration, especially in the summer heat. They'd need water—a lot more than the liter she carried in her get-home bag. "Charlie, keep your eyes open for a backpack, shopping bag, or anything we can use to carry stuff."

"Okay," Charlie said. He stepped over and peered inside the abandoned vehicle he was passing.

"Anything?"

"Nope," Charlie said, rejoining her on the shoulder of the road.

Cody, who was twenty feet ahead of them, stopped and peered inside the back of a pickup truck. He reached in and retrieved a short metal pipe, tossing the heavy tire iron he had been carrying. He tapped it against the palm of his hand a few times and then kept walking.

"What's he going to do with that?" Charlie asked.

"Self-defense," Lauren said.

As she and Charlie passed the truck, Charlie reached in and pulled out a piece of pipe for himself. Lauren stopped to see whether there was anything else inside that might be useful for their journey. A pry bar was wedged under a spare tire. She pulled on it, but it wouldn't budge. "Charlie, climb in there and lift that tire."

Charlie placed his two cans of soda on the ground and climbed over the tail gate. He lifted the wheel, pulled the Stanley "Fubar" free and held it up. "Whoa! This thing is cool." Charlie gripped the tool in both hands and swung it at the tire. "You gonna use it for self-defense?"

"No. I'm going to use it to smash and pry."

He gave her a questioning glance and then handed her the tool. "I think it'll do the job."

Lauren smiled. "Oh, it will do the job all right." Her gaze searched for Cody, half hoping he'd chosen to leave them behind.

Spotting him thirty yards ahead, she stepped back into the roadway.

"Should we catch up with him? You have a bad feeling about him?" Charlie asked.

Lauren didn't necessarily have a bad feeling about the man, but under the circumstances, she was leery about trusting anyone. "Do you?" she asked.

"I think he's a nice guy. He risked his life to pull me over that guardrail. He didn't have to."

"That doesn't mean we can trust him, though. Even serial killers have been described as nice people by those who knew them."

Charlie shrugged. "You think everyone will become stone-cold killers because the cars and phones died?"

Lauren picked up her pace, feeling the added weight of the Fubar in her hand. "I think people will come together at first, like back there at the wreck site. The crazy stuff will happen after they go days without food and water and then realize help isn't coming."

"What do you really think happened?" Charlie asked.

Lauren thought for a moment, trying to decide how much to tell him. He seemed shaken by what had happened, but not overly so. She wasn't sure how he'd react if she told him it could be a very long time before life resembled anything normal again. "I can't be sure, Charlie. Your dad and Uncle Vince talked about a number of scenarios. What I do know is we need to get home as fast as possible." Lauren grabbed Charlie's arm, stepped around a young couple carrying a small child, and moved to the opposite lane. She continued to examine the contents of vehicles as they passed them.

Charlie nudged her. "Cody is waving us over."

Cody held up an orange canvas tote bag with the University of Tennessee logo. "It's a twofer," he said. As they approached, he unzipped the bag and pulled out a sports drink. He handed the bottle to Charlie and then reached back in and pulled out a pair of ear buds. "We won't need these," he said and dropped them to the ground. He tossed Lauren a protein bar. "It probably smells like these smelly gym shoes."

"Nice find," Lauren said. She didn't care what it smelled like. Food was food.

"It'll help us get home," Cody said.

"How far do you have to travel?" Lauren asked.

"About forty-five miles or so. I was headed home to Bean Station."

Bean Station was about eighty miles west of Unicoi. They'd be splitting up before long.

"How about you?" Cody asked.

"Greeneville. We're headed toward Greeneville."

He cocked his head and glanced skyward. "I can walk with you to Morristown."

That would have Lauren and Charlie walking the last seventy-five miles alone. Sam would find them before then—long before then. "Okay."

"Those don't belong to you," a female voice said.

Lauren pivoted to her right.

"You took those things from that car. They're not yours. You should put them back." A woman in her early twenties wearing a University of Tennessee T-shirt stepped from between two cars. Behind her was a man in a tank top, shorts, and a pair of Nike slide sandals. Lauren hadn't seen them as she walked by. They must have been sitting on the ground on the opposite side of the line of cars.

"Yeah? Well, you should mind your own business, lady," Cody said, stuffing the items back into the tote and placing the strap over his head. He patted the bag as it hung across his chest. "Finders keepers."

The man in the sandals closed the distance between himself and Cody quickly, stopping a few feet from him. His shoulders were back and his chest was puffed out. Stressful situations like the one they were all in seemed to bring out the worst in some people. She wasn't sure whether stress was the reason this guy had decided today was the day to flex—he could have been a jerk every day.

Lauren moved to her left to get a view of the man's hands. She couldn't be sure, but he was holding something. It could have been keys, but she wasn't sure.

"That stuff doesn't belong to you. Put it back," Sandal Man said.

"Listen, bro. Why don't you go back to your Prius, chew some more gummies, and chill! This has nothing to do with you," Cody said.

The young woman rushed to her boyfriend's side. "That's stealing. When the cops get here, I'm going to give them your description. You're going to jail."

"You do whatever you like. Just leave me the hell alone."

Cody had started to turn his back on them when the woman rushed over and shoved him from behind. Cody spun, raising the steel pipe he gripped in his hand. The man leaped at Cody and wrestled him to the ground. They started rolling back and forth, each fighting for control of the pipe. The woman reared back and kicked, striking Cody in the rib cage.

"Stay here, Charlie," Lauren said, unholstering her Peacemaker. "Stop. Get off him," Lauren yelled as she approached. "Stop or I will shoot."

The two men rolled and now Cody was on top. As the woman drew a knife, the sun glinted off its blade. Her boyfriend landed a punch to the side of Cody's head as the woman raised the knife above her head.

Lauren's 357 thundered and the woman dropped to the ground. Cody and Sandal Man let go of each other, startled by the gunshot and Sandal Man rushed over to his girlfriend. He glared up at Lauren with such contempt. Sandal Man shifted his weight, intending to stand and lunge at Lauren, but Cody clocked him over the head with the steel pipe. The man fell, draped over the woman's torso.

Lauren was suddenly aware of Charlie at her side. She grabbed his arm and directed him to the space between two cars on their left. "Wait over there and don't look back, Charlie. Don't look back."

THIRTEEN

Billy Mahon

Corbin Industries Headquarters
Johnson City, Tennessee
Day of Event

When the lights went out, Billy was sitting in the lobby of Corbin Industries waiting for permission to leave. It was dark, with the only light coming from a bank of windows in the main lobby at the front of the building. His long, greasy hair was sticking to the back of his neck. He needed a stiff drink in the worst way. He could have been back at the motel throwing back a cold one, but Emmet had insisted he stick around for further instructions. But then everything went to shit.

Preston Corbin had been napping on the oversized leather sofa in his office. In the confusion after the lights went out, no one had bothered to wake him.

Preston appeared in the lobby. "Where is everyone?"

Billy didn't answer. He backed into an office supply storage room right off the lobby as Preston stepped over to Lisa's desk and picked up her phone's receiver. He put it to his ear and waited for the dial tone. He depressed the switch hook several times and still didn't hear anything. "Lisa! Emmet!" he called out.

Billy debated for several seconds whether to whack the man right then while he had the chance, but he heard footfalls coming down the hall.

Emmet came running in. "What the hell is going on here? Lisa isn't at her desk, the office is dark, and the phones aren't working," Preston barked.

Emmet grabbed Preston's arm. "Something's happened, sir. We need to get you home."

Preston yanked his arm free. "The hell you do. I'm not going anywhere until I know what's going on."

"We don't know yet, sir. All we know is the power is off all over town. The phones and cars aren't working." Emmet was out of breath and sweat beaded on his brow.

"Cars aren't working? What the hell would cause that?"

"Just speculating, sir, but it could be some high-tech Chinese weapon. A laser beam or something."

"You think some foreign entity did this?" Preston asked.

Billy cursed the Russians, Chinese, or whoever had done this. He'd been so close to having everything he wanted. Now, he'd have to switch gears and hold things together until everything returned to normal.

"I don't know what to think, sir. I just know it's got people freaked out. We need to get you home and secure."

"Bring my car around," Preston said.

"Sir, the cars aren't working," Emmet said—and he would know because he had wasted twenty minutes trying every freaking car in the parking lot.

"Well, how am I supposed to get home, then?"

"Billy's motorcycle," Emmet said.

He'd made that decision without even consulting Billy. At first, Emmet planned to take the bike from him and drive the old man home until he realized he didn't even know how to start a motorcycle.

"His what?"

"Billy's vintage motorcycle is the only vehicle that's still working, sir. He's going to drive you home."

"No, he is not. I haven't been on the back of a motorcycle since I was sixteen, but I recall how damn bumpy they are. These old bones of mine can't take that. No. You'll have to come up with something else."

"Sir, we've tried every car in our fleet, and we can't wait any longer."

"Why? Why can't we wait, Emmet?"

"Misty Blue's family was seen on their way here."

"So. Call the police chief."

"The phones are out, sir. I sent someone to the station, but there were only two officers there, and their radios weren't working to call anyone else. Sir, if you would just ride home with Billy, your security team can protect you better."

"All right, fine."

"Billy, where the hell are you?" Emmet called.

Billy stepped out of the supply closet and rushed past Corbin and Emmet. He pulled his bike to a stop in front of Preston, who was waiting at the curb. Billy nearly gagged at the thought of the old man literally breathing down his neck. One look at him, and Billy almost decided to just ride off without him.

Emmet helped Preston throw his leg over the seat and climb on behind Billy. A moment later, they were flying out of the parking lot and heading away from town. By the time Billy stopped at Preston's gated driveway, the old man was moaning in excruciating pain from having every aged bone in his body jarred from the ride. Lyle Kent, Preston's chief of security for the Corbin compound, had to manually open the gate. "Welcome home, sir."

"Get me the hell off of this thing," Corbin barked.

Kent waved over two of the security guards, and they gingerly lifted Preston from the bike and carried him up the driveway to his palatial home. They placed him on the sofa, and Kent fluffed the pillows behind Preston's back. "Lizzie, get Mr. Corbin a scotch and water!" Kent shouted.

"I hear the world has gone to shit and that girl's family wants my head."

"We aren't going to let that happen, sir."

"I want my boy home, and then I want them and everyone involved buried. Do you hear me, Kent? I want them all gone. When you've finished that, I want that trouble-making mayor in Unicoi taken care of. Get it done before things come back on."

"Yes, sir. I'll send a team to take care of the girl's family and then to the Unicoi County jail to fetch Nigel. We haven't heard anything from the teams down in Atlanta, but they reported locating the Hobbs girl just before the lights went out. That detective was with her."

"Good. Have Billy take care of that mayor so we can get things moving."

"Will do, sir. I'll send him that way now," Kent said.

Kent left the room and went outside to talk to Billy. Billy gave Kent a thumbs-up and kicked the old Harley started. "Pop-pop, potato-potato-potato," thundered the old knucklehead as Billy accelerated out of the gate, leaving the Corbin compound.

FOURTEEN

Vince

Taylor Residence
Unicoi, Tennessee
Day of Event

A shirtless Buddy French was grilling something out on his front lawn next door as Vince pulled into Sam and Lauren's driveway. He threw a hand in the air like it was just any other day. He likely thought it was just another day. Vince knew better. He also knew it was people like Buddy who would become a problem for folks in the coming days and weeks.

"I'm going in with you. I need to ask Bill something," Vince said. He put the truck into park, turned off the key, and hit the kill switch under his dash. He'd installed the kill switch right after he bought the vintage truck to keep it from being stolen. The vintage Wagoneer was a coveted collector's vehicle. It was an even hotter commodity now that all the newer vehicles weren't working.

Angela, the nurse, answered the door. She looked relieved to see them.

"We just dropped by to see if Bill and Edna were alright and if they needed anything," Lindsay said, stepping into the foyer of the Taylors' home.

"They're okay. I moved them out to the screened-in porch. It's just too hot in here for them. The generator never kicked in after the electricity went out. I tried to call, but none of the phones were working. Buddy said...."

"We know." Vince touched her arm. "Something's happened. Don't panic, but we have reason to believe that they won't come back on for a while." He didn't have time to ease her into the reality of the situation. He needed to be on the road headed toward Knoxville. "Are you good to stay here with them today? Lindsay is going to help you, but I have to go to Knoxville and get Lauren and Charlie."

Angela nodded. "Yes, but I don't understand...."

"Lindsay will explain everything. I need to have a word with Bill."

Vince left Angela and Lindsay in the foyer and made his way to the family room. Bill was in his wheelchair facing his wife. In his frail, wrinkled hand was a cardboard fan. He was waving it in front of his wife.

"Bill, Edna—how are you two doing?"

"Hey there, Vince. Nice of you to drop by. It's been a while," Bill said, turning his chair to face him.

"I just wanted to see if you needed anything. I know Lauren and Sam are out of town."

"Yeah, Sam's chasing some witness down in Atlanta, so Lauren went to pick up Charlie at the airport." Bill touched his wife's hand. "We're looking forward to having Charlie here for the summer. It's always so good to have children in the house."

"He was flying into Knoxville, right?" Vince asked.

"That's what Lauren said."

"Okay. I've gotta run. Lindsay is going to hang out with you until Lauren and Sam get back."

Bill patted his wife's hand. "That will be nice. Won't it Edna?"

"Did she get suspended from school again? She's such a bad influence on Lauren. I'm not sure we should let them be friends, Bill," Edna said.

Vince wanted to laugh. Lauren and Lindsay were quite the pair back in their school days and likely contributed to a lot of Ms. Edna's grey hairs.

"I'll see you two later," Vince said, turning toward the door.

"Vince."

"Yeah, Bill?"

"Something strange is happening, isn't it?" Bill asked.

Vince turned slowly. Bill was old, but his mind was still as sharp as a tack. He couldn't sugarcoat things for him. "I believe we've experienced an electromagnetic pulse. It could have been a coronal mass ejection, but I think we would have heard something about solar flares on the news prior to a major solar event. We've been planning for something like this, though, Bill. Sam, Lauren, and I—lots of others in the community, too. We'll get through it."

"You're going to look for Lauren, aren't you?"

"I am. Sam's driving his Bronco, so he should be back home later this evening. I'm gonna run over to the airport in Knoxville, pick up Lauren and Charlie, and probably be back here about the same time as Sam. We'll figure things out from there. Okay?"

"Sounds like a solid plan, Vince," Bill said.

"Be safe out there," Edna said.

"I intend to, ma'am."

Vince wasn't sure how much Edna understood of that conversation. Her dementia made it difficult to know.

Vince found Lindsay and Angela in the kitchen, pulling items from the refrigerator and stacking them on the table. "We're going to cook up and store as much as we can," Lindsay said as he entered the room.

"I'm heading out. Keep the doors locked and your pistol on you," Vince said.

"You know I will." Lindsay stepped in front of Vince and planted a kiss on his lips. "You don't take stupid risks out there."

"I don't do stupid," Vince said.

∽

Vince's first stop was just outside of Unicoi at his buddy Dave's home. Vince saw smoke coming from the side yard before he even pulled into the gravel driveway. Dave had the smoker going already. Vince stopped the truck in front of the huge wood-planked smokehouse. He and Dave had built the enormous walk-in smokehouse two years prior. Dave did a lot of hunting and his freezers were always full. He'd needed the huge smoker to preserve large quantities of meat if the lights ever went out for good. Dave was leaning over a folding table, poking holes in a slab of meat and running white oak sticks through it. His teenage cousin was hanging them from one of the rafters of the structure's overhang.

"Busy, I see," Vince said, getting out of his Wagoneer.

"I've got twenty pounds of pork to smoke. When the stuff in the freezer starts thawing, I'll have three hundred pounds of deer, beef, and fish to prepare, too. But you didn't come to help me. What's up?"

"Nah, I need a favor."

Dave placed the stick he held onto the table and removed his leather gloves. "What do you need?"

Dave was one of those friends you could always count on. Recently single, he'd been spending more and more time out at the gun range. Vince had put him to work teaching some of the survival classes to keep him busy and his mind off his ex-wife. Vince knew Dave would drop everything to help him.

"I need you to get your gear and take a ride to Knoxville with me."

∽

Dave donned his tactical gear and left his cousin in charge of smokehouse duties. He was in the Wagoneer and they were headed to Steve's house in less than thirty minutes.

Steve lived in a small trailer on a windy, one-lane road five miles out of town. Vince and Dave had to stop twice to push cars out of the roadway just to reach Steve's house. When they arrived, the trailer's door popped open. Steve exited carrying duffle bags in each hand.

"Where you headed?" Dave stuck his head out of the window and asked as they drove up.

"To the compound." Steve stopped and his gaze shifted from Dave to Vince. "That was the plan, right? We're all supposed to pack up and get to the compound."

"Yes, that's the plan," Vince said.

"Then what the hell are you two doing here? My truck runs."

"We need you to take a ride with us over to Knoxville," Vince said.

"Lauren?"

"Yeah."

"Millie said she'd headed there to pick up Charlie. I figured Sam would go get her."

"Sam's in Atlanta."

"Shit!" Steve said. He removed his grungy ball cap and rubbed the top of his prematurely balding head. "They've got bad timing."

"The worst," Dave replied.

"You in?" Vince asked. He didn't have time to be standing around chit-chatting.

"I guess so. I'll leave a note for Millie. She's supposed to go straight to the compound, but she might stop here first. That chick never does what I tell her," Steve said.

"You have a lot to learn about women, Steve," Dave said.

Steve laughed. "Well I sure ain't gonna learn nothing from you."

"True, dat," Dave said, cracking a smile.

Vince jabbed a thumb over his shoulder, pointing to the back seat of the Wagoneer. "Throw your shit in the back and let's get down the road already."

Two hours had passed since Vince had first learned about the EMP. Depending on how many cars blocked the road, it would take another hour and a half or more to get to Knoxville. It would be dark by then. That would make it very difficult to locate Lauren and Charlie. This mission would make spending all that extra dough on high-quality night vision goggles worth it.

Lauren was smart. She'd follow the highway, expecting Sam to come find her. She'd park herself where she could be seen from the roadway, unless things got too crazy, too quickly. Hopefully, people hadn't gotten too crazy there yet. She should be able to travel ten or twelve miles by the time he got to her. Vince knew it wasn't going to be as easy as that if he ran into trouble. But he was determined to find Lauren and Charlie and get them back to Unicoi. Failure was not an option for the Wallace brothers.

FIFTEEN

Lauren

Interstate 40
Knoxville, Tennessee
Day of Event

No one spoke as Lauren, Charlie, and Cody fast-walked, putting distance between them and the young couple they'd killed. Lauren knew she should say something to Charlie about it, but she couldn't. Her mind went blank. Some primal protective part of her psyche seemed to take over, allowing her to continue focusing on getting home and putting one foot in front of the other. All she thought of was getting Charlie to safety and making it home to her parents. No one was going to stand in the way of that goal. No one.

Lauren increased her pace but walked in a daze for the next few miles, unaware whether Charlie and Cody were following. As her feet ate up the miles, her mind replayed that fateful day when she had received the knock on the door that every cop's wife fears. She had opened the door, thinking it was a Fed Ex delivery driver, to find Sam's boss standing on her porch. She couldn't recall his exact words to her. "Is he alive?" was her question. He had survived, but his partner, Jon, had not. To her, Sam was never the same after that day. She had naturally been hesitant about him returning to the job, but Sam was a cop. He lived to hunt bad guys. He was driven to catch murderers and bring justice to grieving families. Lauren had been so relieved when he'd taken the job at the DA's office and she no longer had to fear that knock on the door. But then came the Corbin case and Tara Hobbs.

Sam, you better make it home to me.

Lauren detected movement to her right as Cody came up beside her.

"Thank you," he whispered.

She said nothing, counting her steps over and over again—one, two, three, four. One, two, three, four. Charlie sneezed, startling her. How long had he been by her side? The Colt felt heavy in her hand. She hadn't realized she was still holding it. Somewhere in the melee, she'd lost the Fubar. She holstered the weapon as she kept walking.

Cody continued his search of the abandoned vehicles they passed, seemingly unfazed by the deadly encounter. He was twenty yards ahead of Lauren and Charlie when he reached into the back hatch of an SUV, removed a gallon jug of water, and held it in the air. "Lauren, you're gonna want to see this."

Lauren and Charlie walked quickly toward the vehicle. Lauren stopped with her mouth gaping. Dozens of plastic shopping bags filled with someone's groceries filled the back seat of the vehicle. They had abandoned their car filled with at least a week's worth of food in the back. Lauren's eyes fixed on the cans of tuna. There was enough to sustain them for the entire trip home. The Lord had smiled upon them despite the sin they'd just committed. "Charlie, we need to go through those bags and take everything edible."

Charlie nodded without looking at her. Should she say something to him? Should she try to explain? Should she apologize for taking a life in front of him? Damn it, Sam! He knew she sucked with kids. A lump formed in her throat. For a second, fear that she'd never see Sam again washed over her. How would she possibly raise his son without him?

"This is a good haul, huh?" Cody said, stuffing cans of peaches into his sports duffle bag.

"Yeah," was all Lauren could choke out.

She should have been more excited. They had enough resources to make it all the way to Unicoi. But she only felt numb. They were only hours into the apocalypse and she'd already killed someone. Shooting at paper targets was one thing, but actually pulling the trigger on a living, breathing person was something else. She'd heard Sam and his fellow officers talk about it in what she'd considered at the time a dispassionate manner, but now she understood. She'd made a choice. She'd chosen Cody's life over the young woman's. She'd taken a life to save a life. The woman could have killed Cody and then spun around to attack Charlie. Lauren had done what she had to do. It was the right thing, but it felt so wrong.

∼

Charlie stopped and stared at the sign indicating the exit for the Knoxville Zoo. Lauren and Sam had taken him there on one of his trips to Tennessee. He'd been so thrilled to be spending quality time with his dad.

Oh Sam, how can I do this without you?

Charlie needed his dad now more than ever. He would have to grow up fast. Fighting to survive would do that to him. What did she know about becoming a man? How could she help him grow into a man of integrity in the face of the violence he would encounter in the days, weeks, and months ahead?

"How long does it take to drive from Atlanta?" Charlie asked.

"About four hours," Lauren said.

As they continued walking, she searched for something more to say to reassure him. A few moments later, she said, "He'll come for us."

"I know."

Charlie seemed so different from the little boy she'd first met five years ago. This situation had already changed him. She could see it in his eyes.

Cody disappeared from around the front bumper of a semi-tractor-trailer. Lauren heard a scream. It was a female voice—not Cody. Charlie took two steps in that direction, but Lauren grabbed his arm. "No." Lauren wasn't willing to risk Charlie's life for Cody. She pushed Charlie behind her and moved toward the semi. Putting her back to the trailer, she continued on to the cab. As she rounded the front bumper, the feet of a man came into view followed by the rest of his tall, burly body. He was gripping the hair of a young woman. She wore blue track shorts and a white crop top. Her running shoes dragged the ground as the broad-shouldered man yanked her toward the driver's door of his rig.

"I told you to stay inside the truck."

"Help me, please!" the girl yelled.

Cody took two steps toward them. "Hey, man. What's going on here? Who is she to you?"

"Mind your own business."

Lauren flashed back to Cody's struggle with the young couple and the woman she'd killed to save him. Lauren could already see Cody had a knack for finding trouble.

"Let me go!" the girl screamed.

Lauren stepped in front of the truck. The girl glanced her way, her eyes wide and pleading. "I want to go home."

"Stay here, Charlie," Lauren said as she moved closer to the man and the girl. Now, she could see the girl was, indeed, just a kid. From her clothing, it hadn't been apparent at first. She recognized the look. She dressed like the girls who flopped at the Unicoi Inn—the young girls trafficked by Billy Mahon. But her face gave away her age. She couldn't have been more than fourteen, if that.

Rage boiled inside her. Lauren drew her revolver. Through gritted teeth, she said, "Let her go."

The man slowly released his grip on the girl's hair and raised his hands into the air. "Fine. You can have her. I was done with her, anyway." He said it as if she was property—something to use up and throw away. How else could someone do such a thing to a child?

As Lauren's anger increased, there was the weight of a hand on her shoulder. "He said she could go," Charlie said.

Lauren lowered her pistol. The animal in front of her deserved to die—she knew she would have been saving some other young girl by pulling the trigger. No doubt he was a danger to every woman he would come across from now on. She lowered the weapon, and an overwhelming sadness enveloped her. What must Charlie think of her? He was too young to understand what a man like this could do in a lawless world. These kinds of men would have to be put down without hesitation from now on.

The young girl ran over to Cody, throwing herself into his arms. Cody pushed the girl behind him and backed away from the burly truck driver, holding the steel pipe out in front of him, prepared to defend the girl. She had her white knight. He looked comfortable in the role. How far would he go to protect her? It might be hard to convince her she didn't need him, but Lauren intended to try before she ditched Cody.

"Let's go, Charlie," Lauren said, cautiously moving away from the man.

～

The girl clung to Cody and whimpered. Lauren moved to Cody's left side. "We need to get off the interstate at the next exit."

"Eleven East?"

"Yeah."

"We should stop under the overpass and take a break," Cody said.

"A short one," Lauren said, and then glanced over at Charlie. His face was flushed and sweat beaded on his forehead. He needed a break, even if she didn't. "Maybe fifteen or twenty minutes."

∼

Sitting in the shade was refreshing. Cody handed Lauren a bottle of water they'd found earlier, and she tried to drink it, but her stomach was queasy. She rolled the bottle across her forehead, searching for some relief, but found none. She opened the lid and poured the liquid into the palm of her hand, then splashed it onto her face. It felt good, but it was a waste of a precious resource. She forced herself to drink, knowing dehydration was dangerous and could happen quickly if she didn't continually hydrate.

Charlie guzzled his water and then stretched out on the ground with his hands behind his head like a pillow. Lauren watched the rise and fall of his chest. He seemed to be breathing better. She hoped it was enough to prevent another major asthma attack. He really needed his medication. Bekka had sent a three-month supply to their house two weeks prior in anticipation of Charlie's summer-long visit. Thankfully, he'd be good for a while once they reached home.

Cody handed the young girl a bottle of water. "I'm Cody. That's Lauren and Charlie. What's your name?"

She hesitated before answering. "Casey," she said, taking the bottle.

"Where are you from, Casey?" Cody asked her.

"Kentucky. Daviess County, Kentucky."

As Cody and Casey exchanged small talk, Lauren attempted to calculate the number of miles between them and Unicoi. She was already spent. She was dehydrated and her head was pounding. She felt like she'd been run over by a Mack truck.

When they returned to the road and got back on their way, inching closer and closer toward Unicoi, Lauren thought about the girls and young women being trafficked out of the Unicoi Inn. What would become of them now that the world had gone to shit? She knew one thing: Billy Mahon was going to meet justice. There was no way in hell she would allow him to remain in her town. She'd solve that problem with the two Bs—a bullet and a backhoe.

SIXTEEN

Sam

Centers for Disease Control
Atlanta, Georgia
Day of Event

As they approached the drive leading to the Centers for Disease Control campus, Sam gripped his Unicoi County credentials in his left hand, ready to show the gate guard. He expected to see the chaos or commotion that had led to the shots fired, but all seemed relatively normal. Tara wasn't convinced and walked behind him, apparently making good use of the protection she had rejected earlier.

"Samuel Wallace with the Unicoi County, Tennessee, District Attorney's office. I would like to speak with Mateo Cruz."

The guard stepped from his booth and studied Sam's ID. "Tennessee?"

"Yes," Sam responded.

"What do you want with Cruz?"

"He's a friend?"

The kid looked like he was fresh out of college, five foot ten inches and at least one hundred and ninety pounds. His gaze shifted to Sam. "He's on duty right now."

Sam released a sigh of relief. That had been among his top concerns. If Matt had had the day off, Sam would never have found him.

"I won't take much of his time. It's important."

The guard didn't seem to care.

Sam decided to lie. "It's about his family." He tried to appear solemn.

The guard thought for a moment and then stepped back into his guard shack. A moment later, a second guard appeared and ran off at a jog to the south toward the back of the campus.

"Simmons is going to try to find him for you. I'd radio, but something has disrupted the signal."

"EMP," Sam said.

"What?"

"An electromagnetic pulse."

The guard stepped closer to the fence. "How did you know about that?"

"It's the only thing that makes sense. Cars stalled, electric grid down, electronics fried. Sounds like an electromagnetic pulse to me."

The guard didn't flinch.

"Did you know about this before it happened?" Sam moved closer and put his fingers through the fence. "Were you guys warned?"

The guard stepped away. "I'm not allowed to talk about that."

They were warned ahead of time. Had the National Security Agency picked up chatter? Of course, they had.

Sam and Tara waited for several minutes before the second guard reappeared. "He's on his way." The guard moved closer. "What's it like out there? We keep hearing gunfire."

"Just a lot of confusion right now. People don't know what has happened. They're just trying to get home for the most part. After a few days, panic will set in when they realize things aren't going back to normal."

The young guard wiped sweat from his forehead. "Which way did you come from?"

"Just southwest of here a few miles," Tara said.

The guard smiled at her and looked her up and down. "I have family west of here. I was just wondering what it was like out that way."

"It's not too bad, yet."

"I can't get through to nobody."

Tara approached the fence. The guard took a step closer. "You should go home and look out for them," Tara said. "Things are getting bad and they are only gonna get worse. You know what's going to happen when the sun goes down."

"I'll get fired if I leave." He glanced back at the buildings behind him. "We can't afford for any of the shit inside there to get into the wrong hands. I best stay here and make sure no one gets through these gates."

Tara peered over the young man's shoulder. "I understand."

Sam was glad the man was able to look at the bigger picture and put others first. The headhunters had done an excellent job in recruiting this kid.

As Matt Cruz ran toward them, Tara took two steps back. Matt was even more musclebound than the last time Sam had seen him. That had been nearly eight years ago. They'd met for a reunion of sorts with other guys from their unit. They talked mostly about their time in Afghanistan and about their families. Just before saying their goodbyes, Matt had confided that he'd been struggling with nightmares. He and Sam had kept in touch, often helping each other through rough times when thoughts of ending it all came calling. They'd shared things they never spoke about to anyone else on earth—at least Sam never had. They'd lost touch after Sam made detective. The long hours and back-to-back shifts made it hard to touch base with one another. They'd emailed a few times, though—that's how Sam had known about Matt's new job at the CDC.

It was good to see Matt in the flesh again. Memories of their time in the Afghan sandbox flooded his mind as Matt ran up to greet them.

"Hey, buddy!" Sam said. Matt wasn't smiling.

"Sam?" Matt drew near to the gate. "What are you doing here?"

"I came to Atlanta on business. I'm sorry. I was going to call, but...."

"This isn't the time, Sam. It's a damn shit show around here at the moment. Things are really crazy."

"I know—the EMP."

"You know about that?"

Sam nodded. "I need your help, buddy."

"I don't know what I can do. I'm stuck here until things get back to normal."

"I hate to tell you, Matt, but things are never going back to normal. Do you know what an EMP does to things?"

Matt wore a blank expression.

"The electric grid is fried. That means the large transformers are down, and the local substations are fried. They will all have to be replaced. The computers and electronics that control everything are fried. Do you know where their replacement parts come from? China. It's going to get bad out here. Millions of people are going to die before the country recovers from this—if it recovers at all."

Matt looked like he'd been sucker punched. His skin was pale, and he looked as if he might throw up.

"I need your help, Matt. I need to get home before people realize how bad it is. You know what I mean?"

Matt was staring at the ground, thinking, then his training kicked in. Sam could see it. He was evaluating the information and attempting to form a plan. Matt's gaze flitted from the ground to Tara. He nodded. "I understand. How can I help?"

Tara hung out near the guard gate as Sam and Matt moved to the shade of the trees along the parking lot. Sam explained that they were trying to get back to Tennessee and needed transportation. Matt removed a pen from his uniform shirt pocket.

"I'll draw you a map to my house in Lawrenceville," he said.

"You should come to my place in Tennessee when you wrap things up here. We're prepared and we can survive this thing there," Sam said.

Matt peered back over his shoulder at the buildings. "I wish I could do that right now, man. I have to see this through. After, I'll come find you, if that's okay."

"Absolutely." Matt would be a great addition to their survival group.

"You got paper?" Matt asked.

Sam unsnapped a side pocket on his get-home bag, pulled out a soggy note pad and let it drop to the ground. Matt's lips formed something resembling a grin.

"Rogers, tear me off a blank sheet from the logbook," Matt yelled to the other guard. Matt drew the map, and Sam studied the drawing like his life depended upon memorizing it.

"My extra key is on top of the light near the patio door," Matt said, returning the pen to his pocket.

"A little too obvious, don't you think?" Sam said.

"My girlfriend loses hers weekly. I got tired of getting calls at work. If I didn't keep it there, she'd never get in."

Sam chuckled. "A girlfriend—good for you."

"She's real pretty too," Matt said.

Sam could tell by Matt's expression that he was serious about her.

"You're in love? And she's in love with you?"

"Pretty sure." He smiled.

"You can understand then why I'm so desperate to get home."

"Sure. Lauren's a lovely girl. Where's Charlie?"

Sam lowered his head and closed his eyes. Charlie was on a plane heading to Knoxville. Sam couldn't bring himself to think about it now. He kept telling himself that Charlie had made it to Knoxville and that he and Lauren were at home in Unicoi.

"He's in Tennessee. He arrived for his summer visit today."

"One less thing," Matt said. "At least you won't have to make a trip to Ohio to get him."

Sam had thought about that scenario many times. He knew he'd have to leave Lauren with her parents to go find Charlie had this happened during the school year. It would have been an agonizing decision even knowing that Vince and the rest of their group would look after Lauren and his in-laws.

"One less thing," Sam replied.

Matt poked a thumb over his shoulder. "What about her?"

"What about her?" Sam asked.

Matt pivoted toward Tara. "She a cop, too? She doesn't look like a cop."

"She's not. She's a witness. I came down to get her for a case I'm on."

"You planning on taking her back with you now? You said things were going to get bad."

Sam studied her. He was ashamed to admit he'd thought a time or two about leaving her behind.

"I just need to drop her off in Gainesville and then race home to Unicoi County."

"You'd definitely travel faster without her. She's a huge liability. You never know what civilians will do when bullets start flying."

"She does okay—better than some."

"You already had to use that thing?" Matt asked, pointing to Sam's pistol.

"A few times."

"It's that bad already?"

"The guy she's supposed to testify against doesn't want her to make it back to Tennessee."

"Shit! You get 'em? How many did they send?"

"Three. I got one."

"One? Then you'll have to watch your ass for the other two."

"We lost them back in Cabbagetown," Sam said. "I don't think they were able to follow."

"I hate to say this, Sam, but you need to dump that girl as soon as possible. You got a wife and kid to get home to. They're gonna need you to make it home alive."

Sam grew quiet.

"Think of Charlie. You know what it's like to grow up without an old man. Imagine trying to do that in this shit show." He waved his hand in the air.

Sam dropped his gaze and stared at a shiny object on the ground just beyond the fence.

"If you can't bring yourself to dump her ass, you better teach her to shoot real damn fast," Matt said, stepping back onto the concrete drive.

Sam glanced in Tara's direction to see whether she'd heard Matt. If she had, she didn't react as she continued her conversation with the gate guard.

"You really think old cars still run?" Matt asked.

"My Bronco did. No electronics. That old Camaro of yours might start right up."

"The car key is hanging on a hook by the back door."

A 1977 Camaro wouldn't have been Sam's first choice for a bug-out vehicle, but he knew Matt took excellent care of his high school relict. It would get him home. That's all he needed.

"The Camaro doesn't have fuel. You'll need to find some. There's a gas can in the garage somewhere, but I don't know how much fuel is in it. It won't get you far, though." Matt smiled. "Take care of her. I just got a new paint job. I don't want to find her all beat up when I get to your place."

Sam didn't ask how Matt planned to get to Tennessee since he was loaning them his only running vehicle. Sam's throat tightened. This was likely the last time he would see his friend. Sam stepped closer, doing his best to wrangle his emotions, and held out his hand. Matt grabbed it and pulled Sam into a bear hug. "You be safe out there. Don't play the effing hero, okay?" Matt focused his gaze on Tara.

"You know me. I'm no hero," Sam said. Heroes were the ones who never made it home. Sam had every intention of making it home to Lauren and Charlie.

"Yeah, bro, I know you. I know you too well. If you're going to make it home, dude, you have to close your eyes to what's going on out there on the road. Just walk away. Don't take the risk. Think of Charlie."

"I'll try."

"Say hi to Lauren and Charlie for me when you get back to Tennessee," Matt said. He turned like he was going inside the fence and then turned back. "Sam, take whatever you need from my house." Matt glanced back over his shoulder, scanning the fence line and the multistory buildings beyond. "I won't be going back there."

SEVENTEEN

Sam

Centers for Disease Control
Atlanta, Georgia
Day of Event

"So, what's the plan now?" Tara asked as they headed northwest, away from the CDC.

"The plan is we get you safely to Gainesville, if that's still where you want to go; then I head home to Unicoi County."

Sam's mind was busy planning routes to Matt's house in Johns Creek, then to Gainesville, and thinking about where to obtain fuel for the Camaro. His focus was on how to get back to his wife and son. Tara had made her decision not to return with him, and he'd respect it. From all he'd seen, he was sure her testimony would no longer be necessary to put Nigel Corbin behind bars. There would be no trial. If there was to be any justice for Misty Blue, it would likely have to come from her loved ones taking matters into their own hands now. He imagined there would be a lot of vigilante justice meted out in the vacuum left by a lack of law enforcement.

"I mean, how are we getting to your friend's house?"

"Same way we got here—walk," Sam said.

"How far is it?" Tara asked.

He stared at the hand-drawn map in his hand. "Matt said his place was about twenty miles from here."

Tara stopped walking for a moment. "That far?"

"We can make it in about seven hours, I'd say."

"You really think we can make it all the way to your friend's house on foot. How are we going to do that?"

"There are a number of ways to do that—even without electricity and technology. I'm inventorying our supplies and evaluating our options."

"How much food and water do you have in that pack?"

"Not enough, but I've got something else," he said, "Follow me." He pulled a tree branch out of the way, snuck behind a fence along the sidewalk, and pulled an M6 Air Crew Survival rifle from his pack.

"You're dangerous, you know," Tara said.

"That's good. I hope everyone we come across thinks so, too." Sam held the rifle at his side. "Now, I want you to listen to me. You don't have to like guns—but you do need to know how to use them to protect yourself, and maybe even to find yourself some dinner in the wild."

"I'm never going to shoot anyone—and I'm never going to shoot an innocent wild animal," Tara said.

"I admire your resolve, but just in case you change your mind for some strange reason, this weapon works like this. You pop it open here," Sam said, pointing to a latch on the side of the rifle. "You load rounds into each barrel here and here. It takes .410 shotgun shells here, and .22 Hornet rounds here. The rounds are kept here in the stock, and I have some more in my pack. Here—open and close the action like I just showed you."

"No way, man. Forget it," Tara said, folding her arms and shaking her head.

"All right. I'll just demonstrate for now. This is a 1911 pistol," Sam said, pulling his Commander Classic Bobtail from its holster.

"Put that thing away—are you crazy?"

"Tara, I've been trained by the military and as a police officer. I know how to use these weapons safely to protect the public. This pistol has a magazine that holds its .45 caliber rounds," he said, ejecting the magazine and showing her the rounds in it. "If you ever have a need to use this, all you have to do is point it, snick off the safety, and squeeze the trigger."

"Whatever. I'm never going to snick off shit or pull a trigger."

"Squeeze the trigger—not pull the trigger," Sam said, holstering the pistol. "I hope you never have to. I keep extra ammo for the weapons here in these pill bottles." Sam reached into his pack and withdrew two large plastic pill bottles, shook them, then tossed them back into the pack.

"Whatever."

Sam understood Tara's increasing stress was fear—anger equals fear, so he decided to change the subject. He glanced down at Tara's feet. The Y-shaped strap that was supposed to go between her toes and attach to the sole of the sandal had broken. "You can't make it like that."

She sighed. "I have to, unless you got a pair of shoes in that big ass pack, too."

"No, but I may have something to help."

Sam dropped the get-home bag to the ground and gestured for Tara to take a seat in the grass. He unclipped a small roll of duct tape from a D-ring attached to his pack. "Give me your foot. I don't want to listen to you whine all the way there."

"Wait? Why? What are you going to do with that?" Tara said, pointing to the roll of duct tape.

"Just give me your foot," Sam said.

She huffed and started to jiggle the zipper at the back of her heel. Sam bent and grabbed her foot, placed it on his thigh, and wrapped the duct tape from the top of Tara's foot around the sole of the sandal and back again, leaving the tips of her toes exposed.

"What are you doing to me?"

Sam released her foot and straightened. "Try that."

Tara stood and took a few steps. She spun around, wearing a wide grin. "It worked. My shoe isn't flapping anymore. Thank you."

Sam wished he'd thought of it earlier. It might have saved her a few blisters. "We need to find you a suitable pair of shoes." She needed running shoes like the ones he had bought for Lauren when they hiked the section of the Appalachian Trail near Unicoi.

His mind immediately went to his wife. Lauren kept a pair of get-home shoes in her car, along with her get-home bag. She'd need them both now. He chastised himself for not fighting harder to get her to drive a more EMP-proof vehicle. Lauren wouldn't hear of it, preferring all the bells and whistles of a late model SUV instead. Her argument had been that she was never more than five miles from home these days. Days like today were a rarity for them. They had rarely both been away at the same time and left her parents in the care of their nurse. She must be beside herself with worry for them.

Not knowing whether his son's plane had landed safely was killing Sam. It was nearly debilitating, but he knew from years of training how to compartmentalize and continue on with his mission. When he'd served in Afghanistan, he couldn't just pick up a phone and call home.

"Let's get going again," Sam said.

Sam turned his attention back to Tara's footwear. He'd keep an eye out for a shoe store. He reached back and retrieved his wallet, thumbed through the dollar bills, and counted. Three hundred twenty-two dollars. He had enough for a good pair of trail runners.

"You think shoe stores will be open?" Tara said, her tone sarcastic.

"Maybe. If not, there are more places to find shoes than in stores."

"Like where?"

Sam pointed to an Amazon package delivery van.

Tara scoffed.

"If we had time, it might be worth taking a look. There could be some really useful stuff inside there," Sam said.

"You're a cop and you're advocating breaking into a vehicle and stealing?"

"I not a cop anymore. My career ended the moment someone set off a nuke in the atmosphere. Now, all I am is a husband and father who's determined to get home to his family," Sam said.

"Now you know how it feels," Tara said.

Sam stopped walking. "How what feels?"

"To have to do whatever it takes to survive," Tara said.

"Before all this, people had other options. They didn't have to commit crimes to survive," Sam said.

This time, Tara stopped and spun on her heel to face Sam. Her face was contorted in anger. "You think I had other options? You think I chose to have someone own me and sell me like I wasn't even a person?"

Sam said nothing. He hadn't been thinking of Tara and her situation with the Corbins when he made the comment.

Tara continued walking, pumping her arms like doing so would get her away from him faster. "Do you think Misty Blue had other options, too?" she called over her shoulder.

That stung. Sam picked up the pace and caught up to her.

"I'm sorry. That was insensitive of me."

"You and people like you are clueless."

"I wasn't judging you, Tara."

"Sure you were. But now you're learning how it is, aren't you? You see now what it's like when there's no one to call for help and you're on your own. You do whatever it takes or you sit down and die."

"I've been there before," Sam said. He fought the flashbacks of his platoon being pinned down in a remote village by an Afghan sniper and cut off from their unit. They had been told there would be no air support, and they were on their own for the following six hours until ground forces could reach them. They were on their own. He'd done then what he needed to do to get back home to his family.

"How long do you think it will take to get to Gainesville?" Tara asked, changing the subject.

"Once we get to Matt's house and get the car running, we should be in Gainesville in an hour."

Tara looked to the sky. "It will be dark before we get to Matt's."

"Probably."

They walked in silence for several blocks. Tara was doing her best to keep up with Sam's pace, but her footwear was slowing them both down. An hour later, Sam spotted a shoe store inside a strip mall.

"There," he said, pointing. "Let's get you proper shoes."

The door was locked, but Sam could clearly see a store clerk inside. "I've got cash," Sam said, holding up his wallet. The store clerk shook his head. Sam rapped on the glass. "It won't take but five minutes. I'll pay extra." He opened the wallet and slapped a fifty-dollar bill against the window.

A few seconds later, a thin man in jeans wearing a graphic T-shirt and a baseball hat turned the lock and opened the door. Sam gestured for Tara to enter and then followed her inside the store. The clerk quickly shut the door behind them and turned the lock.

"Make it quick before someone sees you, bro. I ain't trying to get robbed today." He snatched the fifty from Sam's hand and turned to Tara's feet. "Girl, what the hell are you wearing?" He gestured for her to take a seat on a leather bench. He took her non-duct-taped shoe off and placed her foot inside the Brannock foot measuring device against the cold metal. "What kind of shoe were you looking for?"

Tara glanced up at Sam. "What kind of shoes am I looking for?"

"She needs a trail runner. You got any Altra Lone Peaks?" Sam said.

"No. I got Brooks and Hokas."

Both brands were adequate. "Let's try her in both and see which fit best," Sam said.

"I'll need you to get that mess off so I can measure both feet," the clerk said.

Sam dropped his pack, took out his pocketknife, and began cutting the tape. After measuring both of Tara's feet, the clerk disappeared into the back to retrieve the shoes.

Sam grabbed a pair of wool socks from a rack and handed them to Tara.

"Wool? This is Georgia. I can't wear those."

"You'll need them to keep from getting blisters."

Five minutes later, Tara was wearing her new Hoka Speedgoats. Sam knelt and laced them using a lacing technique called a surgeon's knot to keep her heel from slipping and her foot from sliding forward.

Tara smiled as she walked around the store, trying out her new shoes. "They feel great."

A group of teens stepped onto the sidewalk two stores over. Sam turned to the clerk. "I'd lock up and head home if I were you. It's about to get rough before long."

"Bro, this store is all I got. I worked my ass off to get where I am today. I ain't letting no thugs come take it from me now."

"Is it really worth your life?"

"I ain't got nothing else," the man said.

Sam paid the clerk, and he and Tara exited the store just as the teens approached the shoe shop. He felt sorry for the guy. He wanted to explain to him that his shoe inventory was basically worthless now. Thugs would indeed come and take them right after they put a bullet in his head. Sam ran his hand under Tara's forearm and guided her into the parking lot. He didn't look back. There was nothing he could do for the man.

A few minutes later, they stopped at an intersection while Sam checked the map. When Sam stepped off the curb, Tara grabbed his arm. "Sam."

"What is it, Tara?" he asked, thinking she had seen something he had missed.

"I'm scared."

Sam stopped and turned to face her. When he did, Tara burst into tears and collapsed in his arms. Sam felt awkward at first, unsure of what to do. But his humanity kicked in. Of course, she was scared. You'd have to be nuts not to be. The unknown could be terrifying. This unknown even had Sam rattled.

"I'm not going to lie to you, Tara. This is bad, and it's going to get a whole hell of a lot worse before it gets better." Sam took both her hands in his. "You need to come back to Tennessee with me. You can't make it here by yourself."

Tara lost it, nearly crumpling to the ground in tears. This was not what Sam needed at the moment. He had never been good at consoling victims or their family members. It was the part of the job he'd liked least. He placed his hand on her shoulder as she knelt, sobbing at his side.

"Nigel won't get to you. I promise. I won't let that happen."

"I'm not worried about Nigel—not now," Tara said.

"You aren't?"

"Misty's family will take care of him if he's released."

"What are you afraid of, then?" Sam asked, reaching down and pulling Tara to her feet.

"All the evil that will take place now that there's no one to stop it."

"You have to decide. You have to settle in your own mind whether you're going to give up or fight to survive."

Her green eyes filled with tears. "I'm going to fight. I've been fighting all my life. I don't know how to quit."

Sam smiled. "Good. Me, either." Sam's gaze swept the street ahead. "I'd appreciate it if you'd have our six and carry a pistol as we go."

Tara glance at the weapon. "I don't think so. No, you're the gun guy."

"You might change your mind if we run into more trouble."

"I doubt it," Tara said.

EIGHTEEN

Vince

Unicoi Town Hall
Unicoi, Tennessee
Day of Event

"I need to stop at city hall," Vince said, pulling the Wagoneer into the parking lot.

"What the hell for?" Dave said, turning in his seat and glaring at Steve.

"I need to talk to Millie," Vince said.

"We're taking Steve's girlfriend with us?" Dave said.

"Why would we do that?" Steve asked.

"You two sit here and watch the Wagoneer and gear. I won't be long," Vince said.

As Vince approached the building, he could hear yelling even before opening the door. Town Council members, Ralph Cross and Gretchen Rhodes, were at each other's throats.

"Well, I say we let the travel center deal with their own security issues. We have to send our officers to guard the bank and the cash advance shop," Ralph said.

Millie greeted Vince at the door. She was wearing a knee-length dress with running shoes. "I was just leaving," she said. She should have already been at the compound hours ago if she had been following the plan.

"I'm not here about that." Vince pointed down the hall. "Are all four of them in there?"

"Yes."

Without Lauren there to rein them in, there was no telling what kind of trouble those four could get the town into. But that wasn't his concern. Not yet. He knew the town's issues could eventually become their own. His most pressing concern was to get his sister-in-law back to town. She could deal with the mess.

"Who's winning?" Vince asked.

Millie raised both eyebrows. "I'm not sure."

"Steve is going with me to Knoxville to find Lauren."

"He is?" Millie asked, a look of concern on her face.

"When was the last time you spoke to Lauren?"

"This morning, before she left for Knoxville. Benny talked to her after she got there, though."

"Where is he?"

"He and the other officers headed to the truck stop," Millie said.

"Is there trouble there?"

"The travel center was having trouble with stranded motorists. They were demanding food and water."

"I dropped Lindsay off over at Bill and Edna's place. If you want to go there and wait, we'll be back when we find Lauren and Charlie," Vince said.

"Okay. Be careful." She forced a smile. "Try not to get my new boyfriend killed."

Vince wasn't in a joking mood and nothing about this mission was funny. He turned and walked out the door without acknowledging what she'd said.

Vince found Benny at the intersection of Unicoi Drive Highway 173. He and several of the locals were standing in the roadway. Park Ranger Jack Sullivan from the Watauga Ranger Station had positioned his truck in the middle of the roadway, blocking much of the road in both directions.

"Chief Avery is sitting over there at the bank," Dave said.

"I'm sure that was the first thing Ralph wanted protected. I bet Corbin's branch manager ran down to the police station the second the lights went out," Steve said.

"You think they couldn't get the vault locked back up with the electricity off?" Dave asked.

"I don't know, but with all these strangers pouring into town, I can see where they'd be concerned," Steve said.

"What they should be concerned about are the grocery stores. Pretty soon, all the money in the world won't save folks from starving to death," Vince said.

Vince stopped ten yards from the intersection and stuck his head out his driver's side window. "Benny. A word, please."

Benny said something to one of the men with him before hurrying over to Vince's Wagoneer. "Hey, Vince." He took a step back and surveyed the Wagoneer. "I see this old war wagon is running." He was eyeing it like a kid in a candy store.

"Don't get any ideas. I'm heading to Knoxville."

"You going to get Lauren and Charlie?" Benny asked, resting his hands on his duty belt.

"Yeah. Millie said you spoke with Lauren this afternoon."

"I did. We got cut off just before the lights went out and everything went crazy."

"Did she say exactly where she was?"

"Not exactly. She'd just picked up Charlie from the airport. I could hear the planes in the background."

"How much time passed between you losing cell phone

connection with Lauren and when the lights went out?" Vince asked. Depending on how fast Lauren was moving, she could have traveled quite a long way. Being able to narrow down an area would be very beneficial in locating her and Charlie.

"Well, I'd say about the same time," Benny said.

"That helps. Thanks, Benny. I'll check in with you when we get back."

"Okay. Stay safe." Benny started to turn and go.

"Hey, Benny. I'd have Rogers bring that old backhoe of his over and grab some of those jersey barriers from Unicoi Trailer. Stagger them to make a checkpoint."

"Good idea." Benny turned and headed back to the intersection, yelling Liam Rogers' name.

As Vince pulled onto the shoulder of the road, Chief Avery stood. Vince waved at him as he drove away.

"There's going to be trouble with that one," Steve said.

"I'm afraid so," Vince replied.

The bad blood between Vince and John Avery went way back. John Avery had been a bully in school, and because of his family's connections, he'd gotten away with it. Vince hadn't given a rat's ass about the Avery family or their connections. He'd put John Avery on his ass every time Avery had ever started shit with him. Vince wasn't afraid of being suspended from school or Avery's dad's threats of lawsuits. The Wallace family didn't have a pot to piss in to start with, so he wouldn't have gotten much from them.

Vince steered the Wagoneer around the park ranger's vehicle and turned onto Highway 173, heading toward the interstate. He slowed as he passed the truck stop. Just from a quick count of the vehicles and semis in the parking lot, Vince knew the town was going to have a hard time controlling that many stranded motorists.

Two men sitting on the hood of a sedan spotted the Wagoneer and hopped down from their vehicle. Vince sped up, quickly passing the truck port and nearing the Interstate. People were sitting under the Interstate 26 overpass. They stood as the Wagoneer approached.

Dave leaned out of the passenger side window. "I'd stay where you are if I were you," he yelled to them.

When the one guy in the group stepped forward, Dave brandished his pistol, resting it against the windshield pillar.

"We need to conserve ammo, Dave," Vince reminded him.

"We don't want to lose the Wagoneer before we even get out of town, do we?" Dave said.

"We won't. Put the gun away."

The man stepped back and stared at them as they passed. Vince knew the rest of the trip wouldn't be so easy. As more time passed, people would soon realize something monumental had occurred, and they'd start to panic. That was when they'd need to worry about losing the Wagoneer.

They passed a man and woman wearing backpacks and carrying trekking poles near the turn for the Pinnacle Tower trailhead. The trail led to the fire tower observation platform, which provided a three hundred and sixty-degree panoramic view of Buffalo Mountain. Vince hoped the couple had packed for more than the ten mile round-trip hike.

Vince doubted the looting had started yet in Erwin. There were lots of people in the Wal-Mart parking lot in Erwin, but they were probably waiting for someone to tell them what to do. If the police went in there with a bull horn and told everyone to start walking home, most would likely comply.

From Erwin, Vince pointed the Wagoneer southwest toward Knoxville along Highway 107. Although the number of stalled vehicles on the roadway was lighter on the two-lane roads, it was slower and more dangerous as there were no shoulders for vehicles to drive around slower traffic, causing Vince to have to go off-roading several times.

"Okay, guys. Look alive. This could get hairy," Vince said as he navigated the twists and turns of the windy road that ran along the Nolichucky River.

As Vince approached Crossroads Country Store, he slowed, scanning the parking lot, trying to determine whether there was any way to buy gas there. The store clerk and several older gentlemen were standing outside the door.

"Dave, holler at them and ask if they're selling fuel," Vince said.

"Hey, are you able to sell gasoline or diesel? We got cash," Dave asked.

"Electricity is off. The pumps aren't working," the clerk said, moving toward the truck. Vince accelerated, watching the man in his rearview mirror. He wasn't about to risk losing the Wagoneer or his cash.

They passed a large field of tomato plants. It reminded Vince of the commercial tomato farms in Unicoi. That fertile land would feed a lot of people if it was sown with the right seed. He made a mental note to address it with his group. They could harvest the tomatoes and then plant a fall garden of carrots, beets, cabbage, turnips, and anything that might keep well over the winter.

～

After coming around a tight turn, Vince was forced to slam on the brakes to avoid an elderly couple standing in the middle of the road. The man stepped in front of the woman, but they both remained in the roadway. The Wagoneer came to a stop just five feet from them.

"What are you doing, old man?" Vince yelled out of his window.

"Getting you to stop," the elderly man said.

"Get out of the way," Vince said.

The man began walking toward the vehicle.

Dave sat up straighter in his seat. "Vince?"

"Hold tight, Dave."

"I don't see no weapon," Steve said, leaning in between the seats. "Just looks like an old couple to me."

"Nothing is as it seems anymore, Steve. You better learn that quick or you're gonna get dead," Dave said.

"What do you want, sir?" Vince asked.

"Me and my missus need a ride down the road. We've been walking for two hours and she just can't go no farther. I need to get her home," the man said.

Vince glanced over at Dave and then back at Steve. Steve shrugged his shoulders. Turning back to the elderly man, Vince asked. "How far up the road?"

"About five miles. What's your name, son?"

"Vince," he said. "That's Dave, and the guy in the back giving up his seat for you two is Steve."

Steve hopped over the rear seat and sat down, leaning back on one of the duffle bags. "Nice to meet you."

They loaded up the elderly couple and headed down the road.

"I'm Ernest and this here is my wife, Mabel. Where are you boys from?"

Steve gave them a vague answer, following Vince's rule of not divulging too much information.

"We've lived at our place for nearly fifty years. It was my grand pappy's before me," Ernest said.

They rounded a tight curve about two miles down the road and were confronted with a pickup and a trailer blocking the road. A man in his late fifties had unloaded an old tractor off the trailer and was attempting to winch his newer model truck onto it. The old boy had gotten lucky. At least he had some mode of transportation to get him home. As Vince pulled into the opposite lane to pass him, the man threw a hand in the air and waved. Ernest returned the wave.

"Bobby Joe would have his hide if he left that brand new truck out on the highway," the wife said.

"He's lucky he was hauling that old tractor," Steve said.

"So what do you reckon happened? The people who passed us on the road so far all said their cars and handheld telephones weren't working. My wife's phone won't even power on now. Is it the Russian hackers?"

Vince explained his theory and what he'd gleaned from listening to the Ham radio operators. The old couple didn't seem all that upset about the prospect of returning to the old ways.

"We'll make do. We always have. We got a spring and momma's canning will last the two of us for years."

Vince didn't have the heart to tell them that someone younger and stronger would likely come and take everything from them. He knew he couldn't protect everyone. But if circumstances allowed, he'd come back for these two. They deserved to live out what life they had left in peace, rather than dying because of someone else's greed or desperation. The rest of his group might not understand his reasons for bringing in two people who seemed to have so little to contribute, but he didn't care. The knowledge the two held in their brains about how to survive without modern technology was more valuable to Vince than crates of ammo or their basement full of canning.

∽

"Take a right on that road coming up," Ernest said.

Vince took the turn and traveled nearly three miles before reaching a dead end where the road turned to dirt.

"That's us there, the driveway to the left," Ernest said.

Vince pulled the Wagoneer up between a white-clapboard house on the right and an old wooden barn on the left. He opened his door and got out to open the driver's side rear passenger door to help Mabel out of the vehicle. She was old and brittle so he took his time with the nice old woman. He held her hand and escorted her to the back of the Wagoneer, then let go. "You two take care now," Vince said as he turned, went back, and got into the driver's seat. He looked over toward the area beyond the barn. It looked like there were corrals and a hay ring for cattle, but he saw no cows. He glanced back when he heard the back passenger door shut, expecting to see Steve in the back seat. Instead, a kid no more than eleven or twelve had gotten into the vehicle and curled himself into a ball on the floorboard behind his seat. He stared up at Vince.

"What the hell are you doing, kid?" Vince asked.

"Please, mister. I just want to get out of here. Please." He drew out the syllables in a desperate tone.

"What the hell is going on here?" Vince asked.

"I'd stomp on the gas and get the hell out of here right now if I were you," the boy said.

NINETEEN

Sam

I-85 Frontage Road
South of DeKalb-Peachtree Airport
Atlanta, Georgia
Day of Event

Tara pointed. "What's that smoke from?"

"Not sure. Could be a house or business on fire," Sam said.

The smoke grew thicker and blacker as they approached the Interstate 85 overpass. There was an unusual odor. The customers at the Sam's Club warehouse just north of Interstate 85 were standing in the middle of the parking lot staring north. The woods were on fire. The smell was putrid, forcing Sam to cover his nose and mouth with the tail of his shirt.

Tara stopped near a young couple holding a child. "What's burning?"

"A small plane. It was trying to make a landing at the airport."

Sam's heart sank and his stomach flip-flopped.

Don't go there, Wallace. Charlie made it. His plane landed safely, and he's with Lauren right now.

He couldn't afford to let despair derail him. He had too many people depending on him.

"Let's double time it, Tara. We need to get away from here before another one drops."

"Mister, do you know what happened? Was it terrorists?" the young mother asked.

"Something like that. You should start walking and get home as fast as possible. Help isn't coming and things are going to get really bad very soon."

"We were attacked?" the man asked.

"I believe so." Sam turned to face the man and looked him in the eyes. "The electricity isn't coming back on anytime soon. If I were you, I'd get your lady and child out of this city as fast and far as you can."

Sam and Tara left the young couple standing there with their mouths open. They traversed the retail warehouse club's parking lot and headed east toward the Interstate 85 frontage road. Sam set a quick pace, wanting to get as far from the downed plane and the airport's flight path as possible. He occupied his frantic mind with mission planning. He thought about how they'd approach Matt's neighborhood, get into his house, and start the Camaro. The sound of the engine might attract attention from anyone nearby, but there was nothing he could do about that. He'd make sure the garage door was up and Tara was buckled in before he turned the key and started the vehicle. They'd race away from there, hopefully before anyone figured out where the sound was coming from. Next would be…

"Are you okay?" Tara asked.

"Fine. Keep walking," Sam said.

Next, he would search for fuel. That would be the tricky part. Stopping long enough to search for fuel could be deadly—for someone.

"You seem upset," Tara said. "What's wrong? I deserve to know if it puts us both in danger."

"Nothing's wrong. We just need to keep moving. I'd like to make it to Matt's before dark."

"Okay. Don't tell me then," Tara said.

She was lagging behind and it was pissing Sam off.

"I need to think. I have to figure out where to find fuel after we get the Camaro."

"That is a problem. Will gas pumps work without electricity?"

"No. We'll have to get gas from another vehicle."

"You know how to do that?" Tara asked.

"Puncture the gas tank. We'll need fuel cans."

A mile away, a small group of young men sat on the hoods of two cars outside a Mexican restaurant. "Let's cross over," Sam said, guiding Tara to a row of abandoned cars and out of sight of the men. Sureños gang graffiti tagged the concrete divider wall between the feeder road and the interstate. The Mexican gang had staked out this territory for themselves. This could be a problem should they decide to defend it against Sam and Tara.

A block away, two teens were outside a shop. One leaned against the brick wall while the other sat on a stack of wooden pallets. The one standing passed the other boy a cigarette or maybe a blunt. Sam slowed enough for Tara to catch up to him.

"Stay low and keep these vehicles between you and those kids," Sam said.

"Trouble?" Tara asked.

"Could be. I'm not taking chances."

Sam had dealt with tiny locos before. Latin gangs often used young teens to run drugs, fight, rob, even kill a rival gang member. They could be just as dangerous. Sam wasn't about to stick around and find out.

Sam led Tara from vehicle to vehicle, keeping a keen eye on the boys. He moved to the far shoulder, putting two lanes of stalled vehicles between them and the two teens, hoping they weren't spotted. A lowered GTO was sideways on the shoulder, nearly touching the retaining wall separating the frontage road from the interstate. There wasn't enough room to slip through. They had to walk around it in the open. As they did, Sam glanced back. One of the boys jumped down from the stack of pallets and took a step toward them. He nudged his companion and pointed their direction.

"Give me your hand," Sam said, reaching for Tara. "We're going to have to run." Sam attempted to weave between a pickup truck and a Jeep, but as he tugged on Tara's hand, she tripped and let loose of his hand. As he turned and bent to help her, the two teens started running toward them. Sam grabbed Tara's outstretched hand, yanked her to her feet, and put himself between the teens and Tara.

"That your piece, man? Can I see it?" the teen with the pock-marked face asked, in broken English,

Instinctively, Sam noted his physical description. Blue jersey, black jeans, five foot two, one hundred and five pounds, tanned skin, straight dark hair, dark brown eyes. Sam stopped. There would be no call for backup. He wouldn't have to put the kids' description on a police report.

Sam unholstered his pistol and pointed the weapon at the kid. "Back off." Sam didn't have time for a couple of gangbanger wannabes looking to make a name for themselves, but he didn't want to have to kill a kid either.

The husky teen produced a knife and began waving it back and forth in front of him. "You gonna shoot me, gringo?"

"Let's get out of here, Luis," the skinny kid said.

"This is our block, Juan. We can't let these gringos pass through without paying."

"He looks like a cop. Let's go. We'll go tell Marco."

"I ain't got to tell Marco nothing. I can handle this dude myself," the chubby kid said.

Juan turned and took off, running in the opposite direction.

"You should follow your friend," Sam said, keeping his eyes on Luis' hands.

The chunky teen puffed out his chest. "I ain't scared of you, gringo. I've been shot before."

"I don't want to shoot you, kid. I just want you to leave me and my friend alone."

Sam felt Tara's hand on his back. "Sam!"

The teen raised his right hand from his side to the front of his thigh.

"Don't do it, kid. Don't make me shoot you. Just back away and go find your friend."

The teen stared Sam down for a long moment before turning and running off.

"You best get out of my hood, puto," the kid called over his shoulder.

Sam exhaled loudly and relaxed his shoulders, relieved he didn't have to add killing a kid to the list of things he'd regret about this day.

After running for several blocks to put distance between themselves and the teens, Sam and Tara turned north into a more residential area. Sam slowed his pace, allowing Tara something of a break. When he spotted a bus stop bench, he crossed over, weaving between a mid-size sedan and an SUV. A door swung open and a woman and small child got out of the back passenger side of the sedan.

"Mister, do you have a phone I could use to call my husband? My child is hungry," the woman asked, lifting her child onto her hip.

Tara walked past the young mother. "Phones don't work anymore, the lights are out for good, and you should get to walking now."

The woman looked as if Tara had slapped her across the face. Instead of stopping at the bus stop, Sam kept walking. He did not need to add a mother and child to his list of responsibilities.

"People are really clueless, aren't they?" Tara said.

"They don't want to believe what's really happening. It's a bit much for the brain to handle. Don't you think?" Sam asked.

"That's an understatement. But all this is too much to ignore or explain away. You've got to know by now that something strange is going on and start to head home on your own."

"Some people freeze. They don't know what to do, so they sit and wait for someone to tell them."

"People like that won't last long," Tara said.

"Unfortunately not. But some will. After the initial shock is over, they'll rise to the occasion. Look at you." Sam smiled.

Tara wasn't smiling.

TWENTY

Vince

Highway 107
Erwin, Tennessee
Day of Event

Vince was staring at the frightened kid curled between the seats when he heard Mabel yell at him from outside his driver's window.

"Get out of the car!" the old woman spat.

Before he could turn back around, Vince caught sight of Dave in the periphery of his vision. He had his hands in the air and a shotgun at his back. Vince moved his hand from the Wagoneer's gear shift to his holster. He calculated his odds. He had no idea where Steve was, but he had to be in a similar situation from the lack of bullets flying.

"What?" he asked. "What is this about?" Vince glanced to his left. The elderly woman stood outside his door holding a 9mm pistol in her frail right hand. It shook as she spoke. Her hands may have been shaky, but her gaze was fierce. She meant business. "Okay, lady," Vince said. "Put down the pistol."

Before opening the door to exit the vehicle, Vince reached

under the dash and flicked the kill switch, disabling the Wagoneer. Unless they could figure out it had a kill switch installed—and then find it—the Wagoneer wasn't going anywhere.

Vince maintained eye contact with Mabel as he stepped out. "What's this all about?" he asked, moving to his left and shutting the door. She was less than ten feet from him.

He glanced around, searching for Steve to assess their situation further. Steve was at the rear of the Wagoneer. Mabel's husband, Ernest, pointed a revolver at Steve's chest. Vince took two steps to his left to get a clearer view of the third person—the man with the shotgun.

Vince had put his friends in this situation by trying to be a nice guy. He had to get them out of it. They still had a mission to complete. Mabel began barking orders, telling them to drop their weapons.

"Not gonna happen, lady." Vince paused, then said, "Three." Vince closed the distance between him and the woman in one smooth move. He grabbed the barrel of the pistol and twisted it to the right, causing the weapon to pop out of her hand. Vince grabbed the woman's tiny arm and yanked her toward him, pinning her right arm between his chest and her back. He turned to his left, facing Ernest, who immediately spun to face them, pointing his revolver in their direction.

Dave reacted quickly, twisting Ernest's revolver from his hand and pushing him to the ground. Vince and Dave spun toward the man with the shotgun and fired simultaneously as Steve dove to the ground. The shotgun boomed just before the man holding it dropped to the ground next to Steve.

Dave dropped to a crouch and scanned the area to his left and right. Vince spun around, searching in the area in front of the house and barn, searching for other shooters. He saw no movement. No one rushed from the residence or the barn to come to the old couple's aid. "Who else is here?" Vince asked Mabel.

"No one," she said.

"If someone comes out of that house or barn, I'm putting a bullet in your head first before I shoot them. Got it?"

"Yes," she said.

"Don't you move," Dave said to Ernest, "or I'll shoot you in the back."

"Steve?" Vince called out.

"I'm hit, Vince. The asshat shot me," Steve said.

Vince shoved the elderly woman to the ground next to her husband. "Watch them, Dave." He rushed to Steve's side, dropping to his knees in the gravel drive. Steve was holding his abdomen. Blood oozed between his fingers.

"Move your hands. Let me take a look," Vince said.

As soon as Steve moved his hands, Vince could see how bad it was. He placed Steve's hands back over the wound and applied pressure in a futile attempt to staunch the bleeding. Vince knew that even if he somehow managed to stop the blood flowing from his friend's gut, the damage to his organs and intestines would likely kill him. Without medical intervention, Steve was facing a slow, painful death.

"We need to get him to a hospital. Help me load him into the Wagoneer," Vince said.

"What do we do with these two?" Dave asked.

The Wagoneer's left passenger door opened, and the kid climbed out. He rounded the back bumper and stopped a few feet from the elderly couple. "Kill them," he said. "Kill them both."

Dave turned his gaze to Vince. "Who the hell's he?"

"Check them both for weapons and then we'll tie them up," Vince said and turned to Steve. "Just hang in there, buddy. We're going to get you back to Erwin and get you fixed up," Vince said.

"What about me?" the kid asked.

Vince didn't know what had happened there, but he couldn't let it be any of his concern at the moment. He had to get his friend to the hospital.

"What am I going to do?" the boy asked.
"Do you live here?" Vince asked.
"No, I live in Johnson City."
"Who are those people to you?"
"They kidnap kids and hold us 'til some guy comes to get us."
"There are more kids here?" Vince asked.
"Not right now. They took a girl away this morning."
"How many adults are in the house?"
"None. It was just the three of them."
"You're sure?"
"Yes," the kid said.
"He's lying!" Ernest shouted.

The kid spun around and kicked the elderly man in the ribs. "I'm not the liar, you sick asshole."

"We need to get Steve to the hospital. We'll inform the authorities there, and they can come to take care of this mess," Vince said.

"Get in the car, kid. Someone at the hospital can help you get home."

Steve cried out in pain as Vince and Dave lifted him from the ground. They loaded him into the back seat as gently as possible, but the pain proved too much, and he passed out.

"Here," Vince said, ripping a long piece of duct tape from a roll and nodding toward Ernest. "Tape his hands together like we teach." Vince ripped another long piece and secured Mabel.

"We should take Steve to Greeneville. We're closer," Dave said, jumping into the passenger seat and slamming his door as the kid climbed over Steve into the back with the duffle bags.

"Better put your seat belt on, Dave. I'm not stopping for anything," Vince said as they pulled away, leaving Ernest and Mabel tied up next to their dead friend.

∼

Steve drifted in and out of consciousness as Vince wove between stalled vehicles, pulling the Wagoneer to a stop at the hospital parking lot entrance. An ambulance blocked the emergency room entrance. Vince turned off the engine and flicked the kill switch before exiting the Wagoneer.

"Come with us, kid," Vince said. The kid hopped over the back seat, got out of the Wagoneer, and slammed the door.

Dave and Vince carried Steve nearly fifty feet to the emergency room doors. The place was packed with injured people of all ages. "I need a doctor here. I got a guy with a gunshot wound," Vince shouted.

"Make a hole!" Dave yelled at the people milling around in the darkened corridor.

Vince spotted an older man in a white lab coat, and they hurried toward him. "Doctor!"

The doctor and other staff placed Steve on a gurney and wheeled him away. No one came to get his information. The scene was too chaotic. Vince and Dave had so much of Steve's blood on them that a triage nurse passed them twice and stopped, asking about their injuries.

Vince stared at the dim light coming from the end of the long hall. The hospital's emergency generators must have been working. Hopefully, that meant they could still perform surgeries because Steve didn't stand a chance without one. From his research, Vince had discovered it was possible to harden generators from an EMP, and many of the newer medical facilities included such precautions in their building plans or renovations. Vince was relieved this hospital was among them. The injured and ill in the community would receive treatment for a few more days, maybe even a week, before the facility ran out of diesel.

Vince, Dave, and the kid stepped outside the emergency room doors to wait for word about Steve. Vince wasn't aware how much time had passed. Dave nudged him. He glanced up as two cops approached the door to the emergency room carrying an injured woman. Dave grabbed the handle, pulled on the door, and held it open for them to enter.

"Officers," Dave said, following them inside. "We found something you're going to want to see back east of Tusculum."

"You'll have to go to the station and make a report. We're a little busy at the moment."

The three stayed on their heels. As soon as they handed the woman off to the nursing staff, Dave grabbed one of the officer's arms. The officer spun and drew his weapon, pointing it at Dave's chest. Dave's hand flew into the air. Vince stepped up. "We found this kid. He said he was being held by possible human traffickers. My buddy was shot. That's why we're here. I dropped one of the abductors. You'll find the other two tied up in their driveway."

The officer glanced down at the kid. "Is this true? Were you abducted?"

The kid nodded.

"Where was this?" the other officer asked.

Vince removed a notepad and pen from one of his cargo pants pockets and drew the officers a map to the house of horrors.

"Alright, stick with us, kid," one of the officers said.

"How are we going to get there?" the other officer asked. As a nurse walked by, Vince and Dave followed after her, leaving the two cops and the kid to figure out their transportation issue.

"Ma'am, can you tell us how our friend is doing?"

She stopped and faced them. "What's his name?"

"Steve Armstrong," Dave said.

"Oh, the GSW? He's still in surgery. I'll let you know when I hear more."

Steve was alive. There was still hope he could make it.

Vince and Dave checked on the Wagoneer to make sure all their gear was still there. The two cops were at the opposite end of the parking lot where a young couple was clearing their belongings from an older model pickup truck.

"I guess the officers found their transportation," Vince said.

"You think those two gave it up willingly?"

"Probably not."

As they approached the Wagoneer, Vince noticed the wet pavement under the vehicle. He opened the hood to find coolant still dripping from a tear in the radiator hose.

"Shit," they both said in unison. Vince shook his head. He hadn't finished replacing all the hoses when Lindsay had raced up with the news about the EMP. "Dave, start checking for unlocked vehicles—we've got to find another hose. I'll see if I have a flathead and start removing this busted one."

"Roger that," Dave said as he turned to start looking.

It was nearly dark by the time they had found a suitable hose, installed it, and captured enough coolant from a third vehicle to add to the Wagoneer. Vince was topping off the Wagoneer's radiator when Dave returned from checking on Steve's condition for the third time.

"Any word?" Vince asked.

Dave hung his head. "He didn't make it."

Vince had known it was likely Steve wouldn't make it, but hearing the words was still difficult. Dread filled him at the thought of having to tell Steve's girlfriend, Millie, and his family. How many more friends would Vince lose as the apocalypse continued? The sooner he could gather everyone onto the compound, the better he'd feel about their chances of survival.

"How will we find Lauren and Charlie in the dark?" Dave asked.

Vince shook his head. "We can't." He had the night vision

goggles and could see objects and people in the dark, but he wouldn't be able to make out who they were. They would have to stop to confirm whether people on the road were Lauren and Charlie. However, this would put him and Dave at risk. They could be fired upon and lose the Wagoneer. It was too big of a risk—one he was not willing to take—not after losing Steve. "We're going to drive a safe distance out of town and pull off somewhere for the night. We'll head out at first light."

"I hope Lauren and Charlie can find somewhere safe to hold up," Dave said.

"They will. Lauren is a smart woman. Besides, anyone would be a fool to mess with her."

Dave chuckled. "Lauren is scary."

Vince slammed the hood and then tossed his tools into the back of the Wagoneer. They climbed in and sat in the parking lot for a few minutes. Vince wanted to make sure they weren't being watched. He didn't want to be ambushed the moment he started the vehicle. Finally, Vince turned off the kill switch and turned the key.

"And the Wagoneer roars back to life," Dave said, when the engine started.

They looked at each other for a moment. Dave hung his head and Vince looked away, contemplating the irony of the vehicle roaring to "life" as they drove off, leaving their dead friend behind.

～

Vince parked the Wagoneer behind a dumpster at the Volunteer State Speedway just off Interstate 81 south of Bulls Gap, Tennessee. He and Sam had been to the Gap's high-banked dirt oval track many times. They had seen NASCAR Cup Series champion Kyle Larson there once for a late model challenge event.

Vince retrieved his mobile Ham radio microphone from the dashboard.

"We're still fifty miles from Knoxville. You think we're in range for Lauren to pick up a hand-held transmission?" Dave asked.

"Maybe," Vince said.

There were four amateur Ham radio repeaters in the Greeneville area and nearly thirty repeaters in the Knoxville vicinity. Lauren should be able to hear him if she had her radio on. Vince keyed his mic and gave Lauren's call sign, then listened for her response. He heard nothing. He repeated the call sign and gave his own. Knowing Lauren could be just out of range for simplex operation, Vince switched to a repeater frequency that might still be operable after the EMP and transmitted again. Instead of Lauren, another Ham operator responded. He gave a call sign Vince recognized.

"Everything good to go over your way?" Perry Oates asked.

"Just have to round up a hen and her chick first," Vince replied. "Their last known location was near the Knoxville airport yesterday afternoon."

"Big explosions out that way. Some of those big boys must have run out of fuel and tried to glide in for a landing."

"If you hear a female looking for my brother or trying to get to my home base, let her know we're coming for her and to stick to the route, if possible."

"Will do. Stay safe out there. It's going to be one bumpy ride before long."

"Keep your head down and your powder dry," Vince replied.

Vince thought of trying to reach Sam. He had a list of frequencies and repeaters Sam could use on his way home from Atlanta. He could be coming up Interstate 26 and be pretty close to Unicoi by now, if he was able to get out of Atlanta. Vince wanted to alert him that he was already searching for Lauren and Charlie so Sam would be free to go home and look out for Bill and Edna.

Vince pulled out his notepad, ran a finger down the page, found the frequency he was looking for, and then keyed the mic once more. After giving Sam's call sign and his own, Vince listened. He heard some chatter from folks trying to find out what had happened. He decided not to leave a message for Sam as he didn't want to broadcast any more location information to anyone listening. It was too risky.

TWENTY-ONE

Sam

Consulate General of Honduras
Doraville, Georgia
Day of Event

"Smoke again," Tara said, pointing as they neared the Interstate 285 overpass.

Sam pulled Matt's map out and studied it. He couldn't be sure what was on fire ahead or how toxic the smoke might be. They needed an alternate route. He chose one, putting them on the I-285 heading north. Sam was surprised to see the number of motorists still on the roadway. Some still sat in their disabled vehicles. Families with young children sat on blankets in the middle of the interstate as if they were camping. Sam kept his head down and avoided eye contact with them, hoping no one would approach or speak to him. He passed others walking in the opposite direction. Some carried backpacks but none as full as his.

They exited I-285 at the Peachtree Industrial Boulevard exit going north. As they were passing a boarded-up tire store, a group of men entered the parking lot from the back of an office complex that housed Atlanta's Honduran Consulate. One of the men said something in Spanish and two of the men broke away from the group and ran toward Sam and Tara. Sam knew these men would not be scared off. They'd targeted them, and Sam would have to take them down to stop the men from achieving whatever they had planned. He wouldn't let Tara fall into their hands.

Sam shoved Tara to the ground behind a delivery van. "Stay down." He moved two cars over and waited for the men to get within range. As they approached, the two men drew pistols and began searching between the cars for Sam and Tara. Tara was crying. One of the men heard her and turned. He stopped talking and listened, then pointed to where Tara was hiding.

Sam had no choice. He had to take the shot now. Rising from a crouch, he steadied his aim and squeezed the trigger, dropping the thinner of the two men with a thunderous echoing clap of gunfire. The second man jumped at the sound, then turned to help his friend. He grabbed him by one hand and was attempting to pull him behind a vehicle when Sam fired a second and then a third shot. The man dropped his friend's arm and clutched his chest. His pistol dropped to the ground at his feet, and the man fell face-first to the pavement. Neither man moved. It wouldn't be long before the rest of his friends discovered they'd been the ones shot. Sam needed to grab Tara and get clear of the area.

They ran north as fast as Tara could run with the gang of men yelling behind them. A loud boom startled Tara, causing her to jump and lose her footing. She fell forward, nearly toppling them both, but Sam was able to regain his balance and stop Tara's fall. After rounding the corner of a building, Sam pulled Tara and pointed toward a delivery truck parked in a short alley on the other side of the narrow street. "Get under that truck, crawl to the front, and crouch by the front tire. Keep your head down."

As Tara disappeared under the truck, Sam took cover behind a vehicle on his side of the street, ready to engage the men once they came around the corner of the building. Sam waited until one, two, and then three of the men appeared before opening fire on the closest man who was only about ten feet from him by then. Bang, bang, bang, thundered Sam's 1911, fatally wounding all three men. Each man lay on the ground with his own bloody chest wound.

Sam waited a good twenty seconds for more men to poke their heads out from around the other side of the building, but none did. All three men were still by then. Rather than wait any longer, Sam ran toward Tara and motioned for her to follow him once she was in sight. They crossed over an overpass and continued north where a high concrete barrier wall hid them from the view of any remaining members of the gang. Only then did Sam slow down and allow Tara to catch her breath.

"Damn, that was close," she said through gasps.

"I told you this would happen," Sam said.

"You think you could show me how that gun works again?"

"As soon as we put some distance between that gang and us, that's the first thing I'll do."

Sam stopped where the barrier wall ended and peered around the end of it, searching for the men. Not seeing anyone, he listened for their voices. "I think we lost them."

"Good. Can we slow down now? I'm beat."

"We'll stop in a minute to rest. Here, take a drink. You need to stay hydrated." He handed her a water bottle and she took several sips, then handed the bottle back. "No, drink at least half of it." After Tara had finished drinking, Sam slammed the rest and they continued walking.

In another mile or so, they came upon a two-story office complex. On the opposite side of the parking lot, there was a wooded area blocked by a high earth berm. "There," Sam said, pointing. "We'll rest there for a bit."

"How much farther to your friend's house?" Tara asked.

"About ten miles or so."

Sam dropped his pack and retrieved the small black faraday bag containing his Boefeng handheld Ham radio. He could tell as soon as he opened the bag that it had been damaged in the wreck. He pulled it out and turned the knob. Nothing happened. It was too damaged. He wouldn't be able to use it to reach home. There'd be no way to find out about Charlie and Lauren or let his family know he was on his way. He would have to locate another Ham somewhere along the way.

He returned it to the pack and retrieved a map of Atlanta from a side pocket. spread it out on the grass and placed a small rock on their location. "I want you to commit this route and a couple of alternatives to memory."

"Why?"

Sam clenched his jaw. He was tired and emotionally drained from the day. He needed some downtime to rest his mind and body. He didn't want to have to explain everything to her in detail.

"Because you need to know how to get to Matt's if I get killed." As soon as the words left his mouth, Sam regretted how he'd said them. He could see from Tara's expression that he'd been overly harsh. However, he just wasn't feeling that patient at the moment.

"If you get killed?" she asked.

"Just pay attention, please." Sam placed the route his friend had drawn on top of the map and then traced it onto the larger map with a permanent marker. "You can take this road here, but it will add a couple of blocks."

"But you're not planning on me going there alone, right?"

"Of course not. I need that car to make it home to my family. This is just so you'll know how to get there, too. Something could happen where we get separated or I get delayed."

"How? What could happen?"

Sam sighed. She wasn't going to make this quick and easy.

"If we come under attack and I have to cover you while you get away, you shouldn't wait for me to catch up. You can run to Matt's house and wait for me there."

"Oh, okay. I see."

"Study this map," Sam said. "Memorize it, and then stuff it into your pocket." Sam said. He folded up the map of Atlanta and placed it back into his pack. "When it gets dark, we'll need to head out again," he said.

"In the dark? You're crazy. It's dangerous at night around here."

"Yep—you're right. But during the day, people can see you. From now on, we're going to be traveling at night if at all possible."

Tara lowered herself to the ground and pulled her knees to her chest. She wrapped her arms around her legs and rested her chin on her knees.

"You might drink some more water and try to take a nap. I have a feeling it's going to be a long night."

"A nap—right now? Are you serious?"

"Yep."

"You're nuts."

"Suit yourself. I'm going to try to get some shut-eye—maybe an hour of sleep. We're in a pretty secluded area right here. Please don't go anywhere."

"What if I have to go to the bathroom?"

"Wake me up and I'll help you."

"I don't need help—I know how to go to the bathroom."

"I mean help you by standing guard if you don't feel comfortable going right around here if I turn my back," Sam said, dropping the magazine from his 1911 and replacing it with a full one.

Tara said nothing.

Sam leaned back and rested his head on his pack. "You should get some rest," he said.

"I can't sleep on the ground. There are bugs and stuff."

"I've got a sweatshirt in here you can use as a pillow if you'd like."

"That won't stop bugs from crawling on me."

"Okay," Sam said. He closed his eyes and started thinking about his route home from Gainesville.

"I do think I'd like to use that sweatshirt, if you don't mind."

Sam sat up, retrieved the compression bag containing extra clothing, pulled out a black sweatshirt, and handed it to Tara. She wadded it up and used it as a pillow for her head.

***

When Sam woke up just before the sun set behind the buildings, Tara was incredulous. She was sitting on a boulder staring out through the trees.

"Well, welcome back," Tara said.

Sam fixed his gaze on her and scratched his head. "Did you get any shut-eye?"

"I've been in a car wreck, shot at twice, and almost drowned in a creek—all in one afternoon," she said. "No, I didn't get any shut-eye."

"I know you've been through quite an ordeal today, and I can see how you'd be a bit...."

"Pissed off?" Tara said.

"Yeah. Pissed off."

Anger is fear.

Sam stood up, walked around the berm, and scanned the parking lot. Seeing nothing out of the ordinary, he then returned to his pack. "Let me show you how to handle the pistol now."

Sam pulled his Springfield XD-9 and its paddle holster from his pack. He explained the four laws of gun safety and demonstrated once more how to clear the weapon and hold it properly, then handed it to her.

"A gun is always loaded. Never point it at anything you don't intend to destroy."

"You pointed it at those kids," Tara said.

"As I said, never point it at anything you don't intend to destroy. Keep your finger out of the trigger guard...."

"You were going to kill those two kids?" Tara asked.

"Those boys were just as dangerous as the Russo brothers or the gang of men we just encountered."

"But they were just boys."

"Boys with guns and real bullets, Tara."

Tara studied the gun in her hands.

"Keep your finger out of the trigger guard until you're ready to shoot. Point your trigger finger straight ahead along the slide like this," Sam said, drawing his 1911 and demonstrating.

She listened intently to his instructions and asked appropriate questions, exhibiting an understanding of the seriousness of handling a deadly weapon.

"If you hesitate, it could cost both of us our lives," Sam said, handing Tara an extra magazine. "Put this in your left hand back pocket."

"What if I miss?"

"Keep firing until you're out of rounds, then switch magazines." They had a limited amount of ammunition, but if they got into a situation where Tara needed to fire her weapon, conserving ammo wouldn't be Sam's first concern.

"But I only heard your gun go off three times after I crawled under the truck."

"I have a .45 caliber pistol. The bullets create much more damage than your 9mm bullets."

"I hope so. Did you hit the guy all three times?"

Sam was tired and didn't want to get into this discussion with her, but he realized he needed to be patient. They were now conducting what they used to call an After Action Review back when he was a cop, and it would be beneficial to Tara to know what had gone down. "No. I hit three guys, one time each—right in the chest. I set myself behind the front bumper of a car for cover waiting for them, supported my shots using the hood to stabilize my hands, and just waited until enough of them had rounded the corner and were all within range for me not to miss."

"Holy shit."

"Your pistol is just as deadly, but mine has larger bullets. The larger the bullet, the more damage it will cause—and the more damage, the faster the bad guy will go down and bleed out. If you have to shoot your weapon, I want you to aim and squeeze the trigger—aim and squeeze the trigger—over and over. If we have the opportunity, you can do some target practice later, but you have twice as many rounds in each magazine as I have."

"Yeah—but they're smaller."

"Yeah, but they're just as deadly if you hit your target center mass because they're hollow points—they expand when they hit. Always aim right in the middle of the chest where you'll have the best chance of hitting the target. If you aim and are able to stabilize each shot, your chances are very good—and you have twice as many chances as me to stop a bad guy."

"Or three."

"Or three bad guys."

Dusk had caught up with them. As the sun began to disappear beyond the horizon, Sam pulled two MREs from his pack. "Beef ravioli in meat sauce or cheese tortellini?" he asked.

"How about Grub Hub?"

"Sorry. Our options are limited, I'm afraid."

When Tara didn't respond, Sam held the MREs in the air, waiting for a response.

"I'm not hungry."

"Have you already eaten dinner?"

"I don't think I can eat."

"Okay," Sam said, tearing open the ravioli MRE and tossing the cheese tortellini back into his pack. He squeezed the contents of the packet toward the opening and slurped a big piece of ravioli into his mouth. "Mmmm," he said, smacking his lips while he chewed. Meat sauce slid down the side of his chin.

"You're disgusting."

"Mmmm—mmmm," he said, closing his eyes and acting as if it was the best tasting meal he'd ever had.

"How can you think of food at a time like this?" Tara said, her eyes fixed on the tortellini peeking from his pack.

Sam reached in, dug around, and came out with a different entrée. "How about beef stew?"

Tara's stomach growled loudly, and she fought back a grin as Sam spit a fine spray of ravioli with meat sauce and nearly choked before regaining control.

"Shut up and toss me the cheese tortellini," Tara said, struggling to keep a straight face.

Sam flashed her a grin. "Sure thing—wise choice."

"Didn't your mother teach you not to talk with your mouth full?"

"She tried," Sam said, pulling the MRE entrée from his pack and gently tossed it to her, followed by a bottle of water. He held up a plastic spoon in a clear wrapper. "Mom also failed to get me to use silverware."

Tara held up a hand and Sam tossed her the spoon.

"I can see that. Thanks."

They ate their MREs to the sound of distant sporadic gunfire.

"What's happening out there?"

"Same thing that happens most nights around here, I assume. Maybe a little more now without a law enforcement presence."

"Are you sure it's safer to travel at night?"

"They can't shoot what they can't see. Just stay quiet and we'll be at Matt's before you know it."

After finishing the MRE and stowing the wrapper, he shouldered his pack. "Are you ready?"

Tara stood and brushed herself off. "I'm ready to be in Gainesville already and have this part over."

Sam surveyed the surrounding area to ensure he wasn't leaving anything behind.

"Do me a favor,"

"Sure, what?"

"Jump up and down."

"Why?"

"We need to travel as quietly as possible. I need to check you for rattles and other noises."

"The only thing in my pockets is that heavy ass clip you gave me for the pistol and the map."

"It's called a magazine, not a clip."

"Whatever. It's heavy."

"Just humor me."

Tara jumped into the air a few times and nothing rattled, but the holstered XD-9 made some noise as it slapped against her leg. Sam did the same, pulling on the straps of his pack to tighten them each time he was in the air. Satisfied they weren't going to be announcing their presence as they walked through the night, Sam led Tara back to the frontage road. From there, Sam could see flames off in the distance. It looked as if the heart of Atlanta was on fire.

Tara was unusually quiet, watching the city burn as they walked along. Sam nudged her with his elbow. "Stick close." As he turned north on the frontage road, Tara stepped on the heel of his boot. "Not that close."

"I can't see a thing."

"Hold on to my belt loop, but try not to trip me, okay?"

TWENTY-TWO

Lauren

Interstate 40
Knoxville, Tennessee.
Day of Event

Over the next few miles, Lauren's mind worked overtime, trying to think her way out of the mess that she and Charlie were in as the sun got close to the horizon. She had no doubt Sam would come for them as soon as he was able to get out of Atlanta, but she couldn't just stop and wait on the side of the road for him. They had to do what they could to make it back to Unicoi on their own, but one hundred miles was an incredible distance without transportation, and with Charlie's asthmatic condition, they weren't going to get very far quickly. They didn't have enough food or water for five or six days—not with four people in their little procession.

She had considered hunkering down and staying put until Sam came for them, but how would he find them unless they stayed on the side of the road? It wasn't like they could make a sign directing him to their location. If he could find them, so could someone else with ill intentions. Considering the trouble they'd already encountered, anything could happen.

Lauren wasn't sure which option was the least dangerous. However, her most pressing worry was getting home to her parents. Angela was an exemplary nurse and had proven reliable in the past, but how long would she stay with Edna and Bill? How would her father care for himself and Edna if their nurse abandoned them?

"It's going to get dark soon. I think we should find somewhere to camp for the night," Cody said.

"There's a Days Inn up the road," Lauren said.

"We can check to see if they're open, I guess," Cody said.

They trudged on, mocked by the sun as it labored to reach the horizon against the constant pull of gravity.

∼

The motel's parking lot was filled with people standing around, sitting on car hoods, and huddled in small groups.

"Wait here. I'll go check it out," Cody said, disappearing into the lobby.

As they waited outside, Lauren eyed the motel's guests. Some wore dirty work boots and t-shirts and looked like construction workers, while others looked like normal travelers. It was noisy. Without the sound of air conditioners and highway traffic, the sound carried. She wasn't at all comfortable waiting around there. Her hand rested on her hip next to her Colt. A little girl stared up at Lauren, wide-eyed. The girl tugged on her mother's shirt tail and then pointed at Lauren. Her mother looked up and her mouth fell open. She grabbed the child and moved away. Lauren was fine with that. She wanted everyone to keep their distance. She was rethinking even staying at the motel, but she didn't have any more miles in her, and neither did Charlie nor Casey.

Lauren estimated they had walked fifteen or sixteen miles,

maybe more. If there were no rooms available inside, they might be able to camp in the woods behind the motel.

Camp?

They had no camping supplies. Everything she would have needed to make a shelter, build a fire, and purify water was in her get-home bag in the back of her demolished SUV.

Lauren checked the sky. The remaining red glow in the west along with the moon hanging in the eastern sky provided a surprising amount of light. Clouds were even visible overhead. It didn't appear like it would rain anytime soon, but she wasn't looking forward to sleeping on the bare ground without some sort of shelter. This was going to suck. Life without modern conveniences was going to be awful.

Lauren was relieved when Cody returned a few minutes later. He stopped in the middle of the walkway and gestured for them to follow him. Cody led them through a lobby filled with people and into the breakfast area. He stopped and pointed. "In here."

"There?" Lauren asked. "They didn't have any rooms with beds?"

"Not unless you have five hundred dollars cash."

"Five hundred dollars? That's price gouging. That's illegal," Lauren said.

Cody lifted his arm and pointed to his wrist. "I had to trade him my watch just to get us in here."

She took a step back toward the lobby, ready to go inform the clerk that what he was doing was illegal, but there was a line of people at the front desk. She surveyed the breakfast room. It was just for one night, and she was so tired she could sleep anywhere. At least they were inside the building.

"I hope it was a cheap Timex," Lauren said, entering the breakfast room.

"It wasn't, but it hasn't worked since the lights went out," Cody said.

An elderly couple sat at one table in the back. Three men and one woman sat at another. A family of five occupied a third table. Six straight-backed chairs lined the wall to Lauren's right. She headed there. She pulled out two chairs and stuck them together. "We might be able to line them up, seats touching and make something to sleep on."

Casey walked to the back corner, pressed her back against the wall and slid down it. She sat on the floor with her legs pulled to her chest and rested her head on her knees. It looked like she'd done that before. Lauren wondered what the young girl had been through in her short life.

"Charlie, you want to help me?" Lauren asked.

Cody disappeared toward the front desk as Charlie and Lauren rearranged the chairs. A few minutes passed, and he returned. In his arms was a stack of towels. "You can roll one up for a pillow and use the rest for blankets."

"Awesome. Thanks, Cody," Charlie said.

Cody approached Casey. She didn't open her eyes. He unfolded a towel and draped it over her back. A picture of his character was beginning to form in Lauren's mind. She liked that he was proactive and seemed to have some common sense. So far, despite his penchant for finding trouble, he had been more of an asset than a liability.

Cody handed Lauren a bottle of apple juice. As she drank it, he began talking about himself and where he was from. She was exhausted and just wanted to let her mind go blank and rest, but she let him continue, listening for any red flags that would indicate he was more of a danger than just being a trouble magnet.

"We take people out on Watauga and South Holston rivers to catch rainbow and brown trout," Cody said with pride in his voice.

She detested small talk. It was one of the reasons she hadn't dated much before Sam. She hated the game of twenty questions. She didn't play it well—not enough patience. She hadn't met very many people with lives interesting enough to keep her attention. She would have ignored Cody at any other time until he quit talking, but she was thinking ten steps ahead and assessing his usefulness.

"How long have you run your fishing guide business?" Lauren asked.

"About ten years. It's grown in the last five years and I had to take on employees. That kind of took the fun out of it for me. Lately, I've had to manage the business while my guys take the clients out on the river."

"So you know all about how to tie flies and where to find fish?"

Cody was all smiles that she was interested in what he did for a living. "Sure do."

Being able to hunt and fish was more than just a hobby now. It was currency. It was life-sustaining. Unicoi needed someone like Cody.

"And what do you do for a living, Lauren?"

She thought for a moment. Her previous profession was useless now. There wouldn't be a need for lawyers without a judicial system. She wasn't even sure whether she'd be useful in her current position as mayor now.

"I take care of my elderly parents," she said.

"What about your husband?"

"Sam? He's an investigator for the county district attorney's office." She sighed. It was so challenging to keep it together when she thought about him down in Atlanta, possibly having to fight his way back to them.

"So, he's in law enforcement."

"Yeah," Lauren nodded, wanting to change the subject. "What are we going to do about her?"

Cody stared at Casey for a long moment before turning back to Lauren. He cracked a slight smile. "I'd hoped you could take her home with you."

Lauren leaned over and whispered to Charlie, "Make sure you keep a hand on your pistol as you sleep so someone doesn't try to take it," she said.

"Okay."

With her hand on her Colt, Lauren closed her eyes, intending only to rest for a moment. She was startled awake when she felt something brush against her arm. She bolted upright, drawing her Peacemaker.

"I'm sorry. You looked cold the way you were hugging herself." Charlie was holding one of the towels in his hand. He held it out to her.

"I'm sorry," Lauren said, taking the towel from him. "I'm a little jumpy after…." She couldn't bring herself to say it.

"No problem," Charlie said.

"How are you feeling? Are you breathing easier now?" Lauren asked him.

"It's better. Thanks for taking me to the hospital. The nebulizer helped."

"If you start having trouble again, let me know as soon as possible. We don't want it to get that bad again."

"I will, but I think the inhaler is working well," Charlie said. He leaned over and stretched out.

Sam would be so proud of his son. He really was a great kid. Sam was looking forward to doing fun stuff this trip and getting in some quality father-son time. When Lauren watched Sam and Charlie together, she sometimes regretted she hadn't started a family with him. However, if things got as bad in the world as he and Vince had foreseen, she was glad she hadn't.

Lauren looked around for Cody. He was near the opposite wall, curled up on four chairs asleep. No one had been watching out for trouble. Sam would have posted a guard or something and set shifts. She wasn't sure what good that would do them in a room full of people. She and Charlie were the only ones with guns, and she wasn't about to give the Glock to Cody. She needed to figure something out. Most of all, she needed sleep. It could take days to get home if Sam didn't come for them. Did her parents have days? Thinking about Sam and her parents was torture.

She needed to find a way to get home. There had to be an old car or truck somewhere—hell, she'd settle for a dirt bike or even a bicycle. Finding transportation would be her goal when daylight came, even if she had to leave Cody and Casey behind.

Lauren lay back on her makeshift pillow and pulled a towel over her arms. Her mind immediately went to Sam. A crushing ache tugged at her heart. She had no idea where he was or what kind of craziness he had encountered. She couldn't quit thinking about how bad things could get for him in Atlanta. She took solace knowing that he had his three-day get-home bag. If the Bronco still ran after the EMP or whatever this was, he'd likely be home right now, caring for her parents and worried sick about her and Charlie. He'd come for them. In the morning. He'd come for them.

Lauren listened to the whispers of the elderly couple for a few minutes before drifting off to sleep. She was awakened by shouting.

"That's mine, asshole. Get your own," a gruff male voice shouted.

"I had it first," a second man said.

Lauren heard scuffling in the dark hallway. One of the big construction workers got up and stepped into the corridor. Someone hit him, and he went down to one knee, then shot to his feet and started throwing his fists at another man. The other two construction workers jumped from their seats and joined in the fight as well.

Lauren stood and put herself between them and Charlie. She turned to Cody. "Maybe we should go."

"They're just drunk. If we mind our own business, they'll settle it and pass out, most likely," Cody said.

Lauren wasn't sure that would work. In her experience, intoxicated or high people could be unpredictable. One thing was certain—she was not going back to sleep.

"What's happening?" Charlie asked.

"It's okay, Charlie," Lauren answered.

Casey opened her eyes but didn't lift her head. Was she used to this kind of commotion? Likely so.

Lauren lifted one of her chairs and turned it upright against the wall before taking a seat. She stared at the doorway until the men moved away.

Cody lay back down but turned to face the entrance to the room.

"Did you sleep?" Lauren asked.

"Some." Cody pointed to her rolled-up towel on the opposite chair. "You can lie back down. I'm watching out."

"Nah, I'm awake now. Why don't you get some shut-eye? I got this." She patted her holstered revolver.

"You sure?"

"I'll wake you if there's a need. You get some rest. We should head out before daybreak and put some distance between us and these people," Lauren said.

Cody stretched out and yawned. "I agree." He was snoring softly in minutes.

The room was dark, stiflingly hot, and the air smelled of body odor. Lauren stretched and twisted, trying to alleviate the pain in her back from sleeping on the chairs. She wiped the sweat from her cheek with the palm of her hand and felt the abrasions. After the plane crash and the semi smashing into her SUV, Lauren hadn't taken the time to assess her injuries. There'd been no time then, but she was feeling them all now. Her knees were scraped, and her hands felt like they had tiny particles of sand and grit embedded in them. She had several abrasions to her forehead above her left brow. On top of this, the hair on the back of her head was sticky with blood. She probed with her index finger and found the gash. It still felt wet. She could use a couple of ibuprofen, but the bottle was in her get-home bag back in her SUV.

Sam and Vince had carefully chosen her get-home bag and its contents. They'd practiced living out of it several times along the section of the Appalachian Trail that ran past Unicoi, to simulate scenarios she'd likely encounter. She was reasonably proficient in setting up her tarp for shelter, along with purifying and heating water to pour into her freeze-dried meal pouches. She was even getting the hang of reading maps and using the compass. But none of that would help her now—not until she found a way to replace the things she had been forced to leave behind. But with or without them, she would make it home. She didn't care what she had to do. She and Charlie would make it home. No one and nothing would stand in her way. Her parents needed her, and she wasn't about to let them down.

TWENTY-THREE

Sam

Doraville, Georgia
Day of Event

Matt's route took them past a strip mall. As Sam and Tara approached in the darkness, they could hear looters shouting. A dumpster was on fire in the middle of an adjacent pharmacy parking lot. They could see people running back and forth from the entrance in the firelight. No one paid any attention to Sam and Tara as they hurried past. A liquor store about a block away was on fire. The doors and windows of a bank had been smashed, and it was on fire as well.

"What the hell is wrong with people?" Tara asked. She pointed to a burning church on their left. "Why did they burn the church?"

"Because they could. Do you see any law enforcement?"

"I didn't expect it to happen this soon."

"I was hoping most people would just stay home and wait to hear something from the authorities."

"I read about looting and stuff during hurricanes. I have a

cousin who lives in Brooklyn, and he said there was looting there immediately after the hurricane and for days and days. He said they even robbed a nursing home and stole their televisions."

"There's one good thing. It looks like everyone is too busy looting to notice us," Sam said.

"I guess," Tara said.

Even though no one bothered them, Sam was relieved when he and Tara left that area behind as they entered a residential area. It was unusually quiet and especially dark under the canopy of the trees that hung over the roadway as Sam and Tara walked through the middle-income neighborhoods where the houses were somewhat spread out. A few dim lights shone through windows where the homeowners had lit candles or were using battery-operated lanterns.

As they walked past a one-story red brick house, a man stood over a charcoal grill cooking dinner. Nothing was tastier than a charcoal-grilled steak or a thick, greasy hamburger. Sam loved that smell. He imagined Vince and his survival group standing around his grill, downing cold beer and discussing their theories on the cause of the event that had brought down the power grid and taken out their modern technology. If he hadn't come to Atlanta to find Tara Hobbs, he'd be sitting around the campfire with his wife and son and Lauren's parents instead of fighting to get home to them.

After turning the corner into Matt's upper-middle-class neighborhood, they wound back and forth past two-story homes clad in a mix of brick and vinyl siding. The farther they walked, the larger and closer together the homes became. At first, it didn't appear anyone was home on Matt's block. No one was out grilling steaks, and no light shone through the windows. Sam felt better about their chances of starting the Camaro and making it out of there without being stopped by nosey neighbors.

Matt's brick-and-vinyl-clad house was at the end of a cul-de-sac. A trash can sat at the curb. They walked past it, around the side of the house, and entered the backyard. He found Matt's spare key above the patio door right where Matt had said it would be and unlocked the back door. Then, he stopped in the doorway and listened for a few seconds. He could feel Tara's warm breath on his arm. She was breathing heavily from their long walk. Before long, she was going to wish she was in better physical shape—they both would.

Hearing no voices or sounds of human presence inside, Sam stepped over the threshold into the kitchen. He waited until Tara was also inside and the door was shut before flicking on his flashlight and illuminating the space. To his left was the door to the garage. Beside it, the light bounced off a metallic key ring. "Stay right here. I'm going to clear the rest of the house before I check the garage."

"You're just going to leave me here by myself?"

"You have your pistol?" Sam asked.

"Yes."

"I'll let you know it's me when I return. Shoot anyone that's not me."

"I'm not going to do that. What if it's Matt or his girlfriend? You can't just shoot people like that."

Sam pulled out a kitchen chair from the dining set and turned it around. "Just sit here and try to be quiet. I'll be a few minutes."

After clearing every room on the main floor, Sam climbed the stairs and cleared the second story.

"Tara, it's Sam. Don't shoot me." he said as he came through the living room heading back to the kitchen.

"Okay. Can you hurry? I just want to get out of here."

As he approached the kitchen, he stopped and called to her again. "Is your pistol in your hand?"

"Yes."

"Is it pointed at the floor?"

"Yes."

"And your finger is away from the trigger guard?" Sam asked.

Tara hesitated before answering. "It is now."

"Your finger never goes inside the trigger guard until you're ready to destroy something. Got it? Never!" Sam said as he shone the flashlight toward the garage.

"Okay!" Tara said.

"Place the weapon on the table." He wasn't taking any chances after that.

Tara sat the pistol on the table with the barrel pointing at her chest.

"No! Always point the barrel in a safe direction—away from people, including yourself."

Tara's eyes grew wide. She spun the gun around with one finger until the barrel faced the wall, then she stood and backed away from it as if it would suddenly fire on its own.

"Leave it there and come hold the flashlight for me," Sam said. He'd need to spend more time with her on gun safety before he felt comfortable with her handling the weapon.

"Stay back while I clear the garage." Sam grabbed the keys from the hook and turned the knob on the door leading to the two-car garage. He cleared the garage and then returned.

"Shine the light against that far wall."

The light bounced off the hood of Matt's pride and joy—a cherry red 1977 Chevy Camaro. It was a big deal that Matt had allowed Sam to drive it, not to mention take it to Tennessee, but Sam and Matt had been through a lot of shit together in Afghanistan. Back then, they'd been as close as brothers.

"You think it will start?" Tara asked, pulling him from his memories.

"It'll start." Sam opened the car door and no interior light came on. He eased himself into the driver's seat, inserted the key into the ignition, and turned it just enough for the dash to light up. That was a good sign. He watched the gas gauge climb to a quarter of a tank. That would get them to Gainesville. It might even get him all the way to the Tennessee state line before he had to refuel, but he wouldn't wait that long to find gasoline. Sam turned off the key, exited the vehicle, and, as quietly as possible, closed the car's door.

"What's wrong?" Tara asked.

"Nothing. I want to refill our water bottles and see if I can find a gas can before we start it and let all Matt's neighbors know we have a running car."

Tara smiled. "That's smart."

"Will you check the refrigerator and pantry for bottled water while I look for a fuel can?" Sam said, unclipping a second flashlight from his pack and flicking it on for her.

While Tara disappeared back into the kitchen, Sam rummaged around under a workbench along the back wall until he located a one-gallon gas can. Finding that it was about half full, Sam unscrewed the nozzle and shone the flashlight's beam inside. Just what he thought—the gasoline had been mixed with oil for use in a weed eater. He placed it back under the table and shone the light along the sidewall. He spotted a lawnmower. Next to it, he located a five-gallon jug. Bingo! After emptying the fuel into the Camaro's gas tank, Sam unlocked the trunk, placed the empty can inside, and left the trunk open. He had one more item to find before starting the vehicle and racing out of town.

As Sam walked through the kitchen, Tara was stacking cases of bottled water onto the table.

"How many should we take?"

"All of them," Sam said.

"All of them? Won't Matt need them?"

"Matt's never coming back here," Sam said.

"Why?"

"He's smart. He won't stop here for a few canned goods and bottled water. By the time he leaves the CDC, he will want to get as far away from Atlanta as possible."

"Should I load them into the car, then?"

"In the back seat. I'll need the trunk for other things," Sam said, heading back toward the stairs.

"What? Where are you going?"

"To find Matt's gun safe."

TWENTY-FOUR

Sam

Matt Cruz's Residence
Lawrenceville, Georgia
Day 2

Sam checked his watch. It was three-thirty in the morning. They had thirty more minutes to wait before starting Matt's Camaro and racing toward Gainesville to drop Tara off at her friend's farm. Most everyone was fast asleep. If they heard the engine's roar, in their groggy state, they might not even remember that cars weren't working anymore and ignore it. At least, that was Sam's hope.

Sam went over the rules of gun safety with Tara again, and she demonstrated loading and clearing the weapon properly. He broached the subject again of her returning to Unicoi County with him.

"It's going to be dangerous out there, Tara. You really don't know what the situation will be when you get there."

Tara was quiet. Sam hoped that meant she was reconsidering her circumstances and would come to a more reasonable solution.

"I'll seek out the neighbors for help. Everett had friends and family in the area. I'll talk to them. We'll work together."

Sam was torn. On the one hand, he felt obliged to keep her safe, but on the other, he was looking forward to traveling the rest of the way home without having the burden of looking out for her. Deep down, he knew his conscience would bother him if he didn't at least try to get Tara to listen to reason.

"Takers are going to come, Tara. Only a strong group will be able to survive for very long."

"I feel more comfortable here in Georgia."

"What about your family back in Unicoi County?"

"My grandma has my aunts and uncles. They don't really want me back there. They're ashamed of me. My uncle Bob said I ruined the family name."

"You could come to stay with my wife and me. We have her parents to care for—and we could use your help. We're going to do our best to secure the town and rally its residents. Lauren's the mayor of Unicoi."

Tara said nothing.

"We could head up Highway 23 and be in Unicoi in about four hours."

"I'd like to go to Everett's place and check it out."

Tara made eye contact with Sam. Her eyes glistened with tears. He couldn't be sure what was on her mind, but it didn't look like anything he'd said to her had made any difference.

"I wouldn't want to be a burden."

"You wouldn't be. You'd be an asset—another person to help with security, food gathering, and with Lauren's parents."

Tara scrunched her face. "Babysit old folks? No thanks." She lowered her head. "I'll only bring you problems if I stay with you. I wouldn't mean to—not on purpose, it just happens. I don't think Nigel or his family will just forget that I turned him in for killing Misty Blue. Billy Mahon and his crew won't either."

Mahon would have to be dealt with whether Tara came back with him, or not—and before he caused more trouble for the town.

"We're all better off if I stay in Gainesville. I can make it there. I want to try, at least."

Sam exhaled loudly. He'd tried, but she was determined. He told himself his conscience was clear. His responsibility to Tara would end when he pulled away from Gainesville. However, he knew he would still feel bad about leaving her, knowing her chances for survival were so low.

Sam made a check of Matt's house one last time, gathering things that might be helpful for Tara. When the Camaro was packed as tightly as he could get it with canned goods, bottled water, and camping supplies, Sam slowly rolled up the garage door, trying to be as quiet as possible, and climbed behind the wheel of his best friend's beloved Camaro. Sam would do his best to honor Matt by not getting it filled with bullet holes like he had with his Bronco.

He inserted the key into the ignition and turned the key. Instead of an aggressive sounding rumble, the engine only turned over. He cranked it again and again, but the engine wouldn't start.

Sam tried to remain calm, but they risked an encounter with the neighbors with each passing second now. Any minute, one of them could be on Matt's front lawn wanting to know why Sam was stealing the car. He opened the driver's door.

"Where are you going?"

"It's not going to start. I'm going to close the garage door before I raise the hood and check a few things."

Tara exited the Camaro and followed Sam. She stuck her head outside and looked around.

"See any lights?" Sam asked.

"No."

"Help me close this door. Go slow and easy," Sam said.

With the garage door closed, Sam returned to the Camaro and popped the hood. "Shine the flashlight over here, please."

Sam checked everything he could think of that might be preventing the car from starting. Matt said it ran great. He drove it around town every weekend. The EMP should not have affected this older car.

The eastern horizon was beginning to get brighter. Light shone through the garage's side window onto the Camaro. The sun was coming up, and their window of opportunity to get out of town under the cover of darkness had almost passed. Sam leaned on the fender and rubbed his sweaty brow with the back of his greasy hand. Nothing was going according to plan. He weighed his options. If the car started, they could take their chances during the day. The risk of encountering people was much greater, though. They could be seen and heard by people who might want to take the vehicle from them. If he lost the Camaro, he'd be on foot and have to walk the two hundred miles back to Unicoi County if even he survived the encounter.

The other option was to wait, hunker down there at Matt's, and sleep. It was a safe middle-class neighborhood. No one should bother them there. They could sleep, eat, get fully hydrated, and pull out around midnight. Midnight. That would mean another eighteen hours before he could leave there and then thirty minutes to Gainesville to drop off Tara. He couldn't just leave her there without at least talking with the family and making sure it was safe for her to stay there. That could take maybe an hour. It would put him leaving Gainesville around two in the morning. He'd arrive in Unicoi around six o'clock.

Could Lauren hold down the fort for another twenty-four hours? Could she take care of Bill and Edna and do all the things she'd need to do to secure their home? So many things ran through Sam's mind. He couldn't bring himself to consider that Charlie hadn't made it or that he and Lauren were in the same boat. The not knowing was torture—and he knew it was clouding his judgment. It set an urgency to getting home that might not be prudent, and the urgency threatened to consume him. As hard as he tried, he could not stop the constant bombardment of thoughts about the safety of his wife and son.

"Hop in and turn the key. We'll try it one more time," Sam said.

Tara climbed behind the wheel of the Camaro and cranked the ignition. This time, the engine roared to life. His heart leapt, and he rushed around to the driver's side and motioned for Tara to move over, but as he started to get in, the engine died. He cranked it over and over. It finally started again and ran for a few seconds but then died once more. The neighbors were bound to have heard the beefy roar of the motor. He really didn't have much choice now. They had to get the car started and get out of there before the neighbors could pinpoint where the sound was coming from.

Sam pumped the gas pedal and turned the key. The motor turned over and purred to life.

"Yay! Let's go!" Tara said.

The exhaust was quickly filling the enclosed space. Sam hurried to get the garage door open and then jumped back behind the wheel. He put the Camaro in reverse, mashed the gas pedal, and sped down the short driveway and into the road. Then he put the car into drive and glanced into the rearview mirror. Matt's next-door neighbor was standing on his front lawn in his white bathrobe.

"We woke the neighbors," Sam said, jutting a thumb over his right shoulder.

Tara pivoted in her seat. "He's heading this way."

"Hold on!" Sam shouted.

Tara placed a hand on the dash and the other on the door grab as Sam punched the gas. The Camaro's wide back tires caught traction, and the car rocketed away. Sam turned a corner a little too fast as they raced through the quiet neighborhood back to the main street without stopping at the traffic sign. He cranked the wheel to the right and sped up, causing the rear end to fishtail for a moment before catching traction again and speeding away.

TWENTY-FIVE

Lauren

Days Inn Motel
Knoxville, Tennessee
Day 2

A few hours passed while Cody, Casey, and Charlie slept. The noise outside grew quieter as people slept. Lauren stood and walked over to a window. She didn't see anyone walking around outside. She pulled her wrist up close to her face to check her watch. It was nearly five a.m., which meant it was time for them to get on the road.

Lauren whispered Cody's name, and he sat upright. "It's five o'clock. We should go," she said.

"Okay."

"Charlie."

"I'm awake," Charlie said.

Lauren moved to the back corner and stood over Casey. "We're heading out. Do you want to come with us?" They hadn't discussed her traveling with them. She wasn't even sure where the girl was from or where she wanted to go. Casey stood, stretched, and moved toward the doorway without a word.

Cody joined her, stuffing towels into his tote bag. Lauren grabbed her towels and threw them over her shoulder. They'd need them if they had to sit or sleep on the ground. Charlie did the same. The four of them stepped over sleeping bodies and exited through a side door into the parking lot. People were sleeping in cars with the doors open for ventilation. Some even slept on the sidewalk.

Lauren scanned the parking lot as she and her small group headed toward the road. She wasn't sure how long the folks back there would stick around the motel before realizing things weren't going back to normal. That was when it would get dangerous to be in public places. Traveling the major highway wasn't ideal, but maybe when they got away from the populated area, it would be better.

They crossed the Holston River and headed east. After about an hour of walking, the sun arrived, bringing with it the intense summer heat.

"We should take a water break," Cody said, pointing to an overpass.

"Sounds good," Lauren said. She, Charlie, and Casey followed Cody under the overpass. Lauren stared up at the concrete incline and bridge girders.

"It's out of the sun, somewhat concealed," he said.

"It's not that bad. I've slept under them before—lots of times," Casey said.

Lauren wanted to ask why but decided it would be better to focus on the journey.

Charlie held his hand out to Casey and helped her climb to the top ledge. It suddenly struck Lauren that the two were likely around the same age. She couldn't imagine Charlie going through the things this girl had gone through.

Lauren followed them to the top and stretched out on the concrete.

It felt cool against her skin. She wasn't at all looking forward to walking in the brutal heat again. If she had night vision goggles, or NVGs as Sam called them, she would have hunkered down during the day and traveled at night while it was cool. It would be less dangerous as fewer people would be out after dark. Purchasing two sets of good NVGs had been on their to-do list as one of their next preparedness purchases. Sam had a specific brand in mind, and they were expensive. Now she wished they'd made the sacrifice and already bought them.

A rumbling in the distance caused Lauren to bolt upright. "Did you hear that?" she asked.

"Sounds like an engine of some kind," Cody said.

Lauren held her breath, straining to hear. In the absence of other man-made noises, the sound stood out. At first, she thought it could be a generator. It would make sense with the electricity out. But there was a slowing down and speeding up of the engine that wouldn't occur with a generator. "I think it's a vehicle."

"I think so, too," Cody said. He was on his feet now and moving down the incline.

"Charlie," Lauren said, motioning for him to join her. She followed Cody back down to the roadway.

Charlie pointed to the east. "It's coming from that direction."

"You think it's on this highway?" Lauren asked.

"Could be," Cody said.

"You think it's help?" Charlie said.

Lauren frowned. "Probably not." Even if it was emergency personnel, there were too many stranded travelers for them to assist everyone. They would stick to their mission—whatever that was now.

"Even if they can't give us a ride, they can let the authorities know we need assistance," Cody said.

"The authorities are overwhelmed with people needing assistance. I'm afraid we're on our own," Lauren said.

"That's pretty much how it's always been, hasn't it?" Casey said.

Lauren could see where she would feel that way. She must have felt hopeless not to have asked for help before yesterday. "Don't try to flag it down—we might get shot at."

"I see something," Charlie said, standing on the tips of his toes. He turned to Lauren. "Isn't that...."

TWENTY-SIX

Vince

Highway 11 West
Greeneville, Tennessee
Day 2

Vince and Dave had taken turns sleeping. Each took a three-hour shift. Dave slept first since Vince was driving and wanted to be fresh in the morning. Vince had fitful dreams of his days of sleeping on a cot outside his Humvee back in the sandbox. He had just drifted off when Dave woke him shortly before sunrise.

The two men ate cold oatmeal out of mylar pouches, and each downed a bottle of water before Vince started the Jeep and headed toward Interstate 81 where they would go south toward Knoxville. If he turned left, he could follow it all the way through to its end at the Canadian border. He'd never drive through New York City again, especially now. That place was bad enough before the lights went out.

"It's unlikely Lauren and Charlie have traveled this far yet, but keep a lookout for them walking and look for her Honda Pilot, too. She might have made it out of Knoxville before the EMP," Vince said, pulling the Jeep onto the southbound lane of the wide interstate.

Dave craned his neck, scanning the northbound lane for signs of Lauren and Charlie. "You do know that every soccer mom in Tennessee drives a white Honda Pilot, right?" Dave asked.

"Every soccer mom?"

"It's a rule or something."

"Lauren's not a soccer mom," Vince said. Vince wasn't sure whether she even wanted kids. He'd never heard Lauren talk about it. Lindsay was forever going on about her biological clock or some shit.

"Shouldn't we be over in the northbound lane?" Dave asked as trees began to block their view of the northbound lanes.

"True. Look for a median to cross over."

Just before the first overpass, Dave pointed to the grassy median between the north and southbound lanes. "Think the Jeep can make it?"

"I'd rather not take the chance of getting her stuck in the mud."

Shortly after passing the weigh station, Dave spotted a gravel crossover. Vince slowed and took the crossover, then turned right going against the flow of traffic, had there been any, and traveled south along the shoulder until he could pull into what would have been the passing lane.

Dave leaned forward in his seat, scanning both sides of the road. Vince's attention was on weaving in and out of stalled cars. At first, he saw no stranded motorists on that stretch of the road. They all must have given up on help arriving and taken off walking at some point.

Twenty minutes later, Dave was the one to spot the first pedestrians. "Two men, thirty yards ahead in the right lane near the green tractor-trailer."

"Copy that. Any weapons?"

"Nope. They aren't carrying anything."

"I'm going to take the opposite shoulder and punch it."

"Roger that," Dave said.

As Vince felt the vibration from the rumble strip, the sound meant to alert inattentive drivers they were veering out of their lane, it caught the pedestrians' attention. The men stopped and turned toward the speeding Jeep. One of the men raised his hand to wave at them as the Jeep sped past. Dave returned the gesture, waving back, and turned in his seat to keep watch on them as Vince sped away.

"That one dude sort of looked like Sam," Dave said, turning his attention back to the front of the vehicle.

"What—was it him?"

"No—just looked kinda like him."

"You sure it wasn't him?

"Yep—sorry."

Vince said nothing. He tried to stay focused on getting Sam's wife and son home safe before worrying too much about Sam.

"What do you think the chances are Sam makes it out of Atlanta?"

Vince's mind painted a picture of chaos and devastation similar to the riots with stores and cars on fire and violence in the streets. Sam had been a cop in Johnson City, Tennessee, for over ten years. In addition to that, he had had at least two years of urban survival tactical training with Vince. Sam knew to get the hell out of the city as fast as possible.

"I think Sam will be sitting on Bill and Edna's sofa when we get back there."

Vince spotted movement about a half-mile ahead.

"There's a small group of people under the overpass," Dave said, pointing at the pedestrians.

"How many?" Vince asked.

"Seven, maybe eight."

"Looks like a bunch of tourists. That one guy has a camera hanging around his neck," Dave said.

They were within the vicinity of Pigeon Forge, Gatlinburg, and

Great Smoky Mountain State Park, with all its stranded tourists. GSMSP had over a million and a half visitors per year, and it was peak tourist season. That could mean thousands of people were in the park. How would the community possibly support all those people? Where would they all go? How many would just remain inside the park? Vince figured most would likely try to make it home. Some would travel north on Interstate 26 past Unicoi. But stopping in Unicoi wouldn't be an option for the tourists—they would encounter roadblocks and be told to keep on walking.

The tourists under the overpass had built a small fire, and an older lady was cooking something. A middle-aged man stepped out from behind a grey minivan. Vince watched his hands. "Don't do it, dude. Don't do it," Vince said. They stared at each another. The man reached around to his back with one arm. Before Vince could even call out, Dave fired, and the man dropped to the ground. Vince stomped on the gas and maneuvered around a pickup truck. A bullet tore through the back glass as they passed the downed man. More rounds pelted the tailgate. Vince feared a round might hit the gas tank or the tires. He weaved in behind a tractor-trailer, shielding them from the incoming bullets.

"What a dumbass. He could have gotten all those women and children killed," Dave said, dropping the AR-15's magazine to reload it.

"I don't think he gave a rat's ass about that. He just wanted the Jeep."

They continued south on Interstate 81 to 40W toward Knoxville. The closer they got to the city, the more cars, trucks, SUVs, and semi-trucks clogged the roadway. At one point, Dave had to get out to push a small sedan off the road so they could continue. As he was heading back to the Jeep, a guy came out of nowhere.

Vince had drawn his pistol to cover Dave before Dave even got out of the vehicle, but Vince couldn't get a bead on the man. "Dave, your six!" Vince yelled out the window. Dave spun around, pointing his rifle at the man. The man's hands shot into the air, and he began backing away.

"That's right, punk, just keep walking," Dave said, climbing back into the Jeep.

Vince was on high alert. They were encountering stranded motorists about every fifteen minutes now, which increased the risk of them having their vehicle stolen or being shot at again. The overpasses were particularly dangerous as people were sheltering under them to get out of the sun.

"Heads up. We're coming up on another overpass."

"Why don't you stop here and let me take a look in the binos?" Dave said.

Vince pulled onto the shoulder and stopped. He turned in his seat to watch for anyone approaching them from the rear. It was difficult because they were searching for two specific people while trying to avoid everyone else.

"People up ahead," Dave said, with the Bushnell binoculars still pressed against his face.

"How many?" Vince asked.

"I count three. No, four. Looks like a husband, wife, and two teenaged kids."

"That ain't Lauren and Charlie. Can you make out any weapons?"

"I can't really see the woman that well yet, but the dude is carrying a wrench or pipe or something."

"You want me to fire a warning shot?" Dave said.

"No!" Vince said. "No warning shots. If they move into our path. I'll stomp on the gas. They'll move."

"They got kids," Dave said.

"Exactly. They'll move."

Vince flashed back to a similar incident in Afghanistan. It was his third tour and he was in a convoy headed to a remote village when the locals came out of nowhere and filled the road in front of them. His driver was freaking out, shouting for someone to tell him what to do. The locals took off running, scattering in every direction. His convoy came under attack a second later, and an RPG took out the HMMWV behind them. Vince ordered the private to stomp on the gas to keep the convoy moving.

"You don't stop. You just don't ever stop if you're fired upon," Vince said.

As they moved toward the overpass, Dave pointed. "That kid looks an awful lot like Charlie."

TWENTY-SEVEN

Sam

Interstate 985
Lawrenceville, Georgia
Day 2

They'd made it. Sam and Tara had managed to get the car started and out of Matt's neighborhood without a confrontation with his neighbors or anyone curious about them having a running vehicle. Now, all they had to do was weave in and out of dead vehicles clogging the roadway and get to Gainesville without stopping.

"Tara, I want you to draw your pistol and hold it in both hands like I taught you. Keep it pointed at the floorboard in front of you. If we encounter anyone trying to flag us down who won't get out of the way or anyone shooting at us, I want you to lean out the window, take aim, and start firing. Doesn't much matter if you hit the person—I just want you to try so the sound of gunfire causes them to take cover instead of firing at us. Do you think you can do that?"

Tara looked at Sam, paused, and said, "Yes. I can do that." She unholstered her pistol and did as she was asked.

"Excellent. You can do this, Tara."

Things were looking up, and to Sam's great delight, the passing lane of Interstate 85 was mostly clear of stalled cars. It appeared most vehicles had been able to coast over onto the shoulder of their lanes before stopping.

Sam was cruising along in the left lane at fifty miles an hour as they approached the sign for their turn onto Interstate 985 north toward Gainesville. There was a tall earth berm dividing the north and southbound lanes of the interstate. A big rig was half on the roadway and half in the grass. It looked like it was about to tip over. Sam moved to the right lane and pulled onto the shoulder to pass a pickup truck, and then moved back into the left lane to make the turn onto I-985 when a short, stocky man stepped into the path of the Camaro.

"There's something in his hands!" Tara yelled.

There was no time for either of them to draw their weapons and fire at the guy. Sam yanked the wheel to the right to avoid hitting the man. As they passed him, Sam glanced into the rearview mirror just as the man took aim at the Camaro. He fired, and the back window exploded, disintegrating into thousands of tiny pieces of glass, completely covering the boxes of canned goods, camping stove, and other items they'd placed in the back seat. The bullet exited out the rear driver's side window.

Tara was screaming and pounding on the car's dashboard. "Drive! Drive! Drive! Get us the hell out of here, Sam!"

∽

It took thirty minutes to travel just eight miles, weaving in and out between the hundreds of vehicles strewn all over the interstate. As a result, Sam was forced to slow to fifteen miles per hour before it opened back up again. He moved into the far left lane as soon as he could and picked up speed.

Tara touched Sam's cheek with her finger and wiped away a spot of blood. "You're bleeding."

Sam felt the side of his face. A small piece of glass must have cut his cheek. "It's nothing." He glanced over at Tara. "Did you get hit by anything?"

"I don't think so." Tara ran her hand through her long brown hair. She bent her head toward the floorboard and shook her head, running her fingers through the strands. "It's in my hair. I need a brush."

She lifted her head and gasped, pointing to a row of abandoned cars. "There's a group of people over there."

About a quarter mile ahead, a pudgy man was leaning into the left-back door of an SUV. He was bent over with his head and torso inside, throwing items of clothing out of the vehicle. A woman stood near the back bumper with a backpack in her hand. Two more men were on the passenger side of the car. They, too, were throwing clothes out of the vehicle.

"Are they rummaging through cars, you think?"

"Maybe."

The group all turned their attention to the Camaro.

Sam unholstered his pistol. "Don't do it!" Sam said. "Don't."

The pudgy man turned and stepped onto the right lane of the roadway.

"Don't think about it, dude. Just don't."

He dropped what he held in his hands and took two more steps toward the center of the road.

"Tara, I'm going to need you to pick up your pistol."

"What? Really?" Tara said, drawing her pistol from its holster. She held it with the barrel pointing at the ground as he'd taught her.

"Lean out your window—you're going to aim it at that jackass's chest. If he moves one more step, shoot his ass."

"I can't. What if I miss?"

"Don't miss—just keep aiming and firing."

Sam aimed his pistol at the man right through the windshield and punched the gas. The man took two steps back. As he did, he dropped his right hand to his waistband. He was going for his gun. Sam squeezed his trigger, and the 1911 produced a deafening, thunderous boom, causing Tara to scream in terror and cower against the passenger door. Sam watched the man fall to the asphalt through the spider-cracked windshield as the Camaro raced past.

"Oh, shit!" Sam said. He stared into the rearview mirror. The first thing he spotted was the revolver near the man's body. The second was the young boy standing next to the dead man. Sam hadn't seen the kid as they'd approached the group. He must have been sitting on the ground on the passenger side of the SUV. Would his presence have made a difference in Sam's decision to fire?

"What?" Tara asked.

"He had a kid."

Tara looked back past the carpet of sparkling glass fragments still hanging where the rear window had once been. She turned back around, slumped in her seat and was quiet for several minutes.

"I'm not sure I want to live in a world of kill or be killed."

"Then you'll die." Sam realized how blunt that statement was, but she needed to decide whether she was willing to do what it took to survive. She had to wake up, or she wasn't going to last long—especially on her own.

As they approached the next overpass, Sam punched the gas and moved onto the shoulder, determined that he would stop for nothing or no one. He'd had enough, and all he wanted was to get Tara safely to Gainesville and make his way home. People were camped out on the sloped embankment of the road just waiting—but for what? It was like they were all just sitting there in the stands at a racetrack watching the Camaro race by. Help was never coming. How long would they sit there before they realized they were on their own?

Images of the young boy leaning over his dead father haunted Sam for the next few miles as he stared at the dime-sized hole in the windshield, then at the roadway ahead. He saw Charlie's face in his mind. He imagined himself lying on the asphalt and Charlie standing over him. Then the constant agonizing need to find his son ripped at his heart once again. He felt sick. Every second that ticked by was like an eternity. It was causing him to be more on edge. He tried to hold it together, but the slow pace was getting to him.

"The Atlanta Falcons trained there," Tara said, pointing to a building complex barely visible through the trees lining the roadway. "I dated one of the trainers once. I picked him up from work when his car was in the shop. I saw their quarterback, Matt Ryan, get into his fancy sports car."

Sam said nothing.

The days of gathering with friends to drink a beer and watch football were over—maybe forever. It was just one more thing in life that he'd lost due to the EMP. He could feel his mood darkening but couldn't pull himself out of it this time. As he drove past the urban forest of the Chicopee Woods Nature Preserve, Sam was deep in thought. His mind was recounting all the things he would miss, like ice cream and cold beer. He was in a rabbit hole, but it took his mind off Lauren and Charlie, the two people he missed most in the world.

Sam slowed as they entered the town. There were very few people out on foot, but many more cars were stopped everywhere. "Keep sharp, Tara. People could come out of anywhere."

Tara leaned forward, scanning each vehicle they passed. As they approached the Perdue Farms processing plant, Sam pointed. "I wonder how many tons of food are rotting inside that warehouse."

"You think it's all bad already? Maybe some of it can be salvaged."

"I don't know. If you do rally your boyfriend's neighbors to work together, you should hit this place first and take as much meat as you can carry."

"What would we do with it, though? It will just go bad without refrigeration."

"You could can it, smoke it, or dehydrate it. There are ways to preserve things. Our ancestors did it without electricity."

"I don't know how to do any of those things," Tara said.

"I bet some old-timers around here still do—hook up with them."

"Everett's grandmother is still alive—at least she was before this."

"A lot of folks think the older generation will be a burden in times like these, but I think the opposite is true. They know skills that we don't. They know how to survive during hard times. That's sure something the younger generations lack."

"Ours is the DoorDash generation," Tara said.

"Yeah. There won't be any more food delivery anytime soon."

"I don't really know how to cook. My grandma tried to teach me, but I wasn't interested."

"You're going to have to learn quickly. You'll be cooking things you thought you'd never eat in your lifetime."

"I really don't want to think about that. I might throw up."

"A lot of people are going to starve to death, Tara. As soon as the canned and ready-made food in the pantry is gone, they won't know how to feed themselves."

"I don't either."

"You should reconsider and come home with me."

Tara took a long moment before answering.

"I can learn. Everett's mom and grandmother can teach me, right?"

"They can," Sam confessed.

Sam slowly exited the interstate and took Highway 129 north. Driving through town was dangerous. But they would have to go miles out of their way to find another bridge to cross Lake Lanier and then drive several miles back to get to Everett's farm. Sam was banking on the urban area being mostly cleared of people. Surely a good number of them would have found their way home by now.

As they drove through town, business owners were busy boarding up their stores like you would if you were preparing for storms. But this storm wasn't going to pass, and those boards wouldn't keep people out for long. One shop owner stopped hammering and turned toward the Camaro. He pointed with his mouth open. Tara waved as they drove past him.

Sam stared up at the large homes on the hill before the bridge crossing Lake Lanier. The EMP had likely done what some activists had attempted to do for years and leveled the wealth gap. The wealthy would find themselves in the same situation as the poor, searching for food and water to survive.

There were people with shopping carts in the grocery store parking lot off Thompson Bridge Road. The doors were propped open. The windows appeared intact.

Tara pointed, "They're open?"

"It appears so. Maybe they're taking cash," Sam said.

"Maybe we should check it out?"

"It's risky." Sam was trying to avoid risky situations. He had a long way yet to travel, so he wanted to avoid as many of them as he could.

Tara twisted and glanced into the back seat. "Yeah, I guess I have enough for a week or so. I can come back with Everett's family."

She kept referring to Everett's family as if she was close to them. Sam hoped that was the case, and she wasn't disappointed. Going it alone would be devastating.

"That's true," Sam said.

"You're going to take that left up by the hardware store," Tara said.

"How far is his place from here?" Sam asked.

"It's about a mile and a half down this road."

⁓

Sam pulled the Camaro into the gravel driveway of a one-story red brick ranch-style house. The drive circled around to a white metal pole barn off to the left of the home. Cattle dotted the pasture beyond. What did Tara know about raising cattle or growing a garden? Had Tara's ex-boyfriend been home, Sam would have liked her chances of survival a lot better.

"Where did you say his folks lived?"

Tara nodded to the house across the road. The old white-clad-sided farmhouse was set off the road a hundred or more feet and surrounded by a white picket fence. The rolling hills made it difficult to see how much cleared land they had, but it was enough to raise livestock.

Sam stopped the Camaro and put it into park. Tara was out of the car and halfway up the front walkway before Sam climbed out of the vehicle. "Tara, wait. I need to clear...."

Shots rang out, striking the Camaro, shattering the windshield, and sending Sam diving for cover. Tara was screaming as she unholstered her pistol and returned fire. Sam quickly crawled to the front tire and poked his head around the bumper to try to return fire and draw the shooter's attention. Tara was firing and running backward toward the Camaro. She tripped over a rock edging and fell backward into a flower bed along the walkway.

Sam spotted a shooter near the right corner of the home and opened fire. "Move, Tara. Stay low and get back in the car," he yelled.

The shooter ducked back around the side of the house, allowing Tara time to scoot on her butt toward the Camaro.

"I don't think that's Everett's family. I don't recognize that dude."

"I do."

"What? Here? They followed us here?" Tara said. She ran around to the driver's side next to Sam.

"It looks like it. They're not the Russo brothers, though. That was Chris Mooney, an employee of Corbin Industries."

"Shit!" Tara said. "I drank with Chris and his brother. They came down here to kill me?"

"They work for the Corbins," Sam said.

"Now what?" Tara said.

"I'm going to need you to fire at the corner of the house while I jump in and get the Camaro started."

"Where is Russ Mooney?"

"I don't know. I haven't seen him yet. But you can bet he's around," Sam said.

As soon as Tara leaned around the bumper to fire, Sam jumped up and yanked open the car door. As he hopped into the driver's seat, Russ Mooney burst out the front door of the home with a shotgun in his hands.

Boom!

Shotgun pellets struck the body of Matt's car, taking out what was left of the windshield. Sam ducked down and reached for the key. He turned it and started the engine. "Jump in, Tara. Hurry!"

The left passenger door opened, and Tara dove on top of the boxes in the back seat as Russ reloaded the shotgun. Sam threw the car into reverse and punched the gas. The car leapt backward and bounced as it hit the pavement, causing Tara to hit the ceiling of the car and cry out. Chris Mooney stepped out from the side of the house and fired, several rounds of which hit the left front quarter panel of the Camaro.

Sam yanked the wheel to the right and stomped the gas pedal, allowing them to speed away from the Mooney boys, but they didn't make it far. The left front tire was the first to go, followed by the right. Sam drove the vehicle as far as it would go, but eventually, he pulled the car to a stop in the middle of the road.

Tara opened the door and crawled out. She and Sam stared at the flat tires for several seconds. "We have to get going, Tara. Empty that backpack and grab as many bottles of water as you can stuff into it," Sam said as he popped the trunk and retrieved his get-home bag.

TWENTY-EIGHT

Vince

Interstate 40
East of Knoxville, Tennessee
Day 2

Vince pulled the Jeep to a stop about fifty feet from Lauren and Charlie and cranked down his window. "You folks need a lift?" He laughed.

"Uncle Vince! What are you doing here?" Charlie asked, running up to the Jeep. "Did my dad send you?"

Vince exited the vehicle. Lauren peered inside and waved to Dave.

"No, Lindsay told us where you were," Vince said.

"Any word from Sam?" Lauren asked.

"Not yet. I'm sure he's on his way home," Vince said. He walked toward Lauren while staring down Cody. "Hey, Lauren. Who are your friends?"

"Vince, this is Cody and Casey. We met them on the road."

Vince nodded a greeting to Cody, then turned his attention to

Casey. "Ma'am." He positioned himself in front of Lauren but kept his eyes trained on Cody and Casey. "Lindsay is with your parents. You ready to go home?"

"Yes!" Lauren said. She spun to face her new companions and then back to Vince. "I'd like to bring them with us if you don't mind. Cody has skills we could use. He runs an outfitter business and guides hunters and fishing trips. We could use someone like that in Unicoi."

"You still planning on staying in town?" Vince asked.

"I can't move my parents, and I can't abandon my town. If I leave, you know who will step into that void. I can't let that happen."

"We can take care of Mahon and his crew," Vince said.

"What about the Corbins? You going to take them on, too?"

"If I have to. Let's load up and get out of here before we attract unwanted attention," Vince said.

"Let me talk to Cody and Casey, and I'll join you in a second," Lauren said.

~

Lauren made her offer to Cody and extended an invitation to Casey to return with her to Unicoi. Although she hadn't discussed it with Vince, she told them about the compound, playing up how well they were supplied and how safe it would be there.

"I guess I could stay for a bit, if it isn't too much trouble," Casey said.

"It's no trouble." Lauren wasn't sure that Vince and the others would agree. They'd spoken of only adding members to the group who had something to contribute. She wasn't sure how she'd convince Vince that taking in a teenage girl was the right thing to do. But down deep, he was as kindhearted as Sam. He wouldn't turn her away.

Cody didn't fully commit to staying but accepted the ride, giving Lauren more time to convince him. She hoped that once he saw the compound and heard her plan, he'd decide to call Unicoi home for the apocalypse.

Everyone crowded into the vehicle and Vince turned the Jeep toward Unicoi.

∼

On the return trip, Vince took every back road he could to avoid people. They met with a roadblock at Greeneville, Tennessee, near the Wal-Mart store that they had turned around to avoid. As Vince tried to navigate onto Highway 107 toward Erwin, a Green County sheriff's deputy stepped into the roadway. Vince stopped about a hundred feet away from him. The deputy approached the Jeep with his service pistol drawn, pointing at the ground.

"Everyone get down," Vince yelled as he threw the Jeep into reverse and punched it.

The deputy yelled something at them as they sped backward. Lauren shielded Charlie as Vince managed to slow the Jeep down and back into a driveway to turn around and accelerate away from the cop. A J-turn maneuver was out of the question as there was so much weight in the vehicle with the six of them stuffed in there along with all their gear.

Vince slowed the vehicle. "I think we're in the clear," he said.

Charlie took two deep puffs of his inhaler. "You okay? Do we need to find an emergency room?" Lauren asked. Her heart was racing. They were so close to home. She felt so helpless. She couldn't control Charlie's asthma, and now they had deputies aiming their weapons at them. What more would they encounter before they made it home?

∼

An hour and a half later, they entered Unicoi County and were greeted with yet another roadblock. The deputies behind the wooden barricades smiled as the Jeep approached. This time, Lauren wasn't concerned.

"Sir, I'm going to have to write you a citation for having too many passengers in your vehicle."

"At least we've got our seat belts on," Vince said, offering the deputy a fist bump. They bumped fists, and the officer peered inside the vehicle. "Well, most of us—there aren't enough seatbelts for everyone."

"Hey, Dave. Madam Mayor. Where are you folks headed?"

"You're a mayor?" Cody asked.

"I am."

"We're headed back to Unicoi. Have you had any trouble around here?" Vince asked the deputy.

"Not to speak of. Just the regular troublemakers. The sheriff had us go ahead and preemptively round them up. They're going to ride out this...." He waved his hand in the air. "Whatever this is, in the jail."

"Probably best," Dave said. He leaned down to make eye contact with the deputy. "Good call."

"I think Benny and Avery have things pretty well under control. One of their officers rode his dirt bike down to headquarters to see if the sheriff knew what was up with the lights and such. We've got deputies out at the travel center to keep folks on the interstate from causing problems."

"Good to hear," Vince said.

Lauren spoke up. "Deputy, do you still have Nigel Corbin in jail?"

He stepped around to Lauren's window. "Yes, ma'am. The DA ran over right after the lights went out and had a conversation with the sheriff about locking him in solitary confinement because they were afraid some of Corbin's men would try something to get him out. Don't you worry about him. He's not going anywhere."

Lauren exhaled in relief. If Nigel was somehow freed, he and Preston Corbin could focus all their attention on causing trouble in Unicoi. She'd rather not have to deal with that just yet, but she knew it was coming. She hoped Sam would be home when it all went down.

TWENTY-NINE

Becky

Becky Shelton's Apartment
Franklin, North Carolina
Day 2

When Becky Shelton invited the handsome hiker into her home, she hadn't known at the time what was wrong with the electricity or the phones, or what had made the cars stop working. But whatever it was, two days later, they still weren't working. The store remained closed, and mister gorgeous was still lounging on her sofa. It was heaven. Becky didn't really care whether those things ever came back on.

"My mom has probably already sent out a search party for me," Deep Dish said. That was the hunky hiker's trail name. Apparently, he loved deep-dish pizza. "I was supposed to check in with her after I arrived at the hostel."

"The guy at the grocery store said he'd heard the power issues had hit the whole east coast—maybe even the Midwest."

"How'd he hear that if the phones are all down?" Deep Dish asked.

"He said his uncle had some type of radio he used to talk to people all over the country. He said they're calling it an EMP, whatever that is."

"An electromagnetic pulse? You're sure that's what he said?"

"No. He said EMP."

Deep Dish dropped his chin to his chest. She hated when someone looked at her like that. It was so condescending. "That's what EMP stands for. If that's the case, we've been attacked by a foreign enemy. This is bad—really, really bad." Deep Dish stood, pulled on his pants, and headed toward the door.

"Where are you going?" Becky asked.

Deep Dish picked up his backpack and shouldered it. "I have to get home."

"How? The cars won't start."

He pointed to his feet. "The same way I intended to get home before. I have to get back on the AT."

The Appalachian Trail ran from north Georgia all the way to Maine. Franklin, Tennessee, was but one of many stops for thru-hikers making the two thousand-mile plus journey.

"You're leaving, then?"

"I need to get home. See ya later, baby," Deep Dish said as he closed the door.

Becky doubted she'd ever see Wolf "Deep Dish" Ellison again, even if everything returned to normal. From the window of her garage apartment, Becky watched her lover walk out of her life. All she had now were her memories of him and the wonderful few days they'd shared.

She felt a crushing pain in her chest as he disappeared from view. She wanted to throw open the door and run after him, but he would have asked if he'd wanted her to go with him. A tear rolled down her cheek as she closed the blackout curtains and returned to the sofa. Becky stared at the empty water bottles on the coffee table. "What am I going to do now?"

She was low on food and only had two more bottles of water

left. Without running water, they'd been doing their business in the woods behind the main house. Becky thought about Deep Dish's reaction to the news she'd brought him. He was college-educated. He knew what an EMP was—and it scared him—she could tell. She stood and looked round her tiny efficiency kitchen. She had to do something. She couldn't continue to wait there for things to return to normal. She needed to find food. The grocery store was closed. Nick, the owner's son, had said they were going to lock the doors after she left. There hadn't been much left on the shelves when she'd gone there that morning. Anyone with cash had already gone in and gotten what they could.

Becky went to the bedroom closet and slid open the door. In the corner was her rifle—a 30-30 left to her by her brother before he went to boot camp and then Afghanistan. They'd often hunted together as kids—more out of necessity than for sport. Money had been tight at their house, and most of their food had come from what they could hunt or fish for themselves. Becky's grandmother had taught her how to forage the forest floor for wild edible plants.

Becky would go back to her old ways of survival. She'd return to the woods. Once she had enough food, she would set out for home. She'd find her way north to the Shelton Laurel Valley, and her childhood home, nestled in the Blue Ridge Mountains.

THIRTY

Billy

Unicoi Motor Inn
Unicoi, Tennessee
Day 2

"Billy, we're out of booze."

Billy opened one eye. The motel room he called home was dark, except for the light peeking around the sides of the blackout curtains. He sat up, flicked his lighter, and held the flame out to see who the hell had the balls to disturb his nap. Sharon, his bottom girl, stood in the doorway. She'd been with him since the early days. He'd got her fresh off the Greyhound bus in Nashville way back in the day.

"What do you want me to do about it?" Billy said as he sat up and spun his legs over the side of the bed.

"Send Jerome over to the truck stop to get more," Sharon said. "We're thirsty."

"Drink water," Billy said, standing and pulling on his pants.

"We can't. The water stopped running hours ago."

"Fine," he said, reaching the doorway. The hall was dark. He called for Jerome, and the skinny man came running. Jerome wasn't a member of Billy's original crew. He'd been assigned to him by Jerome's uncle, Nigel Corbin. Nigel had sent Jerome to Unicoi to learn the trade from the bottom up, or so the prick had said. Billy didn't buy it. He'd sent the kid there to spy on him.

Jerome came running up. "Yes, boss."

"Take some guys and go find us something to drink. Water, beer, wine, whatever you can get," Billy said.

"Um—the cops aren't letting us into town, and the customers at the truck stop already cleaned that place out," Jerome said.

"What do you mean the cops aren't letting you into town?"

"They got a roadblock up, and the cops are sending everybody here."

"Here? They're sending people here—to my motel?" Billy's hands balled into fists, and he bit down on his bottom lip. He could feel a headache coming on. His stomach was twisting. He needed a fix, and then he'd deal with Avery. They had a deal. If Avery couldn't keep the cops and that lady mayor off his back, he was no use to Billy. If he was no use to Billy, he was no use to his new partners, the Russos. He'd have to remind Avery of that fact.

"What about the south end of town, down near the grocery store?" Billy asked.

"They got roadblocks there, too."

"When did all this happen? Did you even talk to Avery?"

"He said that the mayor and council gave him strict orders. He was working on a way to get around it. He asked for more time."

"Find a way in. Get us food and drinks, or don't come back. I'll go deal with Police Chief Avery."

~

Billy hopped on his motorcycle and was just about to crank over the engine when Sharon came running out. "You are not going to believe who is in your motel lobby."

"I'm in no mood to play guessing games, Sharon. I have to go find Avery."

"You're going to want to see this chick," Sharon said.

"You deal with it. That's your job. You handle the girls, remember?" Sharon was good at her job. She had a way of bringing in renegades and making sure no one in his stable decided to screw up.

"She's not someone to add to your stable. It's Tony Russo's wife. She and his kids are in the office looking for a room."

Billy lowered the kickstand and let the bike lean on it.

"Give her your room and make sure she doesn't leave."

"My room? Why...."

"Do what I say, woman. Give her your room, and then have Mad Dog sit outside her room. I don't want no one to go near her, you hear me?"

"Fine," Sharon said, turning and stomping off.

Billy couldn't believe his luck. He would have run straight for the slot machines if the casinos had been open. Billy was on fire. He'd worked out a deal with the Russos for Corbin's cut of the operation, and now, in walks this new bargaining chip. He'd use Tony's wife and kids to sweeten the deal and get a better percentage. He fought the urge to run inside the motel to inspect this new prize. That would have to wait. He had more pressing matters to attend to right now.

Billy walked over and straddled his motorcycle. He needed to have a quiet conversation with Avery before sending someone to Knoxville to let his partner know he was holding his daughter-in-law and grandchildren. He had an opportunity to have all this turn out to his advantage. Billy could have total control of this area and cut out his partners altogether—but only if he played it right. He needed Avery on board—at least until he had things in place. He would need his help to eliminate the mayor and take on Vince's group. After that, he'd off Avery and appoint himself chief of police.

THIRTY-ONE

Sam

Highway 60
Gainesville, Georgia
Day 2

Sam and Tara had left Matt's beloved Camaro—and Sam's only ride home—in the middle of the road two miles from where Tara had planned to survive the apocalypse. They set off walking—again. Both were equally devastated by their prospective losses. Sam was wracking his brain, trying to think of where he could get another running vehicle. There had to be older trucks or sports cars around there somewhere he could steal.

Steal? A thought once so abhorrent to his moral character was now a part of his vocabulary. An act he wouldn't have ever considered before was now something Sam included in his toolbox for daily survival. He wasn't exactly proud of it, but it was what it was. His singular goal now was to get home by whatever means necessary. Sam had spent all of his adult life putting his life on the line for others. He'd sacrificed his life, and time with his loved ones to do so, but now he felt compelled to put his family first. If that meant stealing a vehicle, he was going to do it.

As they walked through a business district, Tara was limping and falling behind, but Sam didn't slow. They had to put distance between themselves and Corbin's men.

Sam veered toward the right side of the road when two men and a woman wearing backpacks stepped from a pharmacy parking lot on their left into the roadway and began walking next to them.

"Blisters?" An older man asked Tara. He was dressed in hiking shorts, a T-shirt, trail runners, and a Panama-style hat.

"Yes," Tara replied.

"I got something that might help," the woman said. "We're thru-hikers. We know all about blisters."

What she said suddenly struck a chord with Sam. He stopped, turned around, and approached them.

"You're thru-hikers? Appalachian Trail thru-hikers?" Sam asked.

"Yes, we just finished our southbound hike. We were heading to Gainesville to catch the Amtrak to the Atlanta airport when our shuttle van just died. We had to walk to town. When we got here, someone said all the cars weren't working, and that phones and electricity were out, too. Do you know what happened?" the older man asked. The man's white hair stuck up as he removed his hat to wipe sweat from his brow.

"An EMP," Sam said matter-of-factly. "Nothing's coming back on anytime soon."

The hikers stared at one another in disbelief. "That's what the shuttle driver said. We didn't believe her," the twenty-something woman said. She took a step toward them, and Sam held out his left arm, palm out, to halt her. His right hand went to his holster, and she stumbled backward.

"I'm Moondust, and this is Professor and Tumbleweed. I'm from New Hampshire, Professor is from Boston, and Tumbleweed is from Arizona."

Tumbleweed was a head taller than the other two and wore a skull cap and a fanny pack.

"That's a long walk," Tara said.

"Over two thousand miles," Moondust said.

Tumbleweed nodded and set his hiking pack on the ground next to him. "Damn, I planned to do a northbound hike someday, but I didn't think I'd turn around and head back to the trail so soon."

Moondust and the older man stared at each another. "I don't know if I have another hike in me," Professor said.

"Do we have another option?" she asked.

He shrugged one shoulder. "It doesn't sound like it."

"You're going to head north on the AT?" Sam asked. Until that moment, Sam hadn't even thought about using it to get home, but now it made perfect sense. A section of the Appalachian Trail went right through Unicoi County. It was the shortest and safest route to walk, and these three, having just traveled it themselves, would know where to find water and the best places to shelter for the night. "I'm going with them, Tara. I think you should come, too."

Tara dropped her gaze to her feet.

"I can help with that," Moondust said.

Moondust took off toward the pharmacy and returned with a hiker's medkit in her hand. She held out a stick of Body Glide anti-chafing stick. "Apply this to your feet, then wipe your feet down with the baby wipes and dry them really well," she said.

"Deodorant?" Tara asked.

"No, it looks like deodorant, but it will prevent more blisters."

Tara made a funny face but applied the stick anyway.

"Now, this athletic tape will help with pain from the blisters you've already got," Moondust said.

"I wear Injinji Toesocks as my base layer and Darn Tough wool socks over those, and I never get blisters anymore," Tumbleweed said.

"A horizontal patterned lacing on those running shoes might

stop your foot from sliding around inside the shoe so much and reduce the friction causing the blisters, too," Professor said.

Within fifteen minutes, the trio of hikers had Tara's feet squared away, and everyone was ready to head toward Springer Mountain, where the trailhead for the Appalachian Trail started.

"Where are you two from?" Moondust asked.

"Georgia," Tara replied. Sam said nothing. He didn't know these people well enough to reveal his personal information to them.

"I met up with Tumbleweed in Maine. We've hiked together ever since. We're not a couple or anything. We just hike together. I think he considers himself my protector from the Bro Culture."

"What's the Bro Culture?" Tara asked.

"Well, it's the guys who think female hikers are only there because they're wild and want to hook up. They throw a hundred questions at you about how far you've hiked, how you carry your bag, put down your gear as inadequate, hit on you, and get offended when you turn them down."

"Sounds like every guy I've ever known—minus the gear questions," Tara said.

Moondust nodded toward Sam. "You with him?"

Sam turned his attention toward the women. If Tara divulged their problem with the Russo brothers, it could cause the hikers to not want to help them.

"Like you and Tumbleweed. He thinks he's protecting me, but I've saved his ass a time or two along the way."

Sam huffed. She had saved him after the Bronco crashed. The Russo brothers could have easily rushed in and shot him while he was unconscious, but he'd put his life on the line more than once to save her.

"We met Professor just before Harper's Ferry. He has a wife back home. That has to be hard. He was a professor at Harvard. That's how he got his trail name. That, and he reads on every break and every night before sleeping. Most of us are too tired to even eat, but he still pulls out a novel or something and loses himself in it."

"He's a little old to be walking two thousand miles," Tara said.

Sam had seen much older hikers on the trail when he had hiked it two years earlier. In fact, there were a lot of retirees on the trail. The hikers ranged in age from college kids on a gap year to folks fresh off retirement. The year Sam had hiked, an eighty-three-year-old man became the oldest person to complete the twenty-two-hundred-mile journey.

"He keeps up. He hasn't taken as many zero days as Tumbleweed and me."

"Zero days?" Tara asked.

"Days that you get zero miles. Usually, they're the days you go into town for resupply."

Sam had only taken one zero day when he section hiked the AT. He'd wanted to make as many miles as he could before being picked up and shuttled back to Unicoi County.

"I wonder if the stores in the towns we normally stop at for supplies will be open. If not, I don't know how we'll get food and supplies. I had to swap shoes four times during my southbound hike. If I can't get new trail runners, I don't know how I'll make it all the way to New Hampshire."

"I don't know," Tara said.

Sam knew. The stores would be closed, but the entire town would also likely be off-limits to non-residents. That's what he'd do if he was in charge.

∽

As they approached an arm of Lake Lanier, Tumbleweed unclipped a red twenty-ounce water bottle from his pack and slipped through the trees toward the shoreline.

"You're not going to drink that water, are you?" Tara asked him.

"It's a long way back to the trailhead," he said, continuing toward the lake.

"Do you see all those houses across the bridge? All the chemicals they put on the lush green lawns drain directly into the lake."

"My Sawyer S3 Select water filter will take care of any chemicals or heavy metals and make it safe to drink," he said in an animated tone and smiling, pointing to his water filter like he was an actor in a TV commercial.

Moondust rolled her eyes and she and Professor took their water filtration bottles and followed him to the lake.

Sam handed Tara one of their twenty-ounce bottles of Aquafina. She took a sip of water and then wiped the perspiration from her brow with the back of her hand. "How far is it to the trailhead?"

"About thirty or so miles," Sam said.

Tara held the bottle up and stared at it. "I'm going to need a lot more than this."

"I have a water filter. We should cross a creek or something before we run out of water. Save your bottles when you empty them. We'll use my filter to fill them up again."

"This is going to be awkward to carry. I wish I had a way to hook it to me like Moondust has hers. It clips to the strap of her backpack."

"You can put yours in my side pouch and grab it when you need a drink."

"You'll carry it for me?"

"Sure," Sam said.

"You're too nice to have been a cop," Tara said.

"You just have a skewed perception of police officers," Sam said.

"Maybe. We were on opposite sides."

Sam didn't know what to say to that. Tara was a victim. She wasn't really on the wrong side of the law. She'd been forced into her position through bad luck. He couldn't tell her that, though. He didn't want her to see herself as a victim right now. He needed her to be the strong, capable woman that she was deep down inside. He'd seen a glimpse of it in her already. She was a survivor. She'd been through hell in life and was still standing.

"Are we ready?" Moondust asked, climbing up the bank.

"Ready as I'll ever be," Tara said.

∽

As they entered Murrayville, smoke rose from a factory that was on fire. Sam covered his mouth and nose, and the group hurried past it.

"I hope that smell doesn't stick in my hair and clothes," Tara said.

It likely would, but Sam didn't tell her that.

As they passed a small pharmacy, Sam noticed the glass in the door had been broken out. "I'm going to check this place out," he said, stepping off the roadway into the parking lot.

"It's closed, Sam," Tara said.

Sam surveyed the area. It was fairly secluded. No one was around to see him go inside. "Tara, stand by the door and keep a lookout."

"It's too dangerous, Sam. Is it really worth the risk?" she asked.

The three hikers stood at the curb, sipping from their water bottles and watching them.

"You guys can walk ahead if you want. We'll catch up."

"You searching for drugs?" Professor asked.

"I'm looking for antibiotics mostly." He pointed toward the broken glass. "I doubt there are any narcotics left inside."

"Probably not," Professor said. He nodded toward the store. "Maybe we should stock up on supplies. There might not be many places left to get them later."

Tumbleweed shrugged his shoulders and took off toward the pharmacy.

"What if the owner's in there?" Moondust asked, following Tumbleweed.

"Then we offer to pay for what we take," Tumbleweed said.

"We should leave cash on the counter. I don't want to become a thief," Moondust said.

"Cash is nothing more than paper in an apocalypse," Professor said.

"Apocalypse? That's a little extreme, don't you think? Everything will be back to normal by the time we make it back to New Hampshire," Moondust said.

"Hopefully," Professor said.

"You guys wait here. I'll go in and make sure it's safe," Sam said, unholstering his pistol.

∽

Sam pulled open the glass door. Straight ahead was a counter with soda fountain-style stools. No one was behind the counter. Sam scanned the left corner of the store and along the wall to the back where the medication was stored on shelves. He stepped over the threshold. Broken glass crunched under his feet. Sam cleared the building, aisle by aisle. No one was in sight, but he still needed to clear the back storeroom.

Sam moved slowly toward the pharmacy counter in the back of the store. He reached and turned the knob of the door leading into the area where the meds were kept. Easing it open, he walked carefully into the room. He cleared each row of shelving and then made his way toward a door in the back corner. He tried the knob, but the door was locked. Sam moved to the office door. Without entering, he could see through the glass that no one was inside.

Sam returned to the front of the store. "All's clear, but let's make it fast. Grab what you can carry and try not to make much noise."

Sam felt uneasy about what he was about to do. It had been his job to protect private property from theft, and now he was the one doing the taking. He tried the rationale that if he didn't, someone else would, and that his family might need the medication in the days, weeks, and months ahead. There wouldn't be any meds to be found if he waited until then, but in his final analysis, he discovered he was still just a taker. Maybe not exactly like the other takers he had encountered since the lights went out, but the difference was minute—however, it was a very thin line.

While Tara and the hikers went for food and snacks, Sam began loading a plastic grocery sack with every corticosteroid he could find, along with bronchodilators like montelukast, zafirlukast, and zileuton. Next, he looked for antibiotics, heart medication, high blood pressure meds, and the cholinesterase inhibitors his mother-in-law took for her dementia.

Professor walked toward him. "How are you planning on carrying all that?"

"I thought I'd just tie the bag to the outside of my backpack. I'll have to consolidate everything later to get it the rest of the way home, though."

He spotted Tara moving from aisle to aisle. She was the only one in the group not wearing a pack. Sam moved to a display rack that contained sheepskin bed pads. He grabbed the twenty-four by thirty pad and ripped open the packaging. He was in the process of folding it to make a pack when Tara screamed.

Sam dropped the sheepskin pad and unholstered his pistol. Crouching, he moved toward the sound of her voice.

A greasy-haired man was holding Tara with a gun pointed at her. Professor, Moondust, and Tumbleweed stood eyes wide and mouths agape beyond the perp. Sam looked past them to a side door, which now stood open. Were there others waiting for them outside? How many more were with them?

"Let go of me, asshole. You best let me go. Sam! Sam, help me!" Tara shouted.

Sam rushed to the end of the aisle, and eased forward to assess the situation, using a display cabinet for concealment. A greasy-haired man in his early twenties was holding Tara by the hair. His clothes were dirty, and his hands were nearly black with grime. From his appearance, Sam considered him an addict.

Tara was flailing her arms and trying to pull away. Sam stepped out, leveling his pistol at the man. "Stop! Police! Let her go!" Sam shouted. It worked. The man threw his arms above his head, and he backed away holding Tara's gun in one hand pointed at the ceiling. Tara stepped away from the tweaker, out of Sam's line of fire. The tweaker was now standing squarely between the three hikers and Sam.

"Robby!" a woman's voice called out. A short, round woman stepped out from an aisle behind Tara to Sam's right, holding a revolver.

"Stop! Put down the weapon!" Sam yelled, but the woman's gun had gone off before he could finish. The bullet ripped through the display cabinet next to Sam. He returned fire, hitting the woman in the chest. She dropped to the floor, and the revolver skidded toward Tara, who pounced on it and leveled the weapon at the fallen woman. Tara's eyes were wild with fear and fury.

"Tara," Sam said. "Are you okay?"

She turned toward Sam. Her eyes filled with tears. "They were going to kill us. They were going to shoot us over some stupid effing drugs."

Sam returned his attention toward the tweaker. "Put the weapon down!" Sam yelled.

Tara spun around pointing the woman's revolver at the tweaker.

"Don't shoot me. Don't shoot me, please. I got a kid," the Tweaker pleaded, slowly lowering Tara's gun to the floor. "We thought you were going to kill us. I got to get back to my little girl. She's all alone. Please don't kill me," he begged. He was crying and wiping snot from his nose with the collar of his shirt.

"Kick it to me," Sam said.

The tweaker kicked the gun, but it spun sideways toward Tara.

Sam saw the next few horrifying seconds play out in his mind even before Tara began moving toward her pistol. Lowering the revolver, she bent to pick up the weapon. Tara was now in Sam's line of fire, as were the three hikers standing behind the perp. Sam took another step forward just as the tweaker bolted toward Tara and lunged, knocking her to the ground. They were a tangle of bodies, and Sam couldn't get a good bead on the man. A shot rang out, and Tara and the tweaker both stopped moving.

THIRTY-TWO

Lauren

Taylor Residence
Unicoi, Tennessee
Day 2

Lauren wasn't happy to see that they could drive right through the town of Unicoi unimpeded. Police Chief John Avery had failed to set up roadblocks on all the incoming routes like some of the other towns. There was no police presence at all as they approached city hall and the police department. Vince continued through town, past the fire department and post office, without Lauren seeing a soul out and about. As they came around the curve just past the realty office, Lauren spotted something in the road.

"Roadblock ahead," Dave called out.

Lauren leaned forward between the seats. "There they all are." She counted three Unicoi police officers standing behind a row of concrete barriers blocking both lanes near the bank.

"We see where Avery's priorities lie," Dave said.

"I figured we'd find him guarding Corbin's bank. I bet the other officers are guarding Corbin's girls at the motel," Vince said.

Vince pulled up to the barrier and stopped as Avery walked up to the vehicle.

"Vince," Avery said. He eyed the Jeep like it was a juicy steak. "What are you doing out running the roads?"

Vince stabbed a thumb over his shoulder. "Bringing your boss home."

Avery leaned down and peered into the back seat. He appeared surprised to see her. "Mayor. I thought you were in Knoxville."

"I was. Now I'm not. Can you get word to the board members? I'm going to get home and check on my parents and then I want to call a special meeting. Have everyone meet me at city hall in about two hours."

Vince pulled onto the grass to drive around the roadblock before Avery could respond. He turned his head to his left as they passed the road leading toward Interstate 26 and the travel center. "There are the good cops. They're stopping the interstate foot traffic from entering the town."

Benny was directing a group of non-residents back toward the travel center. Lauren leaned over Charlie to get a look for herself. That would be her first stop on her way back to city hall, but first things first: get home and out of her stinky clothes.

~

Lauren's shoulders slumped as Vince pulled up to her parents' house. Sam's Bronco wasn't in the driveway. He should have been home by now unless he'd run into trouble. Her mind went crazy, running through all the issues Sam could have encountered on his way out of Atlanta. Bile rose in her throat, and her breathing quickened. Her thoughts raced. All she wanted to do was find her husband and bring him home.

For a long moment, Lauren stared at the front of her childhood home. The brick facade was aging and in need of repairs. The porch railing was sagging, and the concrete was chipped. Her elderly parents were inside with their nurse. She couldn't leave them to fend for themselves while she searched for Sam. He'd expect her to look after his son. What if neither of them had returned? Who would make sure Charlie survived?

"I can't thank you enough…."

Vince cut her off. "You don't have to thank me. You and Charlie are family."

"You risked your life for us," she said.

"Like I said, you're family."

Her gut clenched. He was so much like his brother. She was sure wherever Sam was at the moment, he was putting his life on the line to save someone. He was saving strangers. That was why he hadn't returned yet.

"Tell Lindsay I'll be back for her in a bit," Vince said, then backed down the drive to take Dave, Casey, and Cody to the gun-range-turned-apocalyptic-survival-compound.

∼

Walking through the door, Lauren heard laughter coming from the family room. The sound of dice hitting the coffee table brought back sweet memories. She removed her shoes and placed them by the door before joining her family. Angela was seated on the sofa next to Lindsay and Unicoi City Clerk, Millie Riley. Bill sat across from Lindsay in his wheelchair. Edna was seated next to him in her swivel chair. A board game was stretched out on the table between them—one of the same ones her parents used to play with Lauren and her brother, Josh. A thought came to her. Were the lights out in California? Would she ever see Josh again? She couldn't dwell on it.

Light filtered in through the large, open windows. The wind coming through them caused the gold-colored curtains to billow into the room. Despite the breeze, the room was stiflingly hot. She worried her father would overheat.

"How are you doing, Pop?" Lauren said, walking into the room.

"I'm fine, Lauren," Bill said, spinning his chair around.

Angela had dug out his old manual wheelchair. It didn't have a spot for his oxygen tank, and the cord tangled as he turned. Angela jumped up and grabbed it, moving the bottle around to the opposite side. Lauren touched her fingers to her lips and choked back tears.

"Lauren, you're home," Millie said, rising from the sofa.

Charlie walked around her and entered the living room, his head moving back and forth as if he expected his dad to pop up somewhere. She felt so bad for the kid.

She pointed to the game on the coffee table. "Who's winning?"

Lindsay tilted her head. "Edna."

Her mother smiled.

"Way to go, Mom."

"Come play with us, Josh," she said.

"That's Charlie, Mom, remember? He's Sam's son," Lauren wasn't sure why she had corrected her. It wasn't like she would remember it ten minutes from then. Charlie seemed to understand and didn't mind being called by her brother's name. Edna returned to rolling the dice without a response.

"Did Sam...." Bill paused, wheezing through labored breaths. He pressed a finger to the tubing, bringing oxygen to his lungs from a tank beside his wheelchair, and then continued. "... get back from Atlanta?"

"Not yet," Lauren said.

Bill rolled over, reached for her, and slipped a frail, wrinkled hand into hers. Lauren stared into his pale blue eyes. He resembled nothing of the strong, steady man she'd known as a little girl. It pricked her heart to see him so fragile. "He'll be fine," he said.

"I know," Lauren said.

"He knows how to take care of himself," Bill said.

"Yes, he does," Lauren said. He did. Sam had served six years in the military prior to returning to Unicoi and joining the Johnson

City police force. But the current situation was different from any they had faced before. It was filled with so many unknowns, and not being able to contact him and learn where he was and how he was doing was pure torture.

Lauren knelt on the floor beside her mother and took her hand in hers. "How are you, Mom? Are you too warm? Do you need a drink of water?"

Edna turned her gaze toward the door. "Where's Josh? He better not be skipping school again. I'll take a switch to him." She started to stand, but Lauren placed a hand on her shoulder.

"He didn't skip today, Mom."

Edna eased herself back into her chair. Lauren released her mother's hand and stood. "Let me get you a drink of water."

"Sam will be home tomorrow. You wanna play Yahtzee with us?" Bill asked, flashing a toothy grin.

"I would, Dad, but I have to go to city hall and check on things there," she said.

"You still having trouble with the owner of the Unicoi Inn?" Bill asked.

"I think Benny has that in hand for the moment, but I might need to get him some reinforcement."

"Billy's a hothead. You want to watch out for that one," Bill said, wheezing loudly. He leaned forward in his chair, trying to catch his breath.

"I can handle him."

"Maybe it isn't such a good idea to make enemies, Lauren."

"Don't worry, Dad. I know how to deal with scumbags like Billy Mahon." She patted her dad's hand and turned toward the kitchen.

"Angela, may I have a word with you in the kitchen?" Lauren asked. She didn't want to upset her parents. She'd need to figure out a few things before breaking the news to them about the EMP.

Angela's face went ghostly white as Lauren explained about the EMP and its effects on the lights, phones, and other electronics. "Why are the cars not working either?" she asked with a hitch in her voice.

"The EMP knocked out all the electronics in the newer cars. Some older ones without modern electronics, like the one Vince drove to get Charlie and me, they still run."

"Wait, Sam has that old Bronco," Angela said.

Lauren was trying not to think about Sam and how he'd get home to them. It was more than she could cope with at the moment. She had too many other things that needed her attention. If she allowed herself to give into her rising panic about Sam, Lauren was afraid it would affect the choices she needed to make, and she had to remain focused on securing their home and the town before anything else.

"He does. He'll be home soon."

～

After Vince had returned and picked up Lindsay and Millie, Angela had graciously agreed to stay with Bill and Edna until Lauren could figure something else out. Lauren promised to help her find a way home that didn't include walking the ten miles to get there. She wasn't sure how she would uphold her end of the bargain, but she'd find a way. The best she could come up with at the moment was Charlie's bicycle, but that was how she intended to get back and forth to city hall.

Lauren debated telling her parents the lights weren't coming back on anytime soon. She knew her father would dismiss the notion at first. Bill never believed any of Vince's predictions. He'd had faith the current administration could avert any conflict with foreign adversaries. Obviously, he'd been mistaken because here they were in the dark, facing the biggest threat in modern history.

"You're sure it's not aliens like in the Fifth Wave movie?"

Charlie asked with a straight face. He pulled his inhaler from his pocket and flipped it around in his hand but didn't use it.

Bill snickered.

"Fairly sure," Lauren said. She didn't believe in aliens, but until proven otherwise, everything was on the table. "We haven't seen or heard anything to lead us to that conclusion."

"My dad has the Bronco. He'll be able to get home, right?"

"It should still run just like Vince's Jeep. I'm sure he's on his way home right now."

Charlie was quiet for a moment. He stared at the floor as he spoke. "What about my mom and little sister?"

Lauren hadn't been prepared for the question. What could she say? If Vince was right, Toledo would soon become a lawless wasteland. Sam's ex-wife, Bekka, had moved there with a man she had met online. At the time, Lauren couldn't believe the judge had allowed her to move out of state with Sam's son. Now she and her new husband, and Charlie's new baby sister, would be fighting for their lives within days. Lauren was glad Charlie was with her in northeast Tennessee. Otherwise, Sam would head straight to Ohio to get him. That was a selfish way to think of it, she knew.

Sam, where are you?

"I'm sure the officials in Toledo will take care of things there," she lied.

Charlie lifted his gaze. He had Sam's eyes. "Like you're going to do here?"

She stared back at Charlie, expressionless. She wasn't sure whether he was being sarcastic, or not. It was sometimes hard to tell with him—just like Sam.

"I'm going to do my best."

Charlie looked down at his pistol and began trying to get the holster unclipped from his belt. "Here's your gun back," he said.

"I want you to keep it with you at all times—even here, Charlie. Can you do that for us?"

Charlie stopped fidgeting with the holster and looked up at her with Sam's eyes again. "I can."

"Thank you, Charlie," Lauren said. She left Charlie in the living room and walked down the hall to her and Sam's bedroom. First, she pulled a backpack out of the closet, set it on the bed, and unzipped one of the side pouches. Then, she retrieved a flashlight, flicked it on, and scanned the dark room. Finally, she pulled out a pair of tactical pants, a tank top, a button-up shirt with pockets, and a pair of thick wool socks from her dresser. She stared at the socks for a moment, debating if she really needed them. It was eighty-five degrees out with high humidity. Wearing wool socks might just give her heat stroke.

After dressing in more apocalypse-appropriate attire, Lauren slid her arms through the straps of the pack and headed for the door. She sat in the corner chair and placed her foot on the ottoman to study the two blisters that had already formed on the heel and side of her foot from walking home. Yes, she needed the wool socks. She hoped the wind would be cool enough as she rode to avoid overheating.

"I thought you were going to work? What the heck is in that thing?" Bill wheezed as he rolled into the bedroom.

"Just a few things I might need at city hall."

"Like what?"

She pulled her flashlight from the side pocket of her pants. "Light."

"You got a gun on you?"

Her gaze remained fixed on her feet as she slid on her black trail-running shoes. "I'm bringing my Peacemaker, as usual."

"Good," Bill said and he rolled behind Lauren back down the hallway toward the living room. "And I'm glad you've given Charlie a pistol, too."

Lauren was shocked. He'd been opposed to her carrying. He didn't even want guns in the house.

"Angela, I cannot tell you how grateful I am for you." She

placed a hand on her father's shoulder. "I'll be back sometime tonight, Pop. Don't wait up, though. I'm not sure how long I'll be."

"You should have Benny drive you home," Bill said.

"The police cruisers aren't working either." She leaned over and put her arms around her father's neck. "I love you very much, Daddy."

"I love you too, Lauren Michelle." He patted her arm. "You don't have to be everything to everyone, you know." He paused to catch his breath. "You are only one person. Delegate. The town will pull together in the end. They may balk at first, but in the end, they'll rise to the challenge."

"Thanks, Pop. I'll do my best."

"I know you will. I would never doubt that for a second."

THIRTY-THREE

Lauren

Unicoi City Hall
Unicoi, Tennessee
Day 2

Lauren was drenched in sweat after pedaling Charlie's bike the four miles to city hall. She'd attempted to keep her mind off Sam by working on the speech she planned to give Unicoi's residents about the EMP. She'd been successfully compartmentalizing for the most part, but there was this deep ache in the pit of her stomach that she could not shake. It was a constant battle not to think the worst. She consoled herself by imagining Sam with his get-home bag on his back, walking up Interstate 26 toward Unicoi.

Lauren parked Charlie's bike in the employee outdoor break area behind city hall and approached the side door. Instead of the sweet, cool air conditioning when she pulled open the door, the inside of the municipal building felt like an oven.

Ralph's voice boomed in the dark corridor. "How did you make it back?"

She ignored his question, walked down the short hall, unlocked her office door, and dropped her bag inside. "Is everyone in the conference room?"

"We've been here practically since the lights went out," Ralph said.

Lauren entered the conference room and was relieved to see all four council members seated around the long conference table. Candles lit up the space. Gretchen Rhodes, the alderwoman for Ward Two, looked like she'd slept at city hall. Normally so put-together, her grey hair was a mess, her clothes wrinkled, and mascara was smeared into the crow's feet at the corners of her eyes. Ralph Cross's white V-neck T-shirt stuck to his rotund belly and had sweat stains around the collar and underarms. The long hair he normally combed over to cover his bald spot hung down over his forehead. The aldermen had had a rough twenty-four hours from the looks of things.

"Good to see everyone here. Let's get down to business," Lauren said, pulling out the chair at the head of the long wooden conference table.

Lloyd Beard, the longest-serving alderman, sat at the end of the table with an empty water bottle in front of him. His face was flushed, and he, too, was sweating profusely. Lauren was concerned that the older aldermen might overheat and suffer heat stroke before they could settle their business and adjourn for the day.

"Maybe we should take this meeting outside to the employee picnic table. At least we'd have a breeze," Lauren said.

Ralph was the first to the door. "I don't know why we didn't think of that hours ago."

Lauren was struck by the eerie silence of their small town as the council members gathered around the picnic table. They quickly began talking over one another as they speculated on what may have caused the lights to go out. Alderwoman Maryann Winters' hands were waving wildly as she spoke a mile a minute.

"Quiet down, everyone! Quiet—please!" Lauren held a hand in

the air, trying to gain their attention. "May I have your attention, please?"

Nothing was working.

She stuck two fingers between her lips and blew. The whistle was loud enough to cause everyone to stop and turn toward her. "Okay, now that I have your attention, I believe I know what this is."

"What? How could you know?" Maryann asked. "You weren't even here when it happened! There's been nothing like this in all my sixty-seven years on this earth."

"No, there hasn't. Not here. Not of this magnitude. I believe an EMP or electromagnetic pulse has occurred. We've talked about this, Maryann—including what it could do to the power grid."

"Ours is protected. Tennessee Valley got that grant, and they said...."

"They just started trying to harden it against an EMP attack recently. Only the new equipment that went into their Faraday cage is hardened. None of the old equipment has been retrofitted." She pointed to the electric poles lining the roadway just outside the building. "It just wasn't enough."

"What are we going to do now?" Maryann asked.

"First, we need to make sure the roadblock out by the travel center is manned twenty-four-seven to keep the travelers on the interstate from flooding into the town," Lauren said.

"What roadblock? Why? What do you mean?" Gretchen asked.

"She means we need to stop the freeloaders on the interstate from swarming the city and using up town resources," Ralph said.

Maryann whipped around and placed her hands on her hips.

"Freeloaders. That's unkind. They're travelers in need of assistance. The town of Unicoi doesn't turn its back on visitors to our fair city."

"The optics won't look good if we start turning away stranded motorists, Lauren," Lloyd said.

"We have an obligation to take them in according to our

contract with the Red Cross and our grant for the community center shelter," Gretchen said.

"Well, the Red Cross has an obligation to provide their services to us, and they are just as incapacitated as we are," Lauren countered. She clenched her jaw. They weren't getting it. Stranded tourists were about to become a burden that the town couldn't bear.

Once the resources are gone, the tourists will move on, leaving the residents with bare pantries.

Lauren stared at the sky, trying to think of a tactful way to say they were all idiots. Nothing was coming to her. All she could think about was the grocery stores being overrun with strangers and the children of Unicoi starving to death because these four were more worried about optics and contracts. She exhaled and rolled her shoulders. They were all in this together. She'd need to bring them around to her way of thinking because the alternative would put her parents and Sam's son at risk. No matter how much she wanted to walk away and let the bleeding hearts learn the hard way, she couldn't. Other families would be hurt. She wasn't about to let that happen on her watch. The people of Unicoi had elected her mayor. Lauren knew she needed to find a way to bring the town together if they were to stand a chance of surviving.

"I understand that turning away stranded travelers sounds harsh, and in normal times we would never, ever consider such an option. But here's the deal: the grocery store only has enough food for a couple of days. Even if delivery trucks were still running, they would have to clear the interstate for them to reach us. There is no way that Herman Palsky and his employees at the Shop-and-Save will be able to restock once all the food is gone. That means your families will be the ones going hungry when the travelers move on."

"We can't let people starve, though, Lauren. How are you going to turn them away?" Gretchen asked.

"The state or federal government will step in and provide for them. They have greater resources than we do. They'll activate

FEMA and the Red Cross. They'll help those folks get home." She scanned the table, trying to read their faces. Did they buy that garbage? She hoped so.

"But you just said the Red Cross is as incapacitated as us," Gretchen said.

"My duty is to the town of Unicoi. There are children, the elderly, and the disabled here who do not deserve to starve. My heart goes out to those stranded on the highways far from home." She swallowed hard, almost unable to say the words. "My husband, Sam, is one of them. He's down in Atlanta right now, two hundred miles from home."

Sam had his get-home bag with three days of food and water. He was also driving a vehicle that was supposed to still run after an EMP. He was prepared. Hopefully, he wouldn't be stranded like those on the interstate. She felt a familiar burning in the pit of her stomach and reached into her pocket for an antacid tablet, grateful she'd gotten them out of her bag earlier.

"I understand what I'm asking here. But if we let anyone and everyone into the city and share our resources with them now, we will not survive this—I can guarantee you. Three days from now, when your children's bellies are empty, you'll wish you'd listen to me."

"I think we should take a vote," Ralph said. He glared at Lauren.

Lauren chewed on her bottom lip. The city ordinances gave her the authority to act without their approval in an emergency such as this. She could unilaterally order the police to close the city. It would be the right and prudent thing to do, but she would alienate the aldermen and some of their constituents when they needed to work together. She tried to think about what her father would say to them in this situation. She wished he was there. His leadership was what the town really needed right then. He had the patience to deal with idiots. She didn't.

"I want to make sure you hear me out first, and then I will consider your position. Fair?" Lauren asked.

Ralph's face contorted. "You'll consider our position? Who made you king—I mean, queen?"

"The city charter gives the mayor authority in an emergency," Gretchen said.

Lauren tried her best to provide the aldermen with the statistics she recalled from reading about EMPs and disasters in general. The food supply was particularly vulnerable. The pandemic had shown them how fragile the supply chain was when store shelves were empty due to so many workers being out sick and warehouses being shut down. The just-in-time delivery model had proven to be a weak link. The stores couldn't restock, and people couldn't buy the food they needed to feed their families. It had led some to reconsider how reliant they were on the grocery store, and more people had begun raising some of their own food. That had made things like wire for chicken and rabbit cages scarce. Many things had been on backorder for months. Some home improvement stores had run out of soil, seeds, and gardening supplies. It should have been a wake-up call for everyone, but as time went on and people returned to work, those lessons faded, and everyone became reliant on fast food and grocery stores once again.

"But you still can't be sure this is an EMP and that they won't get the lights back on tomorrow," Maryann said at the conclusion of Lauren's speech.

Lauren shook her head. She didn't know what more she could say to convince them of the seriousness of their situation. She could feel the heat rise into her face. She heard her father's voice in her head. Patience, Lauren Michelle. Patience.

"An EMP is the only thing that makes sense. What do you know that can knock out power to phones and cars?" They were in denial. She had to find a way to get through to them. "We don't have time for indecision. Those people on the interstate will come looking for help at any moment. Once they're here in town, it will be very difficult to get them to leave. They'll be frightened and too afraid to leave the safety and resources of the city as they wait for someone to rescue them."

The aldermen were unusually quiet. Lauren couldn't tell what they were thinking. She was seconds away from going it alone and doing this without their approval. Her frustration with them was building to a breaking point.

"We should call this emergency meeting to order, have Millie take a roll call to confirm we have a quorum. We should debate the issue and hear all sides and then take a vote," Ralph said.

"Agreed," Lauren said.

After Millie had recorded that all members were present, Lauren opened the matter for discussion.

"I vote to close the city," Lloyd said. "I ain't got the strength to fight some mob for my breakfast in the morning."

"I don't want to watch my grandkids starve to death. I'm not willing to take the chance," Ralph said.

Lauren nearly fell off the bench. Was Ralph now on her side? Was this a trick?

"I just can't live with turning people away," Maryann said.

"That's fine, then. You invite them all to your house and share your food. You don't have kids or grandkids to feed. I do. I have seven little people depending on me. I won't let strangers steal from them," Ralph said through gritted teeth.

He had finally grasped what was at stake? She now had one ally, at least as far as locking down the town to strangers. It was a good first step.

"Gretchen, where do you stand?" Maryann asked.

Gretchen was silent. Lauren was sure that meant she was siding with Maryann.

"I have grandkids too, Maryann. I can't watch them go hungry, no matter how much I want to help strangers." She paused and scanned the room. "I'm not totally convinced that this is as dire as the mayor has described. I say we allow the stranded motorists to stay at the Unicoi Inn for a few days, at least, and see if the situation resolves itself." She turned to face Lauren. "You could be wrong. They could get the lights back on."

Lauren knew she wasn't wrong, but if allowing the travelers to stay in the motel near the interstate appeased the alderwoman, she was okay with it. She'd give strict instructions to the officers not to allow any of them into town. Maybe the conditions at the dilapidated motel would encourage them to move on. If not, the building itself and Billy Mahon and his gang would.

"A few days in that hell hole, and I'd opt for sleeping under a tree somewhere," Lloyd said.

"They'll want to get home to their families, eventually, and when they discover the government isn't coming to help, they'll leave," Lauren said. She moved the stack of papers in front of her and interlaced her fingers. "Can I get a motion to allow non-residents to stay at the inn but prohibit their entry into the rest of town?" Lauren asked.

Ralph made the motion, and Lloyd seconded it. The vote was four to one. Maryann voted against it, of course.

"What about the rest of the roads coming into town?" Ralph asked.

"I think we should have checkpoints, but allow folks from the area in. They could have family to check on," Gretchen said.

"And if they don't leave? What about people who work in town but live somewhere else? Do you want to feed them indefinitely?" Ralph asked.

Maryann huffed. Gretchen said nothing.

"I make a motion that we set a curfew, and all non-residents must leave the city by sundown," Ralph said.

"What? We can't do that. What authority do we have for something like that? We have business owners and their employees who don't live here. Are you saying they have to leave town?" Maryann asked.

"If you're talking about the concrete plant, Clifford Anderson is exactly who you don't want in your town in a situation like this. He will bleed this town dry and then move on," Gretchen said. She'd never been a fan of Anderson's and had vehemently opposed the expansion of the concrete plant. It wasn't a surprise she wouldn't want to share resources with them now. "I second the motion. Let's vote." She glared at Maryann, daring her to say more.

Maryann crossed her arms over her chest as the clerk tallied the vote.

"The motion has three yeas and one nay."

"The motion carries," Lauren said.

Maryann snatched up her water bottle and stomped away, likely to go and tell her clique how horrible and heartless the rest of them were.

"Millie, draw up the order and post it as soon as possible."

∽

Chief of Police John Avery was initially against using his officers to block all non-residents from entering the town. Still, when he saw the decision was nearly unanimous, he knew he had no one to back him up, so he followed the order and set to work securing the roads into town. The street department used an older model tractor to move traffic barricades to the entrance and exit ramps of the interstate, and the chief stationed two officers, one at each ramp, to turn back stranded motorists. Another officer directed anyone exiting the interstate toward the motel. Benny and the chief had difficulty clearing the travel center and securing the convenience store. That would prove problematic but absolutely necessary. There were resources there that would prove invaluable to the town's survival.

Lauren was hand-writing an executive order at her desk when Benny poked his head inside her office.

"Lauren, we have an issue you should know about."

Lauren gestured for him to enter and take a seat in one of the chairs opposite her desk. He chose to stand. Benny looked tired. He could have used a shave, and his uniform was dirty and wrinkled.

"What is it, Benny?"

"Well."

He hesitated.

Lauren's first thought was it was Sam or maybe one of her parents. She was almost relieved when the first words out of his mouth were Billy Mahon's name.

"It's about Mahon's crew and the motel," he said. He reached out and gripped the back of the vinyl chair in front of him. "I took Lindsay's sister there."

"Maggie? Why would you take her there?"

"Avery wouldn't let her into town. I was going to drop her and the kids off there and run to get Lindsay, but then something happened."

Lauren pushed her chair back and stood. "Is she hurt?"

He gripped the chair tighter as if steadying himself. "She and the kids are fine, but Lauren, I found out she's married to a Russo."

Lauren's mind went blank for a moment, refusing to process what Benny was telling her. "Lindsay's sister, Maggie, is married to a Russo?" Her voice grew louder. "The Knoxville Russos? The same bunch that Corbin hired to go after Tara Hobbs? Those Russos?"

Benny took a step back toward the door. "I didn't know. Lindsay never said anything."

Lindsay hadn't said anything to Lauren either. Her sister, Maggie, hadn't come up in their conversation since Lauren had been back home. She could see why Lindsay wouldn't have broadcast the news. Everyone knew the Russo and Corbin families were dirty and had their hand in nearly every criminal enterprise in eastern Tennessee. How had a sweet girl like Maggie gotten in with such evil people?

"When I took her to Billy's, I didn't know who she was. She said she had left her husband and needed help. What do you want me to do?"

"They'll come looking for her," Lauren said.

"And Mahon will hand her over to them," Benny said.

"You have to tell Lindsay. No matter what, she's family," Lauren said.

"But you know what will happen," Benny said.

"It's not our call to make. That is between Vince, Lindsay, and her sister."

"Mahon isn't going to let them walk in there and take her. He's too afraid of the Russos."

"We can't spare officers to go there, Benny."

"I know. We're barely holding our own at the checkpoints, as it is."

"Tell Vince if he goes in there, he's on his own. We can't afford to lose officers."

"But it was my mistake that put her there," Benny said.

"Don't beat yourself up, Benny. You couldn't have known."

"She has little kids, Lauren. A baby and a little girl."

Lauren had great confidence in Vince and the group from their compound. She firmly believed that they were likely more capable of handling this situation than the Unicoi police. They weren't restrained by the same rules of engagement.

"I understand. If Vince decides to go in, I'm sure he will do everything within his power to protect Maggie and her children."

THIRTY-FOUR

Billy

Unicoi Asphalt Plant
Unicoi, Tennessee
Day 2

Avery was late. Billy had sent Jerome out to the police roadblock near the motel with instructions for Avery to meet him at the usual spot at the abandoned asphalt plant on the south edge of town near the interstate. Billy was growing impatient and getting more pissed off by the second. By the time Avery arrived, Billy was ready to spit bullets.

"About effing time. It wasn't an invitation, you know. When I tell you to meet me, you drop whatever you're doing."

"Got it. What's the problem?" Avery said.

Billy hated cops, and he especially hated this smug bastard. He couldn't wait until Avery had outlived his usefulness. He would personally be the one to put a bullet in the back of the guy's brain. But for now, he needed him to obey and get the job done.

"The problem?" Billy guffawed. "Look around, bro. The world has gone to shit, or haven't you noticed?"

"Kinda puts a kink in our operation," Avery said.

"Our? There is no 'our' here. This is my operation. You work for me."

Avery stiffened and threw his shoulders back.

"You don't want to challenge me. You do not want to take on the Russos." Billy fingered the pistol in his waistband. He was so itching to put this dog down.

Avery's shoulders dropped, and he looked away. "I wasn't challenging you, Billy. What do you need me to do?"

"That's more like it. I need you to let my guys do their jobs. I need weapons and ammo, food, and booze. I want you to find a way to get Jerome and the crew past your cops and inside the pawnshop and grocery store."

"I'm not sure...."

"I don't want excuses. I want action. I'm sending Hatchet down here. He better come back with my guns."

"Okay, Billy." Avery shook his head.

Billy wanted to whack him right where he stood.

"Okay. Have them meet me here. I'll get them through the roadblock."

∼

Back at the motel, Billy studied the three screw-ups standing in front of him. What he needed were men who weren't strung out on drugs. If they were going to take over the town and then go after that paramilitary group Vince was leading to gain control of all their hoarded food and weapons, he needed to bring in people who could fire a gun without shooting themselves. He had some idea who he would recruit. He just had to put a few more things in place before showing his cards. Once he brought the Z-Nation boys from Erwin onto his crew, the whole town would know. It would make it a lot harder for them to take the city by stealth.

Billy didn't want to waste bullets unless it was absolutely

necessary. First, he had to gain control of the grocery store. Once he did so and was patient, he was confident most of the dead weight in town would leave to find food elsewhere. He needed to have that leverage over the people. But with Pataky and his sons holed up in there with an arsenal of guns, he'd need weapons of his own. The few pistols and the one AR-15 he had on hand weren't going to cut it.

"Don't come back without those weapons," Billy said, handing Pickle his baseball bat.

"What the hell am I supposed to do with this?"

"Knock some heads in if you have to. It has served me well. Look where I am today."

Jerome's eyes scanned the rundown motel. Billy could see the words forming in his mouth.

"Just go steal me those guns. Oh, and Jerome, don't get caught. Your uncle can't bail you out of jail this time."

THIRTY-FIVE

Sam

Highway 60
Gainesville, Georgia
Day 2

Moondust and her two companions stood over Sam as he sat on the floor with his back against the wall, cradling Tara's lifeless body in his arms.

"Is she...?" Moondust asked.

Sam said nothing.

Moondust pivoted and gasped at the sight of two more bodies on the floor nearby. "I'm so sorry," she said, kneeling. She placed a gentle hand on Sam's shoulder. Her kindness amid such violence and loss threatened to break him. Something inside him snapped. "Get away from me. Get the hell out of here."

Moondust backed away like he'd slapped her across the face. Her mouth dropped open and slowly closed. Professor grabbed her arm and was pulling her away. "Let's go."

She yanked her arm free from his grasp and returned to Sam's side. "No, I will not go away. You are in no condition right now to be alone. Tara said you have a family back home. A wife and son."

Sam bristled. All he wanted now was to be left alone. He wasn't about to be responsible for anyone else's safety. From that point on, he would focus on getting home and finding Charlie and Lauren. That was it.

"We need one another now more than any other time in our lives. No one survives alone. No one. You can't help her now. Let us help you." She pointed to Professor and Tumbleweed, who were backing away. "Let us help you get home to your family."

"He doesn't want our help, Moon. Let's just go," Tumbleweed said.

"He does. He's just hurting right now. We're a tramily, aren't we? The trail makes us family. Family sticks together no matter what."

Sam swallowed hard and brushed a strand of Tara's hair from her bloody face. He placed his mouth next to her ear. "I'm sorry," he whispered, and rolled her onto the floor. He stood and stared down at her. "I can't leave her here like this."

"There's a church one block from here. I saw the sign out at the corner there," Tumbleweed said, pointing over his shoulder toward the door. "They probably have a cemetery. We could bury her there."

∼

After laying Tara to rest in a three-foot grave behind the Baptist church, Sam and the three hikers slept in the sanctuary before heading north the following day and pushing on toward the Appalachian trailhead at Springer Mountain. As they walked, the events at the pharmacy replayed over and over in Sam's mind. He struggled to find the words he would say when he told her family back in Unicoi County. He'd make sure to tell them how strong and brave Tara had been.

Sam often stopped, searching parking lots, barns, and businesses for a running vehicle without success. It was getting late in the day as they approached Dahlonega, Georgia. Sam didn't want to travel through the town in the daylight. He was determined to avoid another confrontation at all costs. He was already low on ammunition, and he'd seen enough death. They stopped to resupply their purified water near a bridge over the Chestatee River. Sam splashed the cool water on his face and then removed his shoes and stuck his feet in the water. "I think we should rest here and approach the next town in the dark," he said.

"The dark?" Tumbleweed asked. "How are we going to see in the dark? There won't even be any streetlights."

"That will help us slip in and out of town without being spotted. If the sky's clear, the moon is all we'll need."

"I don't know. Stumbling around in the dark can get you hurt. A twisted ankle could make it impossible for us to get home," Tumbleweed said.

"You'd rather get shot?" Sam asked.

"No."

"Traveling through populated areas is dangerous. We minimize the danger by not being seen."

"I agree," Professor said.

Moondust dropped her pack and lay down to use it as a pillow. "Me, too. I don't want to get shot either."

~

Just after the sun went down, Sam and the hikers packed up and headed toward Dahlonega, Georgia. A dim light shone through the windows of the houses along the highway. Dogs barked, and one even followed them for a short distance, but no one came out of their homes. Sam stopped briefly at an automotive repair shop to check an older model pickup truck. Unable to locate the keys, Sam attempted to hot-wire the truck but couldn't get it started. A half-mile away, Sam stopped to check another vehicle in a restaurant parking lot. He eased open the driver's door, and as he did, the truck's dome light lit up. Yes! That was a good sign the vehicle might run. He pulled the door the rest of the way open, but it squeaked loudly—loud enough that someone inside the restaurant could have heard. He dropped to the ground next to the pickup.

"Sam—someone's inside," Professor said.

A flashlight beam bounced around the parking lot and from side to side as the person searched for the source of the noise. Sam backed away in a crouch without shutting the door. The three hikers were already on the run. He could hear their footfalls on the pavement but could barely make out their forms in the dark. Sam raced to catch up to them. "Get down. Get in the ditch," Sam whispered.

They hid there for several minutes, watching the flashlight beam search the parking lot. When the person gave up and went back inside, they climbed back onto the highway and continued through town. Sam didn't stop to check any other vehicles.

As they walked, they heard laughter coming from a motel on their right and moved quickly past it. He'd avoid trouble wherever possible.

"Have you noticed all the crosses along the road? I know it's pretty curvy and hilly, but how could that many people have died along this stretch so close to town?" Moondust asked.

"Maybe they're for Memorial Day or something like that," Tumbleweed said.

"That was weeks ago," Moondust said.

"Memorial Day or Fourth of July, I'd say," Professor said.

"It's just eerie to see them in the dark. It's like walking in a cemetery," Moondust said.

"Let's try to be quiet. We don't want to attract attention," Sam reminded them.

They came to a crossroads and stopped. "Which way?" Moondust asked.

Sam pointed to their left. "West."

"How many more miles are we going to walk in the dark?" she asked.

"As long as possible. We should rest during the day and move at night until we make it to the trailhead."

"We're not walking the trail in the dark?" Tumbleweed asked.

"No, we can't do that. It would be too dangerous. There are too many rock scrambles and roots for that," Professor said.

"I'm hoping it's late enough in the season that there aren't very many people on the trail at Springer," Sam said.

"Day hikers, section hikers, or flip-flop hikers like us, maybe, but no crazy druggies," Moondust said.

"So we push on in the dark. We can probably make ten or twelve miles tonight, sleep during the day, and do another ten to get to Springer Mountain tomorrow night," Professor said.

"And then maybe another five or so on the trail before we stop. That's about all I can do in a day," Moondust said.

"Okay. We have a plan," Sam said. It eased his mind to know they were going to be moving under the cover of darkness. Soon they'd hit the trail, and the chance of confrontation would be significantly reduced. Once on the AT, he would put his head down and put in as many miles as possible until he reached home, even if that meant leaving the hikers behind.

THIRTY-SIX

Lauren

Taylor Residence
Day 3

At about seven a.m. Benny ran through city hall, yelling Lauren's name. She had been there at her desk for about an hour going over the list of businesses located within the Unicoi city limits, trying to make a list of items and skills that could be utilized to sustain the town—in between praying for Sam and her bouts of crying. Lauren stiffened. The tone of Benny's voice told her he was bringing bad news. He was out of breath by the time he reached Lauren's office.

"Vince and Lindsay are at the motel. They've gone after Maggie."

Lauren stood and walked around to the side of her desk. "How many people do they have with them?"

"I don't know."

"I mean with Vince and Lindsay," Lauren said, standing and moving toward the door.

She could see Benny's brain shift gears. "I don't know. Six or seven, maybe."

"They'll be armed and hit the motel when most people are sleeping or passed out from all the alcohol they stole from the travel center's convenience store. Tell Avery to keep our officers away from there. This is Vince's party. Hopefully, he'll do us all a favor and put Billy and the rest of his dogs down."

"What if he doesn't, and this thing spills over into the town?"

"Then we'll deal with it. Our obligation is to the citizens of Unicoi. That's who we protect. Vince knows what he's doing." He did. Lauren was confident that Vince could execute the mission. He and the others with him were highly trained and well-armed—unlike the druggies they'd be going up against.

"We need to focus on making that truck stop as secure as possible, Benny. I'm working on a plan that involves those tractor-trailers. I want you to make sure that no one goes near them."

Benny tilted his head to one side and narrowed his eyes. "What do you have up your sleeve, Mayor?"

"Something to give our town a chance to survive this mess."

∽

As Benny returned to the truck stop, Lauren moved to the conference room to study the land-use maps as she waited for news about Vince's raid on the motel. After several hours, the news came by way of one of the officers who'd returned to city hall for supplies.

"Any word about the incident at the motel?" Lauren asked.

"Seems they worked out whatever issue they had."

"Body count?" Lauren asked, expecting it to be high and hoping to count Billy Mahon as one of its victims.

"Vince said he left things pretty much as he found them. Billy and most of his crew weren't there."

"They weren't? Where the hell are they?"

"No one knows."

"Something isn't right. They wouldn't just abandon their operation like that. Tell Chief Avery to keep a sharp eye out for them and report back to me when they return to Unicoi," Lauren said.

"Will do, Mayor."

~

Around midday, and with things somewhat squared away in town—at least for the moment—Lauren rode Charlie's bike back home, looking forward to having a meal with her family. As she opened the door from the garage to the kitchen, she heard Charlie yell, "Yahtzee!" His laughter lifted her spirits. She was glad he'd been able to get his mind off his parents and baby sister.

"How was work?" Angela asked, looking up from a pail of water. "I got the water from the water heater like you said. It's not hot now, though."

"We'll have to be really careful with it until we find another source. There is bottled water in the garage for drinking. Let's use up all the paper plates and cups before we dirty any of the dishes."

"I'm using this to help cool your dad down some."

"How's he doing?"

"The heat is getting to him. His breathing is more labored, and his blood pressure is a little low."

The issue with the heat was something Lauren hadn't considered. Her parents had spoken of not having air conditioning as children, but her grandparents' house had what they called a sleeping porch.

"We need to move their bed out to the screened-in porch."

"Good idea. We'll have to move out all the plants and stuff your dad has in there. We should move their chairs out there and have them sit there in the heat of the day, too. It gets shade in the afternoon. It should help some."

"Let's do that. I don't want them getting overheated."

It took much longer than Lauren thought to get everything cleared out of the sun porch and her parents' bed and easy chairs set up in the space. Her mother seemed to handle the transition better than expected and her easy-going father seemed to perk up with the cooler breeze.

∼

"Angela, can you help me with something upstairs?" Lauren asked.
"Sure thing."
At the top of the stairs, Lauren turned right and into what had been her old bedroom. Now it was stacked floor to ceiling with prepping supplies. Five-gallon buckets of beans and rice were stacked on one wall. The other was lined with black totes filled with freeze-dried foods. Over half the room was dedicated to medical supplies for her mother and father. Angela stepped into the room and sucked in a breath.
"Where did you get all this?"
"I've been collecting them," was all Lauren would say. In fact, she had ordered a lot of the stuff from online pharmacies. She had had some of it smuggled in from Mexico and Canada. Vince had a source. It was risky but necessary.
"The machine to refill Dad's oxygen tank requires electricity. The generator at the farm requires diesel, which will only last so long. I either need a secondary source for electricity or additional oxygen tanks," Lauren said.
"Lauren," Angela touched her arm. "Your father doesn't have to have oxygen. It's not required to keep him alive. Dr. Tom only gave it to him to make him more comfortable. It's not really helping him much. With his heart condition, he has a perception of shortness of breath that persists despite oxygen administration."
"What? Are you sure about that? Why would…." She remembered what the doctor had told her—six days to six months. "Take him home and make him comfortable," he had said. No matter what she did, her father didn't have long to live. Lauren stared down at all the medication and supplies she had painstakingly

amassed over the last three years. None of it would change the fact that her father was already in heart failure. None of it would reverse her mother's dementia, either.

Lauren lowered herself onto one of the totes. She felt totally useless. She could do nothing to stop her father's decline or help Sam make it home. She wasn't sure there was anything that would prevent the city from winding up as Sam and Vince had predicted. Her mother required constant supervision to keep her from catching the house on fire or wandering off. Was Lauren kidding herself? Was surviving the apocalypse even possible with so many issues to deal with?

Lauren rubbed her temples. She wanted to curl into a ball and hide, but she didn't have that luxury. Too many people were counting on her. Despite her best efforts to hold them back, tears welled in her eyes and rolled uncontrollably down her cheeks. What would Sam do if he was here? She desperately needed his pragmatic advice. She couldn't do this without him.

Sam, please make it home.

A knock on the door downstairs startled Lauren, as it always did—ever since the knock on the door that informed her Sam had been shot in the line of duty. It was something she imagined she'd never get over. For a moment, Lauren thought it could be Sam at the door—he could have lost his keys.

Lauren and Angela raced down the stairs. Lauren stood on the last step as Angela peered through the window. "It's Benny."

Lauren's shoulders dropped, and she pressed her lips tight together. It wasn't Sam. Her heart was heavy with grief. She wanted to run back upstairs and avoid whatever bad news Benny had brought her. She couldn't face it. Missing Sam and the torment of not knowing how he was at present were taking their toll on her emotions. She didn't want Benny to see her break as Angela just had. She placed a hand on the old stair rail and wiped the tears from her face.

Benny stepped into the foyer. His eyes met Lauren's, and her heart lurched. "Is it Sam?"

"No." His gaze turned to Charlie, who had left his Yahtzee game to see who was at the door, and Lauren immediately regretted asking in front of Sam's son.

"It's trouble at the grocery store. Herman and his boys were able to fend them off until we arrived. I think at least two of the looters were Mahon's crew. I can't spare anyone to go after them. They'll likely be back as soon as we leave."

Lauren dropped her gaze. They only had five officers. They'd been guarding the roadblocks since the lights went out. She didn't know how much longer they could keep things from boiling over into the town.

"We need to ask the citizens for help. They're good folks. They have a stake in what happens now."

"Avery isn't going to go for that. He won't want armed civilians involved," Benny said.

"To hell with Avery. We should never have hired him. He's never given a damn about this community, only what it could do for him."

She wasn't sure whether activating citizens was the answer. It could backfire, and they could lose all control. Things could get out of hand, and they'd be powerless to stop it. Lauren stared at the floor, debating whether she should leave her family. They were her first obligation.

"Go, Lauren. I've got things here," Angela said.

"You sure?" Lauren asked.

"I'll help," Charlie said.

"Okay. Very good. I'll go see what I can do at city hall and be back soon."

As Lauren followed Benny down the driveway, she noticed Allan Mayberry's old truck sitting at the curb. She pointed. "What's that doing here?"

"Chief confiscated it," Benny said, climbing into the driver's seat.

"He did what?"

"He claims that Mayberry was driving around town brandishing a rifle threatening to shoot looters, so he confiscated the truck and his weapons."

"By what authority?"

"Your emergency orders, he said."

"Nothing in my order gave him the authority to seize private property."

"He claims it did. He's confiscating all working vehicles for emergency personnel's use. He took Maggie's Camaro."

"What a shit show. Take me to Avery. Let's get this straightened out before he sets the whole town against us."

THIRTY-SEVEN

Lauren

Unicoi City Hall
Day 3

Lauren had spent most of the night at city hall, doing her best to put out the fires the council members had started in her absence. After hours of trying to come up with a way to bring clean drinking water to the town, Lauren was pretty much out of ideas. Residents had been getting sick from drinking water taken from North Indian Creek, which ran through town. Boiling it wouldn't remove the toxic chemicals that ran into it from the factories and business that bordered the creek. Nothing in the County and City Basic Emergency Operations Plan covered Unicoi not receiving help from the Tri-Cities, Knoxville, or one of the other twenty-six counties that made up the eastern portion of Tennessee. There would be no aid flowing in from Nashville or Memphis. FEMA wouldn't be setting up shelters, and the Tennessee National Guard wouldn't be passing out supplies. The town of Unicoi was on its own. As its mayor, she had to come up with a plan—and soon, or people would start dying from starvation and drinking bad water.

She'd spent hours with the fire chief, who was the town's emergency manager, along with city department heads going over the inventory of city assets. She stared at the list of fuel, equipment, supplies, and personnel she had to work with now. It wasn't enough. They were quickly running out of fuel. The city's supply of potable water was just about depleted. The head of the water department had thrown up his hands in frustration. There was nothing more he could do to pump the water from the city's wells into the water tanks so it could flow to residents' homes. The sewer plant couldn't handle the raw sewage, and it had begun backing up into residences and businesses. Some residents had fled to the church, which was on higher ground. Things were looking dire for the town.

Lauren knew what they had to do if they were going to meet the immediate needs of the town. She just had to find enough people to pull it off. She needed an inventory of how many semis were parked at the truck stop and how many were on the interstate. They could contain thousands of gallons of diesel and maybe even food and bottled water. She wouldn't know until they could get a look inside them. They needed to get to them before someone else did, but it might prove difficult to convince the board of aldermen of the plan. It was a sticky situation. On one hand, she didn't want to be perceived as confiscating private property, but the town needed the fuel and food. If the town didn't take control of those resources, someone else certainly would. She needed to round up people she could trust for this mission, so she began making a list.

Lauren placed her elbows on the table and rested her chin on her palms. Her eyes closed, and images of Sam drifted in. The ache was beyond anything she'd ever experienced. It was constant, unrelenting, and nearly debilitating. Her whole body racked with it. She could see how someone could die of a broken heart.

A door slammed, jolting her awake. Chief Avery appeared in the doorway of the conference room.

"Why aren't you out at the travel center keeping the peace?" Lauren asked.

"I came to get more tear gas and extra ammunition. It's a mess out there—a real mess. We're going to have to do something to get those folks to move on. I don't know how long my guys can hold them back."

"I'm working on that," Lauren said. "What is this I hear about you confiscating Alan Mayberry's guns and vehicle?"

"We need transportation. My guys can't patrol the checkpoints and keep people from looting without running vehicles."

"So you take it upon yourself to confiscate them without proper authority from the board of aldermen or myself?" Lauren knew how her plan for the tractor-trailers would look but when it put food in the residents' bellies, they wouldn't care. On the other hand, taking private property from the citizens of Unicoi could turn the town against the police and city government. It was a tightrope she would need to walk carefully.

Avery turned his back on her and headed toward the door. "My job is to keep the peace and protect the citizens of Unicoi."

Lauren crossed the room and placed her hand on the door before he could leave. "Your job is to follow the laws and orders of this town. Where are Mayberry's weapons?"

"In the trunk of the Camaro."

Lauren cocked her head to one side. "Maggie Russo's Camaro?"

Avery didn't answer her.

"You took Ray Mayberry's weapons without due process? You have to give them back." The town needed the truck. "I bet he would have let you use it if you'd asked him nicely. Bring me his weapons, and I'll fix this." She turned back toward her office.

The chief huffed. "What we don't need is someone like Mayberry running around with loaded guns."

Lauren spun toward him, heat rising in her cheeks. She glared at Avery. Mayberry was a veteran and had served his country in

Iraq and Afghanistan. Mayberry was just what the town needed now. Benny appeared in the doorway.

"I'll go get them," Benny said, holding his hand out for the keys.

Avery slapped them down in the palm of Benny's hand. "I think you're making a mistake that will come back to bite you in the ass, Mayor."

After his stunt, she didn't give a damn what Avery thought. They needed many more people like Mayberry and fewer like Avery if they were going to survive this crisis.

Alan Mayberry appeared shocked to see her when he opened the door to his home. He eased open the screen door and stepped outside. Lauren stared at the toe poking through the man's socks. He took a sip of his beer and said, "What can I do for you, Mayor?"

"On behalf of the board of aldermen, I would like to extend our apologies for the way things were handled by Chief Avery. I want to assure you that your property will be returned to you right away. In fact, I've come to get you and take you to city hall to retrieve them," Lauren said. She glanced around the toy-littered lawn. The house was older, even older than her parents' home. The wood around the windows had rotted. Part of the soffit hung down, and the downspout dangled in the wind.

"Avery had no right to take my truck and guns. I have a constitutional right to keep and bear arms," Mayberry said.

"I agree," Lauren said, pointing to the Camaro. "Come on —follow me."

Mayberry followed her to the vehicle, and Lauren popped the trunk. She was shocked to see it was filled with rifles and boxes of food. Had Avery been taking food from people as well?

"Which ones are yours?" Lauren asked.

Mayberry picked up two rifles and tucked one under each arm. "Avery's been a busy boy," he said.

Lauren stared into the trunk. "This is a problem, for sure." It was one she wasn't sure how to solve. She could make Benny police chief, but how many of the officers would leave with Avery? She wasn't sure. Either way, five officers weren't enough. Not by a long shot.

"Mayberry, you ever thought about joining the police force?"

"Hell, no!" he spat. "I never wanted to be no cop."

He shot his gaze at her and adjusted his ball cap. "Sorry, Mayor. I know Sam was a cop."

"I understand—it's fine. Here's the deal. We have five officers to secure twenty-five square miles. There are thirty or so people staying out in the motel and another twenty camped out in the parking lot. More are sleeping by their vehicles on the interstate. And then there's Billy Mahon. It's only a matter of time...."

"You need someone to man roadblocks and patrol the streets," Mayberry interrupted. "I can spread the word. I know people don't want strangers coming and taking everything they got."

"We can't have hot-headed vigilantes, Mayberry. I haven't exactly spoken to the board about this either. I'm sure Avery will disapprove."

"That sons-a-bitch best just stay away from me and mine for a while. I'll have to...."

"We need to work together. You have every right to be upset, but if we could put that on the back burner and find a way to get through this crisis and protect our town. That's the goal here."

He was quiet. She hoped he was at least considering it and not figuring a way to get even with Avery.

"Okay. I'll hold my tongue—for now."

Lauren thought hard about how to approach the subject of his truck.

"Do you know where we might be able to purchase or rent old trucks that still run? We need to be able to move quickly to hot spots before things get out of hand and to transport trespassers out of the city."

He adjusted his cap and nodded. "I might. Bobby Joe has some older trucks he's working on over behind the garage—and then there's Ellis Wilson's classic car collection. He's got at least ten classic cars that should run."

Lauren smiled. Her plan was working beautifully. "Do you think they might loan them to the city?"

"Won't hurt to ask," Mayberry said.

"Would you mind if we borrow yours, just for a few days, until we get a few of our own?"

He didn't hesitate. "No, that's fine." He cleared his throat. "As long as Benny's the only one driving it. Those other punks don't even know how to drive a stick."

Lauren smiled. "Thanks. It's people like you that will save this city. I've been thinking about all the semis at the truck port and on the interstate. I have a plan, but I need people I can trust. Got anyone in mind for some hard manual labor?"

"You planning to look for food in them?" Mayberry asked.

"And drain the diesel from them. We have a couple of old tractors and an old backhoe. We need lots of diesel to run them."

"Sounds like a lot of work."

"It will be, but it'll be worth it."

"I'll see who I can round up," Mayberry said.

A man ran past the front of the Camaro, crossed Mayberry's front lawn, then rounded the corner of his house. While they were watching him, a second person ran past, followed by a third. They were carrying bats and crowbars. Lauren didn't recognize any of them.

"They must be from the interstate," Lauren said.

"They ain't travelers—they're some of Mahon's crew. That kid with the bat is Nigel Corbin's nephew."

"What? A Corbin? Shit!" The last thing she needed was to deal with the Corbins.

Mayberry dropped one rifle back into the trunk, chambered a round in the other, and took off running after them.

"Mayberry, stop. What are you doing?"

"You said you needed help keeping the peace," he said, disappearing around the side of his house.

Lauren hopped in the Camaro and took off after him. At the end of the alley, Lauren turned right onto the main street. Mayberry was crossing the road near the pawnshop on the corner. "Crap. I bet they're after the guns." Lauren hadn't thought about securing the pawnshop. She'd assumed the owner would take care of that. Lauren raced to the end of the block and screeched to a halt in front of the shop. Her revolver was unholstered, and she was flying out of the Camaro before she even thought about the danger. She ran toward the store.

Mayberry was near the door. "Stay back. I got this," he said.

"I'm not letting you do this alone," Lauren said. "There's three of them."

The window was smashed already, and the three men were inside. Lauren could hear glass display cases breaking. "Is Willie out of town?" she asked. She couldn't fathom why they hadn't been confronted by the owner when they broke the window.

"He took his mom to Nashville for her cancer treatment."

"I remember that," Lauren said. It had been announced by the church's prayer chain.

"I'm going in," Mayberry said.

"Wait!" Lauren stopped next to the door and called, "You inside the store. Come out with your hands in the air." She didn't have police authority, but they didn't have to know that detail.

The looters ignored her order and continued smashing the display cases.

"I need to get in there. Any minute, they are going to have a boatload of weapons and ammo. We can't let that happen." Mayberry ran inside, shouting for them to hit the floor. "Get down, or I'll shoot."

Lauren sucked in a breath and was about to step through the broken window when three shots rang out in quick succession. Lauren dove behind the brick wall and flattened herself against it.

Mayberry re-emerged. "You need to get someone over here to secure these guns."

"The looters? Are they Mahon's crew?" Lauren asked, standing and brushing sand off her knees.

"They were, yeah. They're dead now."

THIRTY-EIGHT

Lauren

Unicoi Pawn
Unicoi, Tennessee
Day 3

After Allan Mayberry graciously agreed to stay behind to secure the pawnshop, Lauren went to get help. With all the officers committed at the roadblocks, she wasn't sure how they were going to go about making sure those weapons didn't end up in the wrong hands. She would have preferred to have her brother-in-law oversee the task of securing the weapons, but with Vince, Lindsay and the others of their group taking care of her and Sam's farm and the survival compound, Lauren couldn't ask them to do more.

She found Ralph alone in the employee break room, stuffing his face with a three-day-old coffee cake.

"Ralph, I need your help," Lauren said.

He turned, wiping crumbs from his mouth. "With what?"

"Come with me."

They stopped by the reception desk on their way to Maggie Russo's Camaro. She was surprised to see Millie there. Vince had taken her with him to the compound. As far as Lauren had known, that was where she was going to remain. "You came back?"

Millie hung her head. "Steve died."

"Who is Steve?"

"My boyfriend. He went with Vince and Dave to find you. He didn't come home."

Lauren lowered her head. "I'm so sorry." What more could she say? At least Millie knew what had happened to Steve. She wouldn't know the agony of waiting for news that may never come.

She didn't have time to console Millie or feel guilty because Steve had died coming to rescue her and Charlie. They had an emergency on their hands. If those guns and ammunition fell into the wrong hands, many residents could die. "Millie, I'm sorry to hear about your boyfriend. I'm grateful that you came in today. I'm sorry to ask, but I'm going to need you to run out to the interstate and get the police chief and send him over to the pawnshop. There's been a break-in. Three men are dead, and we have to secure the scene."

Millie started to push for details, but Lauren stopped her. She didn't have time to explain.

"We're going to see what we can do to secure the weapons until the chief can get there," Lauren said.

"Why don't you just bring the weapons here and secure them in the police armory?" Millie asked.

Lauren stopped halfway out the door.

"Technically, they are evidence of a break-in. We'd be securing them until the owner could reclaim them, right?" Millie continued.

Technically, nothing had been taken in the burglary. The would-be thieves had been stopped before they had had the chance to steal anything. Lauren had no idea when or if the pawnshop owner would return. What she did know was that she did not want those guns in the hands of anyone who could use them against the citizens of the town.

"I suppose you're right. It would be best just to bring them back here. We can't spare people to guard the pawnshop, too. We'll catalog each one of them with serial numbers and everything so when the owner comes to claim them, we'll have a record," Lauren said.

"How many of them are there? That sounds like a lot of work. I have stuff to attend to at home," Ralph said.

"Something more important than making sure unscrupulous people don't get their hands on a gun and come shoot your ass?" Lauren asked. She couldn't help herself. She was tired and needed caffeine—and chocolate.

"Fine, I'll help you load them, but I'm not sticking around to do the inventory."

Lauren refrained from making a snarky comment and choked out a thank you instead.

∽

Allan Mayberry leaned against the wall inside the pawnshop with a rifle resting in the crook of his arms. He nodded to the three bodies on the floor. "Corbin's nephew is one of them. They drew on me as I stepped through. I had to put them down."

Ralph turned and started walking.

"Where are you going?" Lauren asked.

"I ain't getting tangled up in nothing to do with the Corbins."

Lauren stood in the middle of the street with her hands on her hips. She was sick to death of the Corbin family's grip on her town.

"Coward!" Mayberry called after him.

Ralph kept walking.

"I need to get those weapons to the police station and keep them off the streets and out of the hands of those who could do harm."

"We better get busy then before someone walks by and decides the pawnshop is open for business."

Lauren stepped over the body of a young man and grabbed two rifles from the floor beside him. They were slick with the guy's blood. Lauren choked back vomit as she exited the store and headed toward the Camaro.

"The ammo is good, but there's not much of it." Mayberry said as he placed an armload of rifles into the trunk. "Now, this is useful." He picked up a crossbow and tugged on the string. "You should take this, too."

Lauren followed him back inside. "We should take anything that could be a deadly weapon."

"Anything can be a deadly weapon in the right hands," Mayberry said. He stepped over the body of Corbin's nephew and picked up a baseball bat. "This kid could've killed you with one swing."

"Scary."

"What are we going to do with them?" Mayberry asked, pointing to the bodies.

Lauren thought for a moment. The county coroner was in Erwin. Chief Avery would need to conduct an investigation, and then the coroner would have the bodies moved to the county morgue for autopsy—at least that was how it was supposed to work. But that was before the EMP changed everything.

"We'll board up the store and leave the bodies there until Avery can take control of the scene."

She wasn't ready to abandon all legal protocols. If the lights did come back on, she didn't want to be held responsible for botching an investigation into the burglary and deaths. Avery might decide to lock Mayberry up. He had shot the looters. After the disdain Avery had shown to Mayberry, she was concerned for him. She couldn't tell him—at least not yet. She'd tell Benny. He would have to be the chief soon.

It did start her thinking, though—what would they do with lawbreakers now? She sure as hell wasn't going to bring them food or empty their piss buckets. There were so many new dilemmas they'd need to address. It hurt her head just thinking about it. How would they get water? What about the trash that would soon pile up at the curbs? What about when someone got sick—like her father? How would they get them to the hospital in Johnson City?

"We need to get the weapons and ammo to city hall. After that, we need to round up some folks willing to help with the roadblocks. I don't want Mahon and his crew in town causing any more trouble," Lauren said.

"That won't go over well with Avery," Mayberry said.

"Nope, but after this close call, we can't take the risk that someone with ill intentions makes it into town."

As soon as Lauren's feet hit the tile inside city hall, she called Millie's name.

"Millie, I need to call a town assembly. Can you pass the word? It's time I addressed the citizens and told them what's going on. We need the town's cooperation if we're going to right this ship."

THIRTY-NINE

Lauren

Unicoi Community Park
Unicoi, Tennessee
Day 4

A rumble of fear rolled through the crowd as Lauren addressed the town. Standing on a picnic table in the middle of Unicoi Park, she scanned the residents gathered there. From what she could see, nearly everyone had come out to hear her. Lauren took a deep breath as she rubbed her hands together. She wiped the sweat from her brow and attempted to swallow, but her mouth was too dry. She motioned for Millie to hand her a bottle of water, took a sip, handed it back, and then turned to her constituents.

"Thank you for coming out today. I apologize for not addressing you earlier, but as you can imagine, we've been quite busy at city hall."

"Oh yeah, then why the hell are the lights still out?" a cranky old man in the back yelled.

She ignored him.

"As you might have already surmised, this is not a normal

power outage. Something or someone caused an event that has taken down not only the power grid but affected communications and transportation as well. The problem extends—at the very least—throughout eastern Tennessee and perhaps farther."

"What on earth could cause such a thing?" an elderly woman asked.

"I have nothing official, but I can give you my opinion. What I believe has occurred is an electromagnetic pulse or EMP. Another thing that could cause this is a coronal mass ejection from the sun, but either way, we just don't know. Really, the how is not as important to us at the moment as what we're going to have to do to survive this. And we can only do so if we work together."

"What about the water?" a woman shouted.

"And the sewers. My toilet is backed up, and I got no way to flush it. It stinks something awful," another said.

"Without electricity, our water treatment plant and the city wells aren't able to provide water or sewer services," Lauren said.

"When are they coming back on?" someone asked.

"I don't know."

The crowd murmured.

"I know that's not the answer you came to hear, but that's the truth. I owe you the truth. So here it is." Lauren paused, second-guessing herself. Maybe they were better off not knowing. They could panic and turn violent.

She scanned their faces. In the third row was her soccer coach from the time when she was ten years old. To her left was Arthur Bates, who ran the music store on the corner near the Shop 'n Save. Behind him was Betty Utley, her neighbor. She'd grown up around these people. They needed to know what to expect. Decisions they made now could either save or cost them their lives.

"Help from the state and the federal government may not be coming."

A roar of disapproval erupted.

"We have to help ourselves here. In order to do that, we all need to work together."

She was drowned out by their grumblings. Benny stepped up and shouted for them to quiet down. As the noise died down, Lauren continued. "We're working on solutions. We're going to have to haul water up from a nearby stream and distribute it, but that'll take volunteers. Right now, all the city workers are out securing the checkpoints and keeping non-residents from flooding the town and depleting our resources."

"When is the grocery store opening back up? I've only got enough to feed my kids dinner tonight, and then my pantry will be completely bare," a young mother said.

Everyone turned to Herman Pataky.

Lauren scanned the crowd, looking for his two sons. She doubted Herman would leave the grocery store unguarded. He and his sons had been perched on the roof, daring anyone even to enter the parking lot.

He stepped forward. "Mayor, I've been waiting for someone from the city to come tell me what to do. I have a thousand pounds of frozen meat in my freezer right now. In a day or two, it won't be fit to eat. I just need to know how to distribute it. I didn't want to open my doors and deal with no angry mob stampeding to get free food." His Hungarian accent was still thick, even though he'd been in eastern Tennessee since Lauren was a little girl.

"Thank you, Mr. Pataky. We'll work on a plan for distributing your perishable items."

"When? My kids are hungry now," a man yelled.

Others in the crowd chimed in their agreement.

Lauren crossed her arms. The man was offering them free food, and they were acting like this? If she was Herman, she'd be tempted to tell them to go eff themselves. Lauren studied Herman's face, looking for a reaction. He did raise one eyebrow, but other than that, Lauren didn't detect a shred of offense in the man. She was grateful. If he reneged on his offer now, the citizens would likely tear him apart. Lauren nodded to Benny. As the only officer present, there'd be little he could do if the crowd turned ugly. He stood with his chest out and his hand on his taser. For an instant, he reminded her of Sam. She closed her eyes and swallowed back tears. She couldn't bear to think what he might be going through at that very moment. If she was concerned about folks in tiny Unicoi turning violent, how much worse was it in Atlanta?

She continued. "I need to speak to Chief Avery and the board of aldermen. We will come up with a plan. If you all would meet me back here in say...." Lauren searched for the sun. They had maybe another six hours of daylight left. "Meet me back here in four hours. That should give me time to get the details ironed out. You'll have food to take home tonight."

The residents began fanning out to leave, seemingly satisfied with the answer.

"Wait!" Lauren shouted.

A few turned back, but others continued to leave the park. Benny grabbed his whistle and blew it several times in quick succession. "The mayor isn't finished," he shouted.

Lauren waited for everyone to gather back around her.

"I'm sorry. I know you have a lot to do. But give me just a few more minutes of your time. We have some serious issues to address."

"What is it, Mayor?" Kim, her hairdresser, asked.

"First, I have to ask you to do something that I know you aren't going to like. The city water treatment plant isn't operating. That means, very soon, things are going to get very stinky around here. I'm going to have to ask each of you to refrain from using your toilets and put as little water down your pipes as possible."

"We ain't got no water to put down our pipes, lady," a scruffy-looking young man said.

"I understand that. We're going to address that in a moment. But right now, I need you to understand how serious this sewer issue is. If it hasn't already, sewage will soon begin to back up into homes and businesses." She gestured for Chris to join her up on the table. As the hefty man climbed up, the table teetered slightly. Benny grabbed her hand, steadying her. "Go ahead, Chris, tell the folks what the issues are."

"Well...." Chris paused. He stared at his feet, unable to make eye contact with the crowd. "A sewage backup puts physical and airborne contaminants into your home. Besides smelling like shit, inhaling it can make you sick. You'll get cramping, vomiting, fever, and severe forms of gastroenteritis. If you remain in your home after a backup, it could lead to death." Chris stepped down onto the bench and nearly face-planted himself, trying to get down to the ground and away before anyone could ask him questions.

"Thank you, Chris. I think we all get the picture. So, please, as inconvenient as it will be, do not use your toilet. Get rid of water outside in the grass where it can be absorbed. We are discussing a work-around, but for now, please take this seriously."

"What about the porta-potty the street crew uses?" a guy in the back yelled out.

"We've thought of that. Our street department has one porta-potty. One will not serve seven hundred and fifty houses. But Chris knows where we might get a few more. The porta-potty rental company stored the ones from our strawberry festival in the warehouse by the truck port. All we have to do is find a way to get them moved into the residential neighborhoods."

"Gross! I don't want that in front of my house," a thirty-something woman said.

"Would you rather walk a block every time you have to take a dump?" the man behind her asked.

Howard Mills stepped out from the crowd. "I got a thirty-two-foot trailer, but my truck won't start in order to haul it."

A middle-aged man near the front twisted to face him. "My dad's old tractor will haul that trailer, but he lives about twenty miles out of town."

"You can borrow my son's dirt bike to get out there," a young mother said.

"Awesome," Lauren said. "How about the three of you come over here where Chris is seated, and the four of you can work out the details?" Chris was sweating profusely now. He looked like he was going to throw up. She was pushing the shy man out of his comfort zone, but he'd have to get over it. He was a vital member of this effort, and he had a job to do.

Now was the time to broach the subject of the truck stop and the semis on the interstate. It would take a lot of workers to accomplish the task of going through each one and scavenging food, water and supplies they'd need to survive. The task of obtaining the diesel alone would be daunting.

As Lauren laid out the plan, she could see faces in the crowd light up with hope. Several hands went into the air when she asked for volunteers. It warmed her heart to see the town willing to work together. If only Sam were there to see it.

"I also need volunteers to work on bringing water to the community. I have a sign-up sheet right here." She pointed to the pen and paper on the nearby picnic table. Millie held it up and waved it in the air. "Please see Millie if you can help with the water."

Everyone began talking amongst themselves.

"I'll see everyone back here at four o'clock with a plan for food distribution," Lauren shouted over the noise.

"That went better than I expected," Benny said, holding his hand out to help Lauren down from the picnic table.

Immediately, Betty Utley cornered her. "I need one of those potties in my driveway. I have gout, and Tom has bad knees. We can't go traipsing up and down the street every time we have to go."

Lauren started to respond to her and tell her why they couldn't put them in her driveway but thought better of it. "You'll need to talk to Chris. He's in charge of potties." She hated doing that to the man, but they all had their jobs to do, and she needed to stay out of Chris' lane if at all possible.

"Millie, do you have that volunteer roster?"

She took the roster from Millie. Only two people had volunteered to help with the water solution. That wasn't a very good start to Lauren's plan to work together for the good of the community. She read the names out loud. "Alfred Mitford and Orlando Lawless."

Alfred said he had an old Army four hundred-gallon water buffalo. He was going home to see whether he could find the parts to get his old truck started in order to haul it. Orlando said he may have the parts to build a pump to get water from the stream into the tank. He mentioned that he could put a collection box and pipes in the stream and run water directly into town. He would inventory his supplies and see what he needed to accomplish that. Hope rose within her. Bringing water to the town could be their first step to surviving this mess.

Hell, we may even be able to get the electricity back on at this rate.

Lauren had to chuckle at the irony of the situation. The town had been trying to force Mitford to clean up his place and get rid of all his "junk" for years. The very thing that most people had considered an eyesore would likely save their lives.

Mr. Lawless had been Lauren's high school science teacher and an inventor. She smiled. The town had many folks with skills and talents that could be useful to the community now. Her father was right. If the town pulled together, they could overcome many of the obstacles that might appear impossible.

"Lauren, after we empty those tractor-trailers, we should move them to the city limits and construct a barrier wall of sorts with them," Mr. Lawless said.

"Barrier wall?"

"To keep people from walking in and taking what we've got here."

"How would you build a wall with the semis' trailers?" Lauren asked.

"We use the tractors to haul them out where we need them, line them up in a row and push them over onto their sides, wheels facing in so people from the outside couldn't easily climb over. With them and the terrain we could secure the city with fewer people. I can get together with Benny and work out the details."

"Run it by Benny and Derek in public works. He's in charge of the tractors. If they think it will work, let's get it done. I'm all for locking down the town."

"Four hundred gallons?" She tried to do the mental math to determine how many tanks they'd have to haul per day to meet the needs of the three thousand residents of Unicoi, but she was so sleep-deprived and exhausted that the number evaded her. A lot, she decided.

"Benny!" someone shouted. Lauren spun around to see who it was. Officer Cordell was running toward them.

"Benny, Chief says to get your ass over to the Angelos'. We've got trouble with a group from the motel. They're drunker than Cooter Brown and trying to break into the pizza joint."

"What the hell for? Do they want to eat flour? Cause everything else in there is bad by now."

"Booze. Someone mentioned that Angelo's had the best beer on tap, and off they went demanding to be let in."

"Is Angelo still there?" Benny asked, moving toward Officer Cordell.

"He and his boy have been holed up in there since the lights went out."

Benny stopped and pivoted. "Mayor?"

"I'll be fine, Benny. You go take care of that mob."

Lauren spun around to search for Millie and came face to face with Sharon DuBois, Billy Mahon's sex worker, who helped him to recruit girls and keep them in line. Lauren's hands balled into fists. She considered the other girls who "worked" for Mahon to be his victims, but Sharon was older. She could leave if she wanted to.

"What about the motel?" Sharon asked.

Lauren's jaw clenched, and she leaned in. "The big dog is off the porch now, Sharon. If you're smart, you'll run."

Sharon took one step back and squared her shoulders. "What's that supposed to mean?"

Lauren could feel Benny's breath on the back of her neck. She didn't care. He wasn't there to stop her from speaking her mind to lowlife pieces of shit like Sharon.

"It means there's a new way of doing things now. My officers"—she hiked a thumb over her shoulder toward Benny—"no longer have to wait for the district attorney's office to file charges against you and that cankered piece of shit you work for—and I no longer have to wait for a judge to tear that motel down to the effing ground."

Sharon's face contorted. "Do you even know who you're dealing with?" she snorted. "You have no idea. Don't you know? He'll burn this town to the ground before he's done." She turned on her heels and started to walk away before turning back. She jabbed a finger in the air. "Big dog? You're the one who should run." Sharon strode off and joined a group from the motel.

"It's best not to poke the bear, Lauren—at least not until we have time to plan a bear hunt," Benny said.

"I thought you were going to deal with the interstate freeloaders."

"I am." He started to walk off.

"Benny, you and Officer Cordell serve them an eviction notice. Tell them they have twenty-four hours to leave our town."

"That would be poking the bear."

"I don't care. I want those travelers to move on and go home. We have enough on our plates trying to feed our own. I can't have you out breaking up fights and stopping them from causing trouble. We're going to be dealing with our own rowdy crowd soon. You have to make it clear that they aren't welcome, okay?"

"And how do you suggest I do that?"

"You're a resourceful man. Figure it out," Lauren said.

FORTY

Sam

Appalachian Trail
Springer Mountain, Georgia
Day 5

Sam was pretty much in a daze as he and the trio of hikers made their way west toward the southern terminus of the Appalachian Trailhead. He was exhausted, both mentally and physically. His mind wasn't as sharp as it should be, and he was worried his reaction time could be affected by his lack of sleep and food. On top of that, he was dehydrated—a deadly combination. He had to keep reminding himself to drink. His thoughts were two hundred miles away with his wife and son. No matter how hard he tried, he could not compartmentalize and stop worrying about whether they were even alive. His sleep was filled with nightmares. In them, his son hung upside down, still strapped in the seat of the plane, hands dangling, being gnawed on by wild animals—and often zombies. He would wake in a sweat only to return to similar dreams about his wife. It was torture not being there to protect them from a world that wanted to kill them.

It had taken two days to reach Springer Mountain. Sam and the three hikers moved at night and slept during the day. The tactic worked, and they didn't encounter anyone on the trip from Dahlonega to the trailhead. The forestry road leading from the highway up the mountain was just a precursor to what Sam faced on the trail. He was tired when the sun began to rise, and they reached the parking lot at Springer Mountain. The group rested by sitting on the tailgate of a newer model pickup truck someone had abandoned. Sam ate the last of his protein bars. His water bottle was empty.

Moondust was lying on her back in the bed of the truck. "I vote we stop and take a nap at Stover Creek Shelter."

Professor pulled a trail guide from a pouch on his pack and thumbed through it. "If we rest for, say, three hours and push on, we could stop at Hawk Mountain Shelter for the night."

Tumbleweed shook his bag of potato chips in the air. "Man, that's going to be rough on the food supplies we've got. I'm already feeling the drag from a lack of calories."

"I agree. Burning four or five thousand calories a day and only eating one thousand or so is not sustainable," Professor said.

"Maybe we'll luck out and find a trail angel stash."

Tumbleweed laughed, and chips flew from his mouth. "You see—that's how she got her trail name. You're dreaming, girl. By now, bears will have raided any trail magic left out."

"Not the ones hanging in the trees. Remember that stash of Pepsi and chocolate bar trail magic we found hanging near Winding Stair Gap?"

"What the bears haven't eaten, other hikers will have taken. There might not be too many places open to resupply."

Sam was also concerned about the calorie requirements and his lack of food, but he was determined to keep going as long and as far as his body would allow.

They slept for four hours at the first shelter. After filling their water bottles and rehydrating, the emptiness in his stomach didn't hurt as much, but his energy level was dangerously low.

The next day they only made it about seven miles due to having to take frequent rest breaks. Sam was nauseous on top of being exhausted. He'd tripped numerous times on tree roots and loose rocks, cutting his knee and scraping his hand. When they arrived at the Hawk Mountain Shelter, Sam was so exhausted he could barely lift his leg to climb up into the wooden shelter. The three-sided shelter with its wood floor provided little in the way of comfort for his weary bones, but it beat sleeping on the ground.

Tumbleweed walked behind the shelter to a water source to refill their bottles while Moondust hit the privy to relieve herself. Sam didn't have the energy for either activity. Professor spread his sleeping mat out next to Sam and was stretching out to sleep when Moondust's squeals caused him to bolt upright. Sam assessed the sound and figured she'd discovered some of Mother Nature's creatures inside the outhouse, so he didn't rouse from his spot.

"Sweet!" Tumbleweed said. "I call dibs on the Alfredo."

"Food?" Professor called out. "You found food?"

"Food?" Sam said. "How? Where?"

"There's a bear box beside the shelter filled with food," Tumbleweed said.

Moondust looked inside the metal food storage box and removed a large bear canister that looked like a giant plastic mason jar. She unscrewed the lid and pulled from it a handful of freeze-dried meals. "Someone left in a hurry. Why on earth would they leave their food supplies?"

"I don't know, and I don't care. All I know is they're mine now," Tumbleweed said, pulling a freeze-dried meal from the container.

Sam was sure the Lord was watching over them. The bear box filled with freeze-dried meals and protein bars was a godsend. There was enough in it for them to make it another day, maybe two. They were all filled with hope. With his stomach full for the first time in days, Sam sent up a prayer of thanksgiving and one for his wife and son's safety, then fell fast asleep.

He was awakened in the night by the sound of rustling. He realized they'd left their trash just outside the shelter—something every hiker knew not to do, but in their exhausted state, they'd overlooked it. Sam sat up on one elbow, unclipped his flashlight, and shone it into the face of a large black bear. The bear grunted and, upon seeing Sam, reared up, growled, and then ran off down the trail.

"That was close," Moondust said. "That was my second bear encounter. The first was near the Tennessee and North Carolina border."

"I had an encounter near there, myself," Sam said.

"Were you northbound?"

"I was section hiking from my home in Unicoi, Tennessee, to Harper's Ferry in West Virginia."

"I loved Harper's Ferry," Moondust said. She scooted closer to Sam. "You're from Tennessee?"

"Yes. My wife and I have a homestead there, but we are living at my wife's parents house in town at the moment."

"Really? How cool. Folks don't do that much these days."

"My wife didn't want to have to put them in a nursing home. Her father doesn't have much time left."

"That's sad. It's awful to watch. My mom took care of my grandmother until she passed. It was heart-wrenching."

"It is."

"So your wife's in Tennessee? That's where you're heading?"

"It is." Sam didn't see the harm in telling them at this point. He felt somewhat at home on the trail, almost like when he'd last hiked there. There was very much a social aspect to hiking the AT. In stark contrast to the trail's remoteness, rugged features, and solitude was the feeling of community. The relationships hikers made with one another helped them to cope with challenges that arose on the trail.

"I'm not sure if I'll make it home," Moondust said flatly.

"If you stay on the trail, you'll make it," Sam said. He wasn't sure he believed it. She had a long way to go, and the chance of finding more food lying around the trail was slim.

Everyone would have a difficult time finding food, not just the hikers. Lauren had made sure her family had enough food to last at least six months, but when the rest of the town ran out, and children began to go hungry, Sam knew his wife would share what she'd stored.

After all the food was gone, people would turn on one another. Even friends and relatives would do what they needed to feed their starving families. He was determined to be there to help Benny and the other law enforcement officers keep order. If they could provide security, the town had a chance to work together to find food and other resources they needed to survive.

"What's it like, you think? What are people in the cities doing for food and clean drinking water? How will they survive without electricity?" Moondust asked.

"After a week or so, most people will be out of food and water. They'll be forced onto the streets in search of supplies. The takers will have come fairly quickly and taken what they could by force when necessary. Large bands of refugees will eventually be forced to flee the city as starvation causes even law-abiding citizens to do desperate things."

"God! Will I even have a home and family to return to?"

The question pricked his heart. It was the same one that played over and over in his mind. He didn't have an answer for her.

She was quiet for a long time—so long that Sam thought she'd fallen asleep.

"I'd sure like to see the fireflies at the Great Smoky Mountains National Park one last time," Moondust said, breaking the silence.

Sam had taken Charlie to the Elkmont area the first year they'd moved to Tennessee. Witnessing thousands of fireflies flashing throughout the forest had been a sight to behold. "That would be nice," he said.

"Do you think it will be a really long time before things return to normal?" Moondust asked, sadness filling her voice.

Vince had been convinced that life would never be "normal" again in such an event. The country would have to rebuild from the ground up. The first thing to be restored would have to be law and order. At that point, it may very well take a tyrant or a dictator to set the country right again. Sam didn't even want to think what the country would be like under a selfish, power-hungry kind of leader.

FORTY-ONE

Billy

Unicoi Asphalt Plant
Unicoi, Tennessee
Day 6

A sulfurous odor still hung in the air at the abandoned asphalt plant. Billy Mahon rubbed his temples and bent down to just inches from Police Chief John Avery's face. "Where the hell are my guns, Avery? I sent three of my guys into the pawnshop. They should've been in and out. Now, I'm going to have to explain to old man Corbin how I got his grandson killed. You were supposed to make sure something like this didn't happen."

Avery looked up, blood dripping from a three-inch gash over his left brow. "How was I to know the mayor and Mayberry would intervene?" he whined.

"It was your freaking job to know, you moron."

"I was called to deal with an issue...."

Billy struck him across the face with the brass knuckles again, causing Avery to fall to his right. He rolled into a ball like a pill bug as Billy repeatedly kicked him in the ribs.

"Get him up," Billy ordered, and two of his new recruits lifted Avery up by his shirt collar. It had cost Billy a gram of cocaine to add men to his crew. Lucky for him, there were more than enough applicants for the job. Most never even asked what their duties would entail—they relished the opportunity to terrorize their hometown. This one guy, a former high school football star, even started a list of people he would visit to inform them of his new employment. Billy would need to keep an eye on that one. He seemed to have his own agenda. Billy couldn't abide that kind of behavior. The guy had come in handy for the first phase of Billy's operation, though. It took a special kind of crazy to do what would be required to take over the town.

"I'll ask you again, Avery. Where are my guns?"

"I can get them for you. They're at city hall. Lauren is having them inventoried, and then they're supposed to be stored in the police armory."

"Why are my weapons being inventoried at city hall instead of being delivered to my motel?"

"I wasn't…." He stopped mid-sentence.

"You're useless to me." Billy spun, pressed the barrel of his pistol against the back of Avery's skull, and squeezed the trigger. Avery slumped to one side as blood began to stain the concrete floor.

"Take him out and string him up in front of the grocery store. I want everyone in this town to know what happens if you cross me."

Two of Avery's officers lifted him by the arms and dragged him from the building. "When you're done, meet me back at city hall. I'm going to collect my guns and then deal with Herman Pataky and his sons. I will control that store by the end of today."

"Yes, sir," Officer Cordell said.

Billy took a seat behind an old metal desk. He leaned back in the chair and placed his hands behind his head. He was looking forward to moving into his new office at city hall. There would be a leadership vacuum with Lauren Wallace and the city council out of the picture. He intended to step in to fill it. He would rule this town with an iron fist. Instead of a crew of fifteen, he'd have a few thousand. The possibilities with that many people working for him were endless.

Cordell and the other officer stopped in the doorway. "Billy, what about Benny and the two officers?"

"When they show up to defend their precious mayor, take them out."

"Yes, sir."

After seizing control of city hall and the grocery store, Billy knew he'd need to act fast to strike Vince's compound. They'd hit them at night when everyone was sleeping. He couldn't wait to go through all that food. He'd heard they'd stored enough chocolate syrup and powdered milk to supply half the daycare centers in eastern Tennessee. Billy was craving chocolate like mad. He licked his lips.

"Now, let's go pay the mayor a visit."

FORTY-TWO

Sam

Winding Stair Gap
Franklin, North Carolina
Day 6

They were eating roots, berries, and wild plants by the time they reached Mooney Gap. After filtering filling their water bottles from a spring east of the trail, Sam and his trail buddies were barely moving and about ready to collapse by the time they reached Highway 64 at Winding Stair Gap near Franklin, North Carolina.

"Maybe we should go into Franklin and find help. I'm not sure how much farther I can go without food," Moondust said.

"I'm with you," Tumbleweed said. "Franklin is a hiker-friendly town. Someone there will help us."

"If they have food themselves," Professor said.

Sam's stomach agreed with them, but his head knew the dangers. "They won't. Not enough to share. Most people only have a couple of days' to a week's worth of food at home. The stores will have all been looted by now. It's dangerous to go into town now."

"I have to try. I'd rather die trying than lie down beside the trail and have animals pick my bones clean," Tumbleweed said.

Moondust scrunched her face up. "Ew! Do you have to be so graphic?"

"It's ten miles into town. I'm not sure I have another ten miles in me," Professor said.

He leaned back against the guardrail and dropped his pack. Sam did the same. He wasn't willing to risk another deadly encounter in town. He was tired of killing; unfortunately, it was inevitable if they went there. His preparedness group had discussed this very thing. When food was scarce, and people barely had enough to feed their own families, strangers coming into town would be seen as a threat to their very lives.

They'd find no help in Franklin or any other town. They had to stop, rest long enough for him to set a few traps, maybe catch a rabbit or squirrel, and find mushrooms and enough berries and greens to give them the energy to push on to the next shelter. From there, it would be wash, rinse, repeat for Sam until he reached Unicoi County.

"I'm willing to take my chances. I'd rather ride this thing out in town than starve on the trail," Tumbleweed said. He extended his hand to Professor and then to Sam. "It was nice to meet you both."

Professor and Moondust hugged. She wiped a tear from her cheek as she held her arms open in invitation to Sam.

"It's risky what you two are doing. You won't receive the warm welcome you're used to."

"I know you're probably right, but I'm done. I've been on the trail since December. Six months is a long time, and I'm too tired to continue another two thousand miles home. If I die, it will be here," Moondust said.

"I hope you don't," Sam said, pulling her into an embrace.

"I hope you make it home to your wife and son, Wyatt Earp."

She waved to them as she and Tumbleweed set off toward the town of Franklin, North Carolina.

"I'm going to miss those two young folks. It's hard to think I'll never again see them or know if they made it or not," Professor said.

"You can still catch up to them," Sam said, half hoping the old guy would choose to go with his trail family instead of slowing Sam down.

"No. I think I'm just going to sit here a while longer." Professor pulled out a paperback book and opened it.

"I can't. I need to keep moving," Sam said.

"I know. I hope you find your wife and son, Sam."

"You should at least get off the road and back on the trail where you're less likely to be seen."

"I will after I rest a bit and finish my book. I'd like to know how it ends," Professor said. He looked as if he was going to drop dead any moment.

Sam crossed the highway near the Winding Stairs Gap parking lot and had one foot on the wooden steps, ready to climb back onto the trail, when he stopped and turned. Could he leave the old man like that? Could he live with himself if he did? Already knowing the answer to his question, Sam turned back, crossed the highway, grabbed Professor's pack, and ran an arm around the old man's waist. "Let's just go a little farther. You said there was a stream and a campsite up ahead. We can stop there." Sam patted his holster. "Maybe I can catch us a squirrel or something."

Professor chuckled. "There wouldn't be much left of the creature if you hit him with that cannon."

Sam somehow found the strength, and they made it to the stream. Sam used wire from his every-day-carry pouch to set a couple of snares near the water source, hoping to catch something to eat as they rested. He was filtering water while Professor set up camp at the nearby campsite when voices caught his attention. Not other hikers—angry voices. Sam dropped the water bladder and unholstered his pistol as he ran toward the campsite. By the time he broke through the trees, Professor was on the ground. Twenty feet away, three men wearing hunter's camouflage and orange vests were standing over him.

"We just wanted the gear, old man." The hunter bent down and picked up Sam's pack. Sam knew he stood little chance of making it home to Lauren and Charlie without his pack. However, it was three against one. He couldn't take them all on at once. He had to level the playing field somehow. He had to use the element of surprise.

Sam aimed at the man closest to Professor and fired without warning, striking the hunter in the shoulder. He was too far away for an accurate shot with a pistol, and also low on ammo. He couldn't afford to miss, so he fired again, this time hitting the man in the chest. The man dropped to one knee. The man's companions also dropped to the ground and leveled their rifles in Sam's direction.

Sam dove, rolled, adrenaline propelling him, and crawled behind a fallen tree. Rounds kicked up dirt near his foot. Another round punched through the rotten log. Sam needed to move. He had to find more substantial cover.

Splinters of wood struck Sam's right eyelid, blurring his vision. He got up on all fours and hurried to an outcropping of boulders. The men kept firing. Chunks of rocks flew from where bullets had torn into them. Sam dropped his magazine and counted the rounds. One in the chamber and two in the magazine. He had three rounds left. Three rounds for two perps.

He had to make his shots count, or he was going to die there in the woods. Lauren and Charlie would never know how hard he'd tried to get home. He'd never know whether his son had made it off that plane in Knoxville. Sam gritted his teeth and slapped the mag back into his pistol.

I won't be the one dying here today. Not here. Not like this.

When the younger of the two men stepped out from the cover

of a large tree and raised his rifle, Sam fired. The .45 ACP round struck the man in the center of his chest, and he crumpled to the ground at the base of the tree. The second man ran toward Sam, screaming and firing wildly as he did. Sam ducked, but a round ricocheted off one of the boulders, and something struck him in the thigh. He felt a pinch, but the man was still coming. He had to take aim and stop the hunter before the man could squeeze off any more shots. The shooting paused, and Sam rose, steadied his pistol on top of the boulder, and fired. The man dropped and rolled, trying to get to his feet and reach for his weapon. Sam fired his final round into the man's back. The hunter fell forward, landing face-first on his rifle. Sam watched closely to see whether he moved before leaving the cover of the outcropping.

He slowly approached the first man and rolled him over. The man's vacant eyes stared back at him. Sam bent to pick up the dead man's rifle and felt a searing pain in his right thigh. A crimson stain was blooming on his tactical pants six inches above his knee. He'd been hit. He was bleeding profusely. Sam stumbled toward his pack. "No, I will not die here. I'm making it home. I'm not dying here without knowing my family is alright." He was lightheaded. He fell to one knee. He heard Lauren's voice telling him to get up. He shook his head, trying to clear the fog. He drew in a deep, painful breath and coughed. Using the hunter's rifle as a crutch he pushed himself up on one knee and then to his feet.

Sam stumbled over and dropped next to the lifeless body of Professor. A muddy boot print covered the elderly man's left cheek. He'd been stomped to death.

"I'm sorry, old man."

Sam leaned back against a tree to catch his breath. Then he cut a slit in his pants just above the bloodstain with his tactical knife to expose the wound. He could tell immediately that he'd been hit with shrapnel and not a rifle round. There were dozens of tiny wounds next to the two-inch gash and no exit wound. Sam inserted a finger into the gash and nearly passed out from the pain. He wiggled his finger, trying to locate the piece of stone embedded in his thigh, but it was too deep.

There was so much blood. It had hit blood vessels, maybe even an artery. His training kicked in even as he fought the flashbacks from previous bloody gun battles. Sam pulled his bleeding control kit from his left cargo pant pocket, and retrieved a Combat Application Tourniquet. He slid the CAT over his shoe and up his leg, placed it two inches above the gash, pulled it tight, twisted the rod until the bleeding stopped, and locked the windlass rod into place. He glanced at his watch, and then wrote the time of the application on the time strap with the marker.

Now, he had to find a way to make it into Franklin and get medical help. Sam scooted toward the first hunter he'd shot. His arm was draped over Sam's get-home bag. There wasn't anything in there these men needed. He had no food, no ammunition, nothing they didn't already carry in their own bags. Certainly nothing worth killing or dying for. But the bag was everything to Sam. Without it, he stood very little chance of making it home. To him, it was his means to acquire food and water.

Sam pulled the strap of the man's AR-15 over his neck and around onto his back and then searched the hunter's pockets for spare ammunition. He found none. The rifle held everything he now had. Sam crawled to a nearby tree, dragging his bag with one hand. He pulled himself upright, swung the rifle around the front, and hobbled back to where Professor lay to retrieve the elderly man's trekking poles, still attached to the back of his hiking pack.

Sam covered Professor with the canopy from the man's hammock tent. He wished he could have at least placed rocks on top of it or something, but he needed to get to town. He had to find a doctor, or he wasn't going to make it home.

He fought back the memory of the last time he'd been shot. He could still remember the feel of his partner's blood on his face and how minutes had felt like hours as he had watched the life drain from Mike's body. At some point, prior to hearing the sirens of his fellow officers' cars and the ambulance, a sense of peace had washed over Sam. He'd accepted death had come for him, but then he had heard Lauren call his name. He had a wife he adored and a son whom he hadn't really gotten to know. Then, as now, he fought death to remain with them.

"One foot in front of the other. That's how you complete a hike on the AT," Professor had told him.

One foot in front of the other was how he'd make it to Franklin to find medical treatment.

"You can do this. Never give up. Never quit," he told himself as he stepped back onto the highway and turned toward the town of Franklin, North Carolina.

FORTY-THREE

Lauren

Unicoi City Hall
Unicoi, Tennessee
Day 6

After Lauren had given her speech to the residents of Unicoi, she'd been at city hall around the clock to work out the details for the orderly distribution of food and supplies from all the food, water, and hygiene items that had been found inside the tractor-trailers at the truck port and out on the interstate. The city workers were busy trying to move porta-potties into the neighborhoods and helping to haul water to the city park where it could be distributed to the residents. Mayberry and the group that had been going through the semis were moving the trailers from the truck stop to the outskirts of town to be used as a barrier wall.

City hall was quiet—quieter than Lauren had ever experienced. She was going over land records and trying to determine how to turn the public land into cropland. They'd already had at least three tractors donated to the cause. Fuel was the next problem they needed to resolve. There was fuel at the travel center. They just had to have a way to pump it from the tanks. Derek, the head of the public works department, was working on a solution for that. After that, they needed to find a way to get the diesel out of all the semis, but storing it was going to be a problem.

Lauren stretched and rolled her shoulders. A familiar ache gripped her heart. As long as she kept her mind busy and focused on problem-solving, she could manage not to think about Sam and her father's deteriorating medical condition. As soon as she stopped and was quiet for even a moment, the crippling grief hit her again.

It had been six days. Six days of not knowing whether her husband was alive, hurt in a ditch somewhere, or dead. The not knowing was almost too much to bear. Vince had driven the interstate all the way to the Tennessee border looking for Sam and even checked the back roads Sam might have taken without any success.

So many times, she'd wanted to take off and go look for him herself, but she had Charlie, her parents, and the town to think about. Vince had also gone out a few times on horseback looking for his brother, checking the interstate and a few other back roads without luck. She knew Vince would keep looking for as long as he could.

"Millie, I need a break. I'm going to run home and check in on Mom and Dad. Hold down the fort for me? I won't be long," Lauren called from her office.

"Take all the time you need, Lauren. I'll pull the maps and put them on your desk for when you get back."

Lauren had just stepped into the hallway when the sound of breaking glass echoed through the corridor. "Millie?"

"Lauren!" Millie screamed, and then there was the sound of a scuffle. Millie screamed again. There was a guttural noise down the long hallway, first high-pitched then muffled and gurgling.

Lauren ran toward the records room on the west side of the building. "Millie!"

Millie didn't answer her. Billy Mahon did.

"Hi there, Mayor. Nice of you to join us."

"What are...." Lauren stopped in her tracks.

Billy Mahon?

"You three go get the guns. Round up all the ammo. Avery said there were still flashbangs and smoke bombs in there as well. Get it all. I'll deal with our lovely lady mayor," Billy said.

Lauren ran into the conference room and closed the door. There were no windows, and the room was dark. She drew her peacemaker and leveled it at the door.

"Lauren!" It was Charlie's voice. What was he doing here?

"Charlie!" Lauren called out as she threw open the door. "Charlie, get out!"

Lauren was thrown to the ground as soon as she stepped into the corridor. In seconds, Billy Mahon was on top of her, straddling her torso with both his hands on her throat. She couldn't believe this was happening. She reached for her revolver, but it was too far away. Rising carbon dioxide in her body activated the insular cortex, a primal sensory area of the brain that triggered her brain's survival mode, as Lauren fought for her life, clawing at Billy's hands, trying to pry them from her neck. She gouged her fingernails into his hands, face, and eyes as she tried desperately to arch her back, kick, and throw him off her to get a precious breath of life-sustaining air, but Billy was just too big and strong.

Sam!

She was going to die there, never knowing what had happened to her husband. Who would look after Charlie? Who would take care of her parents?

Charlie!

She couldn't let Billy hurt Sam's son. She arched her back once more and tried to pull Billy's hands from her throat with all her strength. Her hands fell next to Billy's knee. She followed his thigh to his groin, found his testicles, and squeezed with all her strength. Billy released his grip on her throat and landed a right cross against her cheekbone. She twisted his sack harder, and he cried out, falling off her and rolling around on his back.

With great difficulty, Lauren forced herself to get up on all fours and crawl to the end of the hall. She drew in quick breaths trying to pull air into her lungs. She tried to call Charlie's name, but nothing came out. The outer door that led to the parking lot stood open. Lauren grabbed the door handle and used it to pull herself upright and into a standing position. She was able to take two steps away from the building before she felt a blow to her back.

As she fell forward over the top of a flower planter, she stretched out her arm to catch herself and landed on her hands and knees. Billy was on her back, his fingers intertwined in her hair. Lauren tried to crawl away, but he pinned her to the ground and pounded his fist into the back of her head. She saw stars with each blow. Strength left her body, and she fell limp. Billy seized the moment and flipped Lauren over onto her back. His long fingers wrapped around her neck, and he once again began squeezing the life from her.

Lauren was lightheaded. She was going to pass out. She knew she would die there in the parking lot if she fell unconscious. Lauren fought with all her strength, but Billy was just too strong. She went limp, staring up at the sky. It was a brilliant blue. Somewhere out there was Sam. The man of her dreams. The man who'd saved her life once, but he wasn't here now. No one was coming to save her. Lauren felt a strange peace wash over her as she closed her eyes and prepared to give herself over to death.

All of a sudden, Billy shifted his weight. The pressure lifted from her chest and then from her throat. Her eyes popped open, and she bolted upright, gasping for air. Her hands flew up to her throat to protect her airway. Benny was screaming for her to run, but she struggled to get to her feet. He was wrestling with Billy, trying to fend off blow after blow to his midsection. Lauren was torn between helping Benny and saving herself.

"Damn it, run, Lauren! Get the hell out of here!" Benny shouted.

Somehow, Lauren managed to get to her feet. She was still lightheaded and stumbled several times, trying to right herself. Finally, fully upright, she took off in what felt more like a fast walk than a run. A shot rang out, and Lauren jumped, stumbled, and fell to one knee. She twisted, crawling backward, searching for the shooter. Benny was standing over the body of her attacker. Behind him was Charlie, holding his pistol with both hands.

Their eyes met. Charlie let the weapon fall and ran to her. He dropped to his knees, and Lauren cradled him in her arms, rocking him softly as he sobbed into her shoulder.

"I had to. He was going to kill Benny and then you. I had to shoot him."

Lauren kissed the top of his head. "I know. Thank you for being so brave. You saved us all. Your dad will be so proud of you."

Lauren heard footfalls on the concrete. She grabbed Charlie, and they ran to where Billy had knocked her revolver from her hand. She snatched it from the ground as she shoved Charlie behind her. She spun to face the approaching threat, revolver aimed and ready to fire. Vince rounded the corner of the building, followed closely by Alan Mayberry and Keith Pataky. Relief washed over her and Lauren lowered the weapon and holstered it.

Vince walked over and rolled Billy's body over with the toe of his boot. He bent and placed two fingers against Billy's neck.

"Is he dead?" Lauren asked.

"As a doornail," Vince said.

Although she'd long wanted to see this moment, she regretted that Charlie had been the one to do it. It wasn't something any child should ever have to do. She wanted to kill Billy all over again for making Charlie do such a thing.

"They attacked the grocery store, but we held them off. Vince arrived just in time," Keith Pataky said.

"Where's the rest of the police force, Benny?"

"Cordell and Owens attacked Wilson and me as we approached city hall. They're dead."

"Where's Wilson?" Lauren asked.

"He's injured. I left him by the Baptist church. Reverend Brown took him to Doctor Wang's office."

"Anyone injured at the store?"

"Just Billy's crew. Some of them were locals he'd recruited. One was Lloyd's grandson."

It concerned Lauren that locals had chosen to join Mahon in attacking the town, and for one of the aldermen's family members to be among them was even more disturbing.

"Where are the bodies?"

"Mostly in the street," Keith said. "Dad mowed a heap of them down before they reached the parking lot."

"Can we get them moved quickly? We need to get ready for a major food distribution there this evening. I don't want residents coming out and seeing that—especially the children."

"I'll get some guys and drag them out past the hardware store. We'll bury them later," Mayberry said.

"Thank you. After you've done that, can you go back to the store and help guard it while Herman gets things ready for distribution?" Lauren asked.

"Sure thing, Mayor. I'll see you at the park."

FORTY-FOUR

Becky

Nantahala National Forest
Franklin, Tennessee
Day 6

Becky went out to hunt and forage every day before first light and returned at dusk. She didn't want anyone to see her carrying in small game and a bag of berries, leaves, roots, and fungi. She didn't have enough to share. Besides, no one had offered her help. Apart from the grocery store clerk, she hadn't spoken to anyone in town since the lights had gone out. Her landlord had been away on vacation when it occurred. He had yet to return.

As more time passed, Becky had considered breaking into his house and collecting what food and drinks he had before someone else got to them first. But she hadn't worked up the courage to do it yet.

She had learned that a shelter had been established at the church just outside town, but the church didn't have indoor plumbing and it was crowded with residents who'd had to leave their homes. Becky had remained in her tiny apartment, perched on the hillside overlooking the Little Tennessee River. She drew water from a creek.

It was getting increasingly harder to find game close to town, so Becky slung her brother's rifle over her shoulder and pushed west toward Winding Stair Gap in search of something larger than a squirrel or rabbit. She wasn't sure what she'd do if she bagged a deer. She wouldn't be able to carry much more than the hindquarters back with her. Becky couldn't abide such waste, especially now. She needed to find a way to get as much of the meat home as possible.

Becky crossed her driveway and walked down the hill to the Wilsons' place. She'd once seen Old Man Wilson hitch one of his ponies to a cart and give his grandchildren rides around their field. Mr. Wilson passed away two days prior. The sheriff had come for his body, but no one had come to care for Wilson's ponies.

"Whoa, Brownie," she said, giving the pony an appropriate name as she slid the harness over its head. "Let's go for a little walk. You'll enjoy it. There will be new things for you to taste along the way." She ran her fingers through Brownie's mane and he gently nudged her forehead with his and exhaled sharply.

"You like that, Brownie?"

The pony nodded on cue in response, and Becky went to work hitching him to the cart. She led him down the drive to the road, and he happily followed. Thirty minutes later, she tied his reins to a tree trunk, ran her fingers through his mane again, and headed off into the woods.

"I'll be back, little Brownie."

She walked and walked, looking for deer rubs and studying the ground ahead of her before spotting a deer trail. Becky squatted by a fallen tree and lowered herself to the ground. Resting the barrel of her rifle on the trunk, she scanned the area through her scope, searching for any sign of deer or other game to feed herself.

To the right of a clump of blackberry bushes, something glinted in the sunlight as Becky got to her feet. She couldn't make out what it was from that distance, but there shouldn't have been anything shiny in the thick woods. Curiosity got the better of her and she made her way over to where she thought the object lay. She spotted a pack leaning against a tall oak tree. The sun glinted off the compass glass in the hand of a man who was face down on the ground.

"You alive, mister?"

The man didn't move.

Becky took a step closer. "Mister? Are you okay?"

He didn't stir. She took another step. Blood pooled near the man's legs. Against her better judgment, she approached him and poked him with the barrel of her rifle. "Mister? You alive?"

He groaned and Becky stumbled backward. Her heart pounded against her rib cage. Gaining her wits, she raised her rifle, pointing it at the man's back as he rolled onto his side.

"Wait!" he shouted. "I've already been shot. I'm no threat to you."

"Shot? By who?"

"Hunters."

"Good ole boys or city slickers like yourself?"

"Does it matter?"

"To me it does. Were you poaching?" Becky asked, still pointing the barrel of the rifle at the man's torso.

"I wasn't poaching. I think it was city guys." He tried to sit up and moaned.

"You should stay down, mister. I don't want to have to put another hole in you."

"I need help."

"I'm not sure I can help you. That wound looks pretty bad. You need a doctor."

"Yes, I need a doctor," the man said.

"We ain't got no doctor. The only one visited the area twice a week, and he hasn't come back since the lights went out."

The man didn't act surprised when Becky mentioned the electricity not working. "Mister, do you know what has happened?"

"The EMP? Yeah. I was in Atlanta when it happened."

"Atlanta? How did you get all the way here?"

"We made it to Greenville, Georgia, and met up with some southbound thru-hikers. After the shit hit the fan, they decided to head back the way they'd came. They let us tag along north on the Appalachian Trail."

Becky spun around in a circle, scanning the woods for the others who he was speaking about. "Where are they?"

"Dead."

"Did you kill them?"

"No."

"Whereabouts did this happen?"

"I'm not sure exactly. Where am I now?"

"Just west of Franklin?"

"Tennessee?"

"No! Franklin, North Carolina. You probably exited the AT Windy Stair Gap," Becky said, her eyes still scanning for the man's shooter. "How long ago did you say this happened to you?"

"Yesterday. Maybe the day before. As I said, I was out for a while." His hand dropped to his leg, where the CAT had been fastened around his thigh.

"Can you feel your leg?" Becky asked.

"Yes. It hurts like hell. I was able to stop the bleeding—mostly. I can't walk."

"How'd you get here then?"

"I have hiking poles and I crawled part of the way." He held up one of the hiking poles he had fallen on.

The man had to have a strong will to survive to manage that. His injury had to hurt like hell.

"Help me, please! I have a kid. I have a wife and kid who need me."

Becky felt a tug inside her chest. His pleas were working on her. But helping out a wounded stranger wasn't part of her plan. What would doing so mean for her getting home to her own family?

"I just need help to get into town. Maybe someone there can help me. A nurse, a dentist, even a veterinarian?"

Becky glanced over her shoulder toward where she'd left Brownie.

"Wait here," she said, backing away from him.

"Where are you going?"

"I'll be right back. Don't you move." Becky didn't take her eyes off him as she made her way the rest of the way down the hill to the stand of cedars where she'd stashed Brownie and his cart. She untied the reins and led the pony back through the woods to the man.

She stopped ten feet from him and pointed the rifle at the ground near his feet. "Can you stand on your own?"

"I can try."

"Get in," she said, swinging the barrel of her rifle toward the cart.

"I'm not going to hurt you," the man said.

"I know. I won't let you."

The man grabbed his hiking pole and pushed himself up into a standing position. His injured leg stuck out to one side. The foot on his injured leg dragged on the ground as he made his way over to the cart. After two attempts, he managed to climb inside. He lay on his side, sweat pouring from his brow.

"You best not try anything. If you do, I'll finish what those ole boys started. Got it?"

"Yes, ma'am."

∼

299

As they approached town, Becky grew increasingly nervous. She was an outsider, and she was bringing in an injured outsider. She wasn't sure how that would play out. "Where you from?" she asked him.

"Tennessee. Unicoi, Tennessee. I live there with my wife and her parents. My wife is the mayor there."

"What's your name?"

"Sam Wallace."

"Well, nice to meet you Sam. I'm Becky."

"What did you do in Unicoi?" Becky asked.

"I was a cop and then a criminal investigator for the district attorney."

A cop. That was a plus. Franklin was a pro-law enforcement town. There were a great many American flags in Franklin with the blue line on them showing their support for law enforcement.

"Have you lived in Franklin all your life?" Sam asked.

The question pricked her heart. It reminded her of all she'd lost.

"No. I moved here a few years ago with my husband."

"Where is he now?"

"In the cemetery," she said flatly.

"I'm so sorry for your loss."

Tears filled Becky's eyes, blurring her vision. She and Brownie stopped the wagon. Sam was the first person to say those words to her since her husband's funeral. Not even Jared's family had attempted to console her with the phrase. "Thank you," she managed to choke out. "He and my brother were killed in Afghanistan."

Becky's throat tightened as Sam shifted and turned to face her.

"I served in Afghanistan. I understand loss. When I was a cop, my partner died sitting right next to me in our patrol car—and I couldn't help him."

Sam reached out a hand to her, and she leaned toward him against the cart. She couldn't contain herself as her loss began to overtake her. Becky's raw, genuine pain drew Sam's grief to the surface and he fought to keep it together. His memories had been working overtime against him since the EMP, and they threatened to release the grief he had held back for so many years. The grief they each carried had been too difficult a burden to successfully manage before the EMP. Now, as each new day unfolded, hopelessness increased at a rate too alarming for the mind to comprehend.

"I feel how weak and fruitless must be any word of mine which should attempt to beguile you from the grief of a loss so overwhelming. But I cannot refrain from tendering you the consolation that may be found in the thanks of the Republic they died to save." Sam was quiet for a long moment. "I pray that our Heavenly Father may assuage the anguish of your bereavement, and leave you only the cherished memory of the loved and lost, and the solemn pride that must be yours to have laid so costly a sacrifice upon the altar of freedom."

"What was that," Becky asked, sobbing.

"Those were the words of President Lincoln to a mother who'd lost five sons during the Civil War," he said. "You, too, have paid a costly price, and I'm sorry you had to pay it."

"Thank you." Becky wiped away her tears and picked up the reins. "Let's get you some help for that leg."

Neither of them spoke again until the doctor's house came into view.

Becky pulled the cart to a stop at the end of the driveway. She waited, hoping someone in the house would see it was her before firing.

"Maybe you should call out and let them know we're here."

"Might not be a bad idea," Becky said. "Doc! I have an injured man here. You mind taking a look at him?"

The front door eased open. Doctor Hammond stood in the doorway. He raised his rifle to his cheek. "I don't recognize him."

"He's a hiker. I found him near the AT," Becky shouted back.

"Oh! Bring him around to the side door."

Franklin, North Carolina, loved their hikers.

"What kind of doctor did you say he was?" Sam asked as Becky pulled the cart up the doctor's driveway.

"He's a veterinarian, livestock mostly."

FORTY-FIVE

Sam

Hammond Veterinary Services
Franklin, North Carolina
Day 11

Although Doctor Hammond was a large animal veterinarian, he did a pretty fine job of repairing the wound to Sam's thigh, but by the third day, infection had set in despite the antibiotic the doctor had graciously given him. Sam was weak and could barely stand, but he was determined to get back on the trail and home to his wife and son.

The doctor had set up a bed in the office attached to the barn where he treated horses and cattle. Although the breeze coming through the window brought some relief from the unrelenting summer heat, the manure smell that accompanied it turned Sam's stomach. Still, he was grateful for the hospitality. Lying around recuperating led to hours upon hours of nothing but thinking about home. His mind imagined horrible scenes. His dreams were filled with images of Charlie, Lauren, and her parents. Some of the memories were pleasant, but they mostly involved their deaths. He was nearly overcome with guilt. He'd let Tara down. He was supposed to have protected her, but he hadn't.

Every day he sat there in Franklin was another day he was failing his family. Lauren needed his help. There would be so much to do to care for her parents without electricity. She'd feel obligated to help as much as she could. And then there was the town. Was Charlie with her? Had they even made it back to Unicoi? There was no way for Sam to know the answers to any of the questions that haunted him. Whatever it took, he had to head home.

Sam grew impatient with the slow pace at which he was healing. He knew that he needed to be up and moving, using his leg as much as he could if he had a chance of getting back on the AT and making it home. He set out walking, trying to strengthen his leg, using the cane Doc Hammond had given him. He made it as far as the end of the veterinarian's driveway before collapsing. Becky found him. To Sam's surprise, she'd stayed to care for him, bringing him deer, rabbit, and squirrel to help him regain his strength.

Becky placed her hand on Sam's forehead. "You have a raging fever, Sam. You have to give the meds time to work. I thought you wanted to make it home to your family?"

"I do. That's what I'm trying to do," Sam said.

"It looks to me like you're trying to kill yourself. Stay here. I'll go get Brownie and the cart."

"You could come with me when I go. You said you wanted to make it home to Shelton Laurel. I could help you. We could help each other."

"We'll discuss that when your fever breaks and you're able to put weight on your leg. Me and Brownie can't carry your heavy ass all the way to Unicoi County."

Mrs. Hammond walked up. She held a basket of berries under one arm. "You probably just ripped all your stitches out." She walked past Sam and then turned back. "I'd hate to think we wasted good antibiotics on someone without common sense." She whipped around and strode up the drive to the front door, letting the screen door slam behind her as she entered.

~

Becky returned with Brownie and helped Sam into the wagon. The bumpy ride up the drive and around to the barn was excruciatingly painful. Sam willingly took a pain pill and fell fast asleep. He awoke to voices outside the veterinarian's office.

"Bring him in here," Doc Hammond said.

A woman was crying, begging the doctor to save her boy.

Sam got to his feet and hobbled to the door. He cracked it open just as two men approached, carrying a teenage boy. He was unconscious and bleeding from his head.

"What happened to him?" the doctor said.

"He was shot," one of the men said.

They carried the kid in and placed him on an exam table next to Sam's bed. Sam stepped outside to give them room. Several minutes later, the woman began to wail. "My boy. My beautiful baby boy!"

"I guess he didn't make it," Becky said, approaching Sam from the open barn doors.

"Doesn't sound like it," Sam said.

"His brother said the boy tried to stop chicken thieves from running off with one of their hens, and they shot him," Becky said.

"Unfortunately, there will be a lot of that going on. When people get hungry, they get desperate," Sam said.

"There's a meeting in town. The police chief and three of his officers were killed the night before last trying to stop looters from entering the grocery store. The three other officers didn't live in Franklin and stopped coming to work about a week ago. The mayor wants to deputize people to patrol the town."

"Might not be a bad idea if those people they deputize are trustworthy folks," Sam said.

"He said we should set up roadblocks and control movement, like curfews and such, so no one is out at night. If anyone breaks the curfew, they could be shot on sight. I just think that's too much."

Sam wasn't in favor of curfews, but under the circumstances, it would help to distinguish the good guys from those with bad intentions. There had been situations where city officials had instituted curfews back in Tennessee. During natural disasters and riots, they had been effective at quelling violence and looting. Officers could arrest people who refused to heed the curfew.

"Are town officials doing anything to provide food and water, or is everyone left to fend for themselves?" Sam asked.

"The emergency supplies were all used up in the first few days. The city council voted to confiscate and distribute what was left of the food and water from the grocery and convenience stores. That lasted another few days. Now they're pretty much out of options," Becky said.

"That's why people have turned to stealing from folks outside of town," Sam said.

"I heard that it wasn't folks from Franklin but some of the tourists that got stranded in town. There are some rowdy dudes that were here on a float trip that had been acting all entitled and pushing their weight around even before the shit hit the fan. I don't know how they can stop those people without ending up like that poor boy in there," Becky said.

"That will be one of the biggest threats. Takers will take. People will need to band together to defend what's theirs."

"Band together how?"

"Form groups. Work together. Set up their own security teams. Whatever it takes to protect their food supply." Sam rubbed his aching leg. It was time for more pain meds, but he decided to hold off. With talk of trouble in town, he wanted to be as sharp as possible.

Sam spent the rest of the afternoon thinking about what he'd discussed with Vince back in Unicoi and how he could approach the topic of security with the doctor and his family. The doctor was well respected in the community. If Sam could convince him to rally people behind working together, they might just stand a chance. Sam would like to avoid trouble spilling over into the countryside as much as possible. If the Hammond farm came under attack, that would be very hard to do. He needed to be able to recuperate and get strong enough for his two hundred-mile hike home.

～

Everyone was quiet as they sat around the picnic table, upwind from the barn. Mrs. Hammond had prepared the rabbits that Becky had hunted that morning and served them over rice and beans. It was delicious, filling, and so much more than most others had to eat. In a way, he felt guilty taking food they would need later, but he had no choice. He'd never make it back to his family if he didn't.

"Doc, I was thinking. Maybe we should speak to some of your neighbors about setting up some type of patrols."

"What for?" Mrs. Hammond asked.

"Safety. To avoid what happened to that boy today," Sam said.

"That was so tragic. Later, I'm taking some of our stew over to the parents," she said. She wiped the sweat from her brow with the hem of her white apron and pushed several loose strands of her grey hair back from her face.

"Might not be a bad idea to talk to Francis and Titus. They're our two closest neighbors. I'm not opposed to helping folks," Dr. Hammond said.

"Folks out here help each other. We always have. It's how country folk live. We need each other. We trade things and lend a hand when needed. That won't change just because the lights went out. Some of the older folks around here grew up without electricity or running water. We know how to make do," Mrs. Hammond said.

"That's great. That's as it should be, but folks in town don't know how to survive without the grocery store. They're going to come here. They're going to want more than you can afford to give. Some will take it by force," Sam said.

Mrs. Hammond placed a hand on her neck, and her eyes grew wide. "Oh my." She turned to her husband. "That won't happen. Franklin is filled with good folks. They won't hurt us."

Dr. Hammond pushed his empty bowl away and stood. "Well, I'm not going to sit back and let them. I'll be at Foster's house. Don't wait up for me. You know how long-winded he can be."

Sam watched Doc Hammond walk across his pasture and through a gate leading to the neighboring field. Sam was surprised they'd been able to avoid trouble this long. He hoped it wasn't too late and that the community would be able to pull together and protect themselves. He prayed Lauren had been successful with all she had to do in Unicoi and, if not, that she, Charlie, and her parents were safe behind the gate on Vince's compound.

Sam rose and grabbed his crutches. "Thank you for the lovely dinner," he said, excusing himself and leaving Mrs. Hammond to clean up the dishes. Becky would bring water from the spring when she returned the next morning and stay to help the elderly couple with chores. Sam felt truly blessed to have been rescued by Becky and for the Hammonds' kindness, but he was ready to get back on the Appalachian Trail and home to his family.

Maybe tomorrow. That was what he told himself, but with the infection in his wound still spreading, he knew that wouldn't happen. Maybe tomorrow or the next day—whatever it took, however long it took—Sam would make it home to Unicoi and his family.

Becky cleared her throat. "Mrs. Hammond, there are two

strangers in town, a man and a woman. They need a place to stay. They're willing to work here and help you. I'll bring extra game for them if I can. They're from the AT and haven't received the warmest of welcomes. They've been staying with me, but there have been threats, especially after the looting. I'm afraid they're going to get blamed, and the town will come after them."

"A man and woman." Sam smiled. "Are their names Moondust and Tumbleweed?"

Becky gave him a puzzled look. "How'd you know?"

"We've met. They're good people."

Doctor Hammond and two of his neighbors appeared at the edge of the lawn. Everyone gathered around the picnic table. "Sam, we all agree that after what happened to the police chief, we need to take some steps to ensure that group doesn't head this way causing trouble. But frankly, we have no idea how to go about protecting our farms," Doc Hammond said.

Sam patted his leg. "Well, I can't do much, but I can tell you how to set up defensive positions and secure a perimeter." Sam gave the group of farmers gathered around the table a list of items they would need. He would supervise the placement of the roadblocks and sandbags. Sam would do what he could until he had healed enough to continue home to his family. He prayed it would be enough.

FORTY-SIX

Lauren

Taylor Residence
Unicoi, Tennessee
Day 12

Another week had passed. It had been twelve days since the life Lauren knew had ended. Sam hadn't made it home yet, but she refused to give up hope. Her heart ached for him.

Vince had set out again that morning down the interstate in hopes of finding Sam. He'd taken Billy Mahon's motorcycle right after they'd cleared everyone out of the motel and sent the last stragglers packing, on foot, down the interstate.

Vince was using fuel they couldn't afford to lose. Folks in town would complain, but Vince didn't care. He wasn't swayed by their opinions of him. That was what he'd said when Lauren had brought it up with him before he left. It was his fuel, and he'd do whatever he damn well pleased with it. Lauren just prayed he'd bring her husband home.

The city had plowed every inch of land that they could and sowed the ground, but although they'd managed to retrieve thousands of gallons of diesel, they were using it very quickly. Just one of the old tractors used over one hundred gallons per day. Soon all the fuel would be gone, no matter how tightly they regulated its use. In addition, they lacked the people to guard the fields when harvest time came around. They were living day to day and sometimes moment by moment, constantly putting out fires, both real and metaphorical. At least the residents of Unicoi were working together well with a few exceptions. Drinking water remained a problem. But Lauren was hopeful they could find enough pipe to run water from the mountain stream into the town.

Mr. Pataky's food distribution and the food they gathered from the trucks had helped to alleviate some of the immediate issues, and most everyone seemed to be getting what they needed. Of course, the same people who showed up to every council meeting to complain also camped themselves on the doorstep of city hall, waiting for someone to hear them gripe about the placement of the porta-potties or how far they had to walk to fill their water jugs. But all in all, things were going better in town than Lauren could have hoped for after Billy and his gang had met their end.

Their major problem now was the constant battle to guard what they had not only from the takers and hordes but from the ones who couldn't help themselves—those outside the walls of Unicoi who were really starving and couldn't find any other way to feed themselves and their families.

No one living these days had ever known a hunger this intense.

Angela poked her head in Lauren's door. "Any word yet?" It was the same question she asked every morning. Every time, it sent daggers through Lauren's heart. It had been twelve days with no sign of Sam. Charlie had grown quiet. He missed Sam, his parents and baby sister, and Lauren was out of comforting words for him.

"Nothing yet."

"Tomorrow, then," Angela said, backing out of the room. "He'll make it home tomorrow."

It was the not knowing that was the hardest. Not knowing the location or status of a loved one was the strangest of feelings. Lauren did her best to keep hope alive. He had his get-home bag. If something had happened to the Bronco and he was on foot, it could take up to two weeks for Sam to walk two hundred fifty miles from Atlanta, but he had only a few days of food. At least he had some fishing line and lures in his bag. He could hunt. He knew which wild plants were edible. He would make it, no matter what.

Today, the plan was to meet with the board of aldermen and those with select specialties and discuss a plan to plant food plots in the park. Residents seemed eager to get started, and ladies from the Master Gardeners club had volunteered to lead the effort.

The entire park was plowed using the old tractors. Everyone pitched in to get the soil ready. Aged cow manure was brought in from a nearby farm to fertilize the soil. Rows were made, and seeds were planted. People were even laughing and singing as they worked. Charlie wore Edna's pink floral gardening gloves as he raked dirt to make a row. Millie brought out filtered drinking water.

Everything appeared to be running smoothly until Benny came rushing across the freshly plowed field toward her.

"What? What is it now?"

"Vince is at city hall. He needs you and the aldermen back there now!"

"Why? What's wrong?"

Lauren knew it didn't have anything to do with Sam. Vince wouldn't need the aldermen present to bring her news about her husband. He had left just that morning searching for Sam. What could he have seen or learned that would have him returning so soon?

Lauren gathered Gretchen and Ralph and met Vince back at city hall. He looked like he'd aged ten years since she'd last seen him earlier in the day. Whatever it was, it had the confident man rattled.

"There's no easy way to say this, so I'll just tell you straight. Nigel Corbin is free. He and Maggie Russo's brother-in-law, Bobby, have some sort of alliance and are working together. They just took over the grocery store in Erwin and killed everyone that had been staying there. I saw them dragging out the bodies," Vince said.

Nigel Corbin was free. Of course, he was. She'd been told the sheriff had released the prisoners, but Lauren had thought Nigel would return to his home in Johnson City. There would be no trial. There would be no reason for him to hang around Erwin.

"I talked to a survivor of the attack. The Corbin and Russo crews have been in Erwin for over a week. After the sheriff released Nigel, the Corbin and Russo crews went and massacred the prosecutor and his entire family. It seems Nigel wants revenge," Vince said.

Lauren felt queasy. "You think they'll come here next?"

"There's something you may not know. Maggie shot Stuart Russo before she escaped. If Tony Russo made it back from Atlanta, he might want revenge. He may want to get Maggie and his kids back. We may have a war on our hands," Vince said.

Lauren knew Vince wouldn't hand over Lindsay's sister and her kids to those madmen. It would be a bloodbath. "Did you learn anything else?" Lauren asked.

"The survivor heard one of Corbin's men say that Unicoi was their next stop."

Thank you for reading Brink of Darkness, book one in the Survive the Collapse series. **The story continues in book two, Brink of Chaos . Order your today at Amazon.com!**

If you enjoyed this book, I'd like to hear from you and hope that you could take a moment and post an honest review on

Amazon. Your support and feedback will help this author improve for future projects. Without the support of readers like yourself, self-publishing would not be possible. **Don't forget to sign up for my spam-free newsletter at www.tlpayne.com to be the first to know of new releases, giveaways, and special offers.**

Acknowledgments

I'd like to thank everyone who helped me with Brink of Darkness.

Randy and Linda Philips for their technical advice regarding thru-hiking and the Appalachian Trail.

Beta Readers Samuel Bradshaw, Sam Stokes, Scott Guilfoyle, Lee Reed, Carolyn Rahnema, Sue Jackson, and Lindsay Smith for their tremendously valuable feedback and suggestions.
The Anderson Family for their love, support, and technical advice.
Dockery for everything you did to make this the best book possible.

Also by T. L. Payne

Survive the Collapse Series

Brink of Darkness

Brink of Chaos

Brink of Panic

Brink of Collapse

Brink of Destruction: A FREE Novelette

The Days of Want Series

Turbulent

Hunted

Turmoil

Uprising

Upheaval

Mayhem

Defiance

The Gateway to Chaos Series

Seeking Safety

Seeking Refuge

Seeking Justice

Seeking Hope

Fall of Houston Series

No Way Out

No Other Choice

No Turning Back

No Surrender

No Man's Land

Desperate Age Series

Panic in the Rockies

Getting Out of Dodge

Surviving Freedom (Coming Soon!)

This We'll Defend: A Desperate Age Novella (Newsletter signup required)

About the Author

T. L. Payne is the author of the several bestselling post-apocalyptic series. T. L. lives and writes in the Osage Hills region of Oklahoma and enjoys many outdoor activities including kayaking, rockhounding, metal detecting, and fishing the many lakes and rivers of the area.

Don't forget to sign up for T. L.'s spam-free newsletter at www.tlpayne.com to be the first to know of new releases, giveaways, and special offers.

T. L. loves to hear from readers. You may email T. L. at contact@tlpayne.com or join the Facebook reader group at https://www.facebook.com/groups/tlpaynereadergroup

Join TL on Social Media

Facebook Author Page
Days of Want Fan Group
Twitter
Instagram
Website: tlpayne.com
Email: contact@tlpayne.com

Made in the USA
Columbia, SC
26 May 2025